MIRROR, MIRROR, ON THE WALL

The dressmaker to whom the Duchess had sent Catherine beamed with pride. Now at last, the woman assured Catherine, the young lady was fit to be seen in public. Catherine looked into the mirror and first paled with shock, then flushed with embarrassment.

The dress was so low in front that even her spanned hand could not cover the naked expanse it showed. She could clearly see her breasts as she had seen them before only when she was in her bath. Below, the folds of the dress clung and draped about her so that she seemed mired in some rich red kelp that outlined all of her lower body.

Then she realized she was not alone in taking in this sight. "Bravo," said the tall, handsome, elegant gentleman lounging in the doorway. "The little country mouse has become a dazzler."

And Catherine knew not where to look—whether into the mirror that showed her shame . . . or into the avid eyes of the Marquis of Bessacarr as they feasted on it. . . .

THE
DISDAINFUL MARQUIS

SIGNET REGENCY ROMANCE
COMING IN JANUARY 1989

Emma Lange
Brighton Intrigue

Jane Ashford
Meddlesome Miranda

Mary Jo Putney
The Controversial Countess

The Disdainful Marquis

by

Edith Layton

A SIGNET BOOK

NEW AMERICAN LIBRARY

**For three particular graces:
Dottie, Gillian, and Renée**

NAL BOOKS ARE AVAILABLE AT QUANTITY DISCOUNTS WHEN USED
TO PROMOTE PRODUCTS OR SERVICES. FOR INFORMATION PLEASE
WRITE TO PREMIUM MARKETING DIVISION, NEW AMERICAN LIBRARY,
1633 BROADWAY, NEW YORK, NEW YORK 10019.

Copyright © 1983 by Edith Layton

All rights reserved

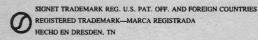

SIGNET TRADEMARK REG. U.S. PAT. OFF. AND FOREIGN COUNTRIES
REGISTERED TRADEMARK—MARCA REGISTRADA
HECHO EN DRESDEN, TN

SIGNET, SIGNET CLASSIC, MENTOR, ONYX, PLUME, MERIDIAN
and NAL BOOKS are published by NAL PENGUIN INC.,
1633 Broadway, New York, New York 10019

First Printing, September, 1983

3 4 5 6 7 8 9 10 11

PRINTED IN THE UNITED STATES OF AMERICA

Chapter 1

The pavements were gray, the houses were gray, the very air was gray with cold October fog. Although it was a damp mizzly dank day in London, the fog did have its capricious moments. Here and there it lifted its skirts, or blew in little skirlish puffs to create small pockets of translucence so that anyone who had to be abroad on such a wretched afternoon had at least some small chance of finding their direction. But they had to be quick about it and gain their bearings to head in the right direction before the fickle mists encompassed them completely again. It was altogether a dreadful day for a stranger to be traversing the city, with the fog being so coy and whimsical.

The inhabitants of the city were used to the weather's vagaries, in much the same way that they might be used to an eccentric aunt's changes of mood. Those who had to be up and about traveled the streets with an air of grim tolerance, and they called comments to each other about how she was a right terror again today. But those who could afford to, avoided the outdoors entirely. And so the fog, most democratically covering the city's length from its most palatial houses to its most wretched stews, ironically only served to point out the undemocratic distribution of wealth and class. The poor groped about the town because they had to, the rich stayed snug at home because they chose to, and the only other travelers were the adventurers.

The occupants of the hired coach that picked its way through the mist-shrouded streets did not feel like adventurers. The rotund gentleman who kept tapping his neat little well-shod foot against the floorboards and consulting his gold watch and emitting periodic stifled sighs felt put upon, and his every ill-concealed gesture of impatience showed it. He was cold; the damp had crept through the floorboards and the ill-fitting windows of the coach into his very bones. He was bored, traveling through the gray city with nothing but gray vapor showing outside the windows. And he was hungry; his watch clearly showed teatime, just as his stomach had been telling him for the last hour. Yet every time his companion glanced at him, he tucked the watch back into his pocket, put on a brave smile of sweet forbearance, and pretended to gaze out the milky windows with active interest.

"Poor Arthur," his companion thought guiltily as she watched him once again check his timepiece and heard another little muffled sigh. She smiled brightly at him and wished again that she felt half so bright as she pretended. In truth, if he felt cold and weary and his every motion showed that he thought himself on a fool's errand, then she felt colder and wearier because the whole day had been a crashing disappointment. Added to that, she knew she was the fool who had sent him on the errand. But he only suffered boredom and hunger. She was enduring the pangs of crushing defeat.

It had seemed so reasonable, Catherine remembered, when she had been back at home, carefully penning all the letters to the London employment bureaus, stating her qualifications and expectations of a position. It had seemed so correct a course to take, seeking some kind of genteel position in Britain's greatest city, so as not to be any further burden upon Arthur or her stepsister now that they were expecting an addition to their family. For despite all their protests to the contrary, she knew that it was not right that they should support not only a new marriage and the coming of a new baby, but also an unwed stepsister as well. And a stepsister who, she felt, could well be able to support herself if only she were not a resident of a little country town. But London! She had been sure she would be able to find a place for herself there. But she hadn't. And now the coach was taking her to her last interview, her last chance to find a post. For she knew Arthur would never again take her to the City, and never allow her to go by herself. It was propriety and duty that had forced him to come so far with her; if she failed, he would be careful not to say "I told you so" more than a dozen times to her, for he was basically a kind man, but he would never be persuaded to leave Kendal on such a mission again.

She glanced down again at the small pasteboard card she held tightly in her little gray glove. "Introducing Miss Catherine

Robins," it stated in flourishing script, "to see Her Grace the Duchess of Crewe in reference to a position on Her Grace's staff." It was signed, with another discrete flourish, "The Misses Parkinson, Employment Counselors." It was the last card she had. The other six lay, crumpled and used, deep in her reticule, mute testimony to her failures in the past two days.

Yesterday, on Catherine's very first call, Mrs. Oliphant had taken her card, taken one look at her, and screeched, "Oh no, my dear, you'll never do. Reely, you won't do at all. Why, just take a look at Mum, just have a look. Why, I can't even lift her when she's a mind to be propped up for tea in bed. How can a slip of a lass like you do it?"

And, in truth, Mrs. Oliphant's mama had just lain there deep in her bed like a beached whale and grinned up in concurrence with her daughter. "Aye," she had puffed, "my arm's just the size of your waist, luv," and she had wheezed with laughter at the look on Catherine's face when she lifted said member and waved it about.

"But," Catherine had gone on gamely, "the agency said you required a lady's companion, not a nurse."

"Nurse!" Mrs. Oliphant replied, affronted. "Mum don't need a nurse. She's sharp as a tack just as she always was, but a lady's companion don't just sip tea and tattle. No, we need someone to shift her, now and again. Get her up out of bed when the weather suits. Dress her and lead her about now that she's not too sure on her feet. No, my dear, you'll never do."

"You don't weigh up, lass," the older woman had cackled, from her bed. "That's all. You'll do when you gain a few stone."

Catherine hadn't "done" for Miss Coleman either. That aged spinster had given Catherine a few sharp looks and then had said in her crackling voice, "Not suitable. Sorry, Miss Robins, but you're too young to have one thing in common with me, and I do like to while away the evenings in friendly chatter."

She had been "too young" for Mrs. Webster's great-aunt, and "too inexperienced" for Sir Stephen's mother-in-law. "Not what we're looking for," Mrs. Bartlett had said succinctly, and Lady Brewer hadn't even given a reason—she had just sighed and said in her fadeaway voice, "Oh, not at all suitable." And Mrs. White had just given her one gimlet-eyed look and snapped, "Not in this house, my girl. Not with three young sons on the premises. We want an older female to companion my aunt."

Catherine sat erect and listened to the horses' muffled tread. This call was her last, she had left it for last because she had felt that a duchess would be far harder to suit than any mere Mrs. Whites or Mrs. Oliphants. In fact, she had thought not to dare try for the position of a duchess's companion. But now she had to—it was her last chance. If she failed at that, it would be back to Kendal, back to Jane and Arthur's little house, there to wait for their children to arrive, to be a dependent till she dwindled to nothing more than a dependent devoted auntie. For she had no finances and no parents, and her birth placed her too high for Kendal's sheep farmers to aspire to, and her dowry too low for anyone higher. Most of Arthur's merchant friends were married and even the vicar had a large and hopeful family. No, the duchess was her last chance, she thought, as she sat up straighter and thought frantically of how she could present herself so that she could at last "suit," and wondered why she had so far failed so ignobly.

The coachman could have told her. But she was a lady, so he didn't dare be so cheeky. But when she had loomed up out of the fog to step into his coach, he had, for one moment waxed poetical and thought that in her muted cherry pelisse she had looked like a little robin redbreast come to cheer up London on a dark winter's day. In that moment's lapse of fog, her well-spaced sapphire eyes had twinkled up at him, and he had drunk in her fresh white complexion and noted, with approval, one saucy nose, two delightfully red lips, and a cluster of ebony curls beneath her gray bonnet. He had warmed for one moment, just looking at her.

Her brother-in-law could have told her. All the fellows he knew had tweaked him, from the moment he had married Jane, about the two dashing-looking females he now housed. Jane was well-enough-looking, they had teased, but to have another smashing-looking female under his wing as well was the outside of enough. He had laughed with them, for they meant no harm, but it did give a fellow a sense of well-being to come home to two delightful young women, to be stared at when he promenaded with them, one on either arm, to be waited on after dinner by two attentive and lovely young women. Not that he thought of his sister-in-law in that way, no, that would be most improper. But it was rather a treat to have her around. He would be glad when this job-hunting nonsense was over and she came back to Kendal with him and they could go on just as before, the three of them. As for ever telling Catherine that she was a stunner, that was a thing that just wasn't done. While Jane might tell him that Catherine took no account of her looks at all, that was too much to ask a fellow to believe.

But of all the reasons for her failure in obtaining a position that Catherine tortured herself with, her looks were not brought into account at all. She thought raven tresses were commonplace, and bright blue eyes unexceptional, and her complexion ordinary, and her overall appearance unfortunate. She conceded she was not ill favored, but that was all. For Mama had been a pale and stately blonde, and her half-sister, Jane, had also the fair hair and light hazel eyes that were Catherine's only standard of true feminine beauty. Papa, she remembered from far back in the dim recesses of memory of childhood, had been dark haired and blue eyed. That was well enough for a male, but it was Mama who had been beautiful and feminine and sought after. And Jane, who seemed from her five years' seniority over Catherine to be the most beautiful of females. Catherine thought of many reasons for her failure as the coach proceeded through the streets of London, things that ranged from wearing the wrong sort of gloves to not speaking clearly or standing straight enough, but never once did the thought of simply being too young and too alarmingly lovely enter her mind. No one, after all, had told her so. Except for Mama and Jane, and they were just being kind. And a few scalawags in the streets over the years, and they were just being rowdy.

"This is the last call," Catherine said to Arthur, as she saw him lift the watch out of his pocket again.

"We'll finish up early then," he said, "and go back to the hotel for some tea. Then we'll leave straight away in the morning, and it won't be long before we're all snug at home again."

Catherine winced.

"There is the possibility that this time I might succeed, Arthur." Only a hint of reproachfulness was in her voice, and Arthur missed it altogether.

"Oh, aye. Of course there's that possibility, but it is unlikely. As I said before, some young gently born females have to go out and toil for their livelihoods, and some do get positions. But only after much privation. And then that is only when they are willing to sacrifice some of their, ah, expectations. They get harder, my dear, and they get more worldly-wise. It's just as well that you discovered this for yourself. Now I think it wasn't such a bad idea, this trip. Once you're done with all that air-dreaming, you'll be happier. As you should be, with a devoted sister, and myself of course, to look after you. You will understand how fortunate you really are, and be content to settle down with us."

"I know I am fortunate in you and Jane," Catherine said as she had said so many times before, "and you do know how grateful I am, but Arthur, can't you see, I just wanted to do something for myself and not be only a burden?"

"Burden? Nonsense," Arthur said, warming to his favorite theme and crossing his hands around his stomach, which Catherine knew was calling for sustenance. She had noticed that Arthur, plump to begin with, was adding to his substance at a pace to almost equal that of Jane, who expected their baby in the spring.

"As if family could ever be a burden. When I met your sister, I knew of your closeness and never did I expect anything other than your coming to live with us when we wed. I made that clear to Jane at the outset. I have often wished for a large family—it was one of the sorrows of my life that I was an only child. Family is the backbone of the nation."

Arthur went on, as he had done so often in the past on the virtues of family, while Catherine looked out the window again, seeing the city slowly pass by, trying to make out the shadowy figures that flitted by on the pavements, and hoping that some wildly wonderful thing would come to pass. Perhaps she might turn out to be the image of dowager duchess's long-lost sister, or perhaps the dowager had a little dog who would rush to her and the dowager would cry, "If FiFi likes you, the matter is settled. You must come to work at once." Or perhaps the dowager would be a sweet little old woman who would offer her tea and say, "I know just how difficult this must be for you. I have been looking for some pleasant young woman to keep me company," or then again she might say . . .

"We're here, miss," the coachman called.

Catherine felt her hands turn to ice. And her heart began a faster beat.

"Arthur. I won't be long. But if I'm delayed, there's no need for you to sit here freezing in the coach. Why don't you go back to the hotel, and I'll take another hackney back and meet you when I'm done."

"Nonsense," Arthur said staunchly, with an air of seeing things through, as she knew he would. "I'll wait right here.

Can't have a young female on the loose alone in London. I'll wait right here. After all, it's your last call.''

Catherine shivered at his words and stepped out to the pavement and stared at the imposing entrance of the house before her. The fog had lifted for a moment, making the entrance of gleaming white steps dramatically clear. Catherine swallowed, only to find she had nothing to swallow, and began to walk toward the steps with much the same gait of someone preparing to mount a gallows. Her gaze was so fixed on the door above the street level, the door with the beautiful fanlight glasswork, the door that might either open onto a new future for her, or onto the end to her hopes of independence, that she almost collided with a pair of gentlemen who emerged suddenly from out of a bank of fog.

"My pardons, miss," said the closer of the two gentlemen, and after a look at her face, he went on more fulsomely, "a hundred pardons. It's this confounded fog. One moment the way is clear, the next I've almost run you down. Are you all right?"

As he had not even brushed against her, Catherine could only reply distractedly, "Why yes, quite all right."

But the gentleman, dressed, Catherine noted absently, in the first stare of fashion, only stood and gazed at her, bemused.

A deeper voice intruded.

"Cyril, the lady is fine. I suggest we move on so that she can reach her destination."

Catherine peered up to the speaker, who was so very tall that the fog, in a show of frivolity, shrouded his face as it might a mountain peak. He was dressed in unobtrusive grays that further blended with the day.

"But, Sinjun," the other gentleman protested, "I might have done her an injury. Or frightened her, looming up like that, out of the fog. Are you sure you're unharmed, miss?"

"Quite sure," Catherine answered, suspicious of the gentleman's inclinations to linger, and wondering if Arthur was watching this incident through the coach window. He might get it into his head that she was being molested and spring from the coach and make a scene, and if the duchess heard the altercation, her interview would be over before it began.

Seeking to end the conversation promptly, and yet not be rude, for these gentlemen might be friends of the duchess, Catherine asked the taller of the two, whom she could not see so well, rather than the shorter, who was staring at her in the most improper fashion, "Is this the Duchess of Crewe's address? In the fog," she temporized, "I cannot be sure."

"Oh yes," the taller gentleman answered in an amused tone, "to be sure it is. Never fear, you have come to the right place."

There was that in his voice, that undercurrent of sarcasm, that made Catherine look at him again. The mist, bored with veiling his face, drifted away, and she found herself looking into a pair of icy gray eyes that seemed as if they still held the depths of the fog in them. He was very handsome, Catherine thought with alarm, lowering her eyes from his frank stare, and very insolent.

As she turned to mount the steps, she heard him say again with amused cynicism, "You have come to exactly the right place, I believe."

"Good day," Catherine said firmly, sure that in some strange way she was being insulted and knowing one did not bandy words with strange men, friends of the duchess or not. She went up the stairs, lifted the door knocker, and rapped more firmly than she would have wanted to, in an effort to escape the two men's attention. But when she turned to look down again at he street, she could only see their shapes receding in the distance.

The butler who took her card almost took her breath away with it. He was old, and large, and impeccable. He looked at her with no expression and yet made her feel as though she were standing in her nightdress. "Yes," he said after he glanced at her card, "come this way." Without further comment he led her into the largest hall she had ever seen. It was floored with marble, and lined with spindly chairs. And each chair held a woman, sitting erect, each with a reticule, and a packet of letters on each lap.

"Oh," Catherine sighed to herself, her spirits sinking further than she had thought possible, for it seemed that every unemployed lady's companion in the kingdom was there waiting to be interviewed, before her.

By the time the clock at the end of the hall had discreetly chimed four times, Catherine had gotten sufficient control of herself to observe the other females in the hall. She had a moment's fleeting thought for Arthur, sitting chilled in the carriage outside, waiting, but she could no more have left than she could have asked the butler to dance. She was here now, she reasoned, and she would see it to the end.

There were twenty-three other females in the hall. Each one studiously ignored the other. Some stared into space. Some busied themselves with bits of needlework and some were browsing through small volumes that they had brought with them. They were representative, Catherine thought with sorrow, of the entire spectrum of women companions. There were some who were elderly and looked like timorous spinsters. Some were motherly-looking women, large in their persons and almost dowdily dressed. One or two were elegant-looking middle-aged females, who looked as though they themselves might be advertising for companions. There was one huge muscular woman who might have easily belonged behind a barrow, hawking turnips. Catherine wondered if she might drop a hint about the elderly Mrs. Oliphant's search for a companion, for that woman looked as though she might be able to turn both her and her daughter in bed without a thought. But the women all sat silently, and she could no more speak to the female beside her than she could have whispered in church. None of the women looked happy, and all, she thought, wondering if there were some truth to Arthur's lectures, looked downtrodden in some fashion. Worst of all was the realization that she alone was under middle age.

Miss Parkinson, Catherine thought frantically, would not have sent her if she felt she would have no chance. It was true that she had looked at Catherine and whispered, "Oh, dear. You are not at all what I expected from your letters." But when Catherine had explained her mission, and convinced her that she had nursed her own late mother through her final illness, Miss Parkinson had said, filling out the cards, "Might as well have a try at it. But," she had cautioned, "a lady's companion is not an easy life, child."

Looking at her fellow applicants, Catherine could well believe that. They all seemed resigned to their waiting, to their very lives.

After the butler had admitted two more prospective companions and seated them, he reappeared.

"The duchess," he intoned, "is ready to begin her interviews." And he motioned for the woman closest to a door at the end of the hall to come with him. She was a spry wiry woman with spectacles. With ill-concealed eagerness, she closed the book she was reading and sprang up to follow him. After a few minutes, in which Catherine had only time to smooth out two of her gloved fingers, the little woman reappeared. She seemed confused and walked the gamut between the outer circle of applicants and disappeared out the front door. "Obviously," muttered a hawk-faced woman in black bombazine, "inferior references."

The next woman to be called, a heavyset elderly woman, left the room after what seemed like moments, looking puzzled. And after that the succeeding applicant stalked out angrily after what could only have been a moment, muttering, "She's mad." The remaining women began to mutter among themselves. One by one the applicants disappeared, only to reappear after an indecently short time.

"She could be deranged," whispered a timid-looking woman sitting near Catherine. "But then," she added with a smug little smile, "my last was quite gone in the head and I stayed with the poor soul until the end."

"I," said one of the elegant women, "shall not work with a mad person. An eccentric perhaps, as my last dear lady was an eccentric, but charming withal. But not a raving lunatic."

One by one the others were shuffled in and out so quickly that Catherine doubted they had the time to present their credentials at all. The duchess, she reasoned, must be relying very heavily upon first impressions. And when the muscular woman went in, and returned so quickly that she must not have had time to have said a single word, Catherine was convinced of it. As she sat and watched, it seemed that only the two more stylish-looking applicants were given time for any decent conversation in their interviews. And yet the last one left very angrily, stating firmly to those who remained, "You are all wasting your time; this whole interview is a farce." And then Catherine was called.

Remembering to remain calm at all costs, Catherine walked slowly across the room in the wake of the butler. He opened a door, and Catherine found herself within a room facing the duchess.

She must be a duchess, Catherine thought dazedly, for I should know her for a duchess anywhere.

The room was small, but richly furnished. It had been the duke's study at one time, and it still had a very masculine air. The duchess stood ramrod straight in back of a huge mirror-polished walnut desk. She stared at Catherine. And Catherine, bereft of speech, could only stare back. The duchess was tall, and thin, and very old. Her hair was white, not the commonplace snowy

white of most elderly persons Catherine had met. It was rather
the color of ice, as were the two direct cold eyes that fastened
upon Catherine. The duchess had a great long imposing nose and
gaunt slightly rouged cheeks. She wore a gray dress and was
altogether the most imposing, imperious woman Catherine had
ever seen. She looked almost as though the title "duchess" was
too insignificant for her; rather, Catherine thought, she should be
addressed as "Your Highness."

"Well," the duchess brayed in a loud nasal voice, quite
shattering the image, "now this is more like it. How did a
poppet like you get in? Who are you, my gel?"

Catherine fumbled her papers out and laid them carefully on
the desk. "Catherine Robins, Your Grace," she said in a low
voice.

"Speak up," the duchess commanded. "If you want to companion me, you must be more forthcoming. Why does a young
thing like you want to be companion to an old woman?"

"I need to find a position, ma'am," Catherine said, in a
clearer voice.

"And how does your family feel about it? Got any family?"

"I have a sister—well, actually a half-sister and a brother-in-
law—in Kendal, ma'am. He, my brother-in-law, does not want
me to go, but my sister does approve—that is, of my desire for
independence." Lord, Catherine thought, I'm making a muddle
of this.

"Can't blame your brother-in-law, he must feel like a fox in a
hen house. Can't blame your sister neither for wanting a good-
looking baggage like yourself out of harm's way." The duchess
chortled.

Catherine wondered whether she should hotly defend Arthur
or Jane or herself, but the duchess was actually smiling benignly
at her now, and she wanted the position so badly she let the
comment pass.

"Tell me, my gel," the duchess asked, unbending enough to
sit, and motioning that Catherine do the same, "got any
experience?"

"Here are my references, ma'am," Catherine said, spreading
out the papers. "From the vicar, and the schoolmaster, and the
others from my home—"

"Not those," the duchess cut her off. "I mean, any experience of life?"

"Well, yes, ma'am," Catherine faltered, not knowing quite what the duchess was getting at.

"You'd travel with me," the duchess went on. "I travel a good bit. I meet a lot of people, all kinds of people—you ain't a shy one, are you?"

"Not at all," Catherine replied, for in truth, she was not a shy person.

"Not frightened of men, are you? Or prudish? I can't stand a prude."

"Not at all," Catherine replied, thinking she was more frightened by the duchess than by any man she had ever met.

"Didn't think you were with a saucy face like yours. So you've come to London to see the queen, eh? And hope to be my companion. Well, you're more in the line of what I'm looking for than any of those biddies out there. You have an air of real gentility. Related to anybody important?"

"My father was a younger son," Catherine said, putting up her chin. "And we were related to the Earl of Dorset."

"Then what are you doing out looking for a position as lady's companion?" the duchess cried out ringingly, looking angry and affronted for no reason Catherine could fathom.

"We never corresponded with the family much after my father's death," Catherine admitted, "and not at all after my mother's remarriage, which they did not approve of."

"Black sheep? Better and better." The duchess smiled.

"What would your family think of you flying across the Continent with me, meeting all sorts of people?" she challenged.

"As I said," Catherine went on, "there's only my sister and brother-in-law, and they want only what would make me happy."

"So they're cutting line from you? Don't blame them. What I'm saying, with no more roundabout," the duchess said, leaning over and looking keenly at Catherine, and cutting off her indignant reply, "is, are you free and footloose? Are you ready for a lark?"

"Yes," Catherine said, wondering why a companion would find life a lark, but feeling that if any came along she'd be quite ready.

"Get up," the duchess suddenly barked, and, startled, Catherine did so.

"Turn, no, turn that way. You are a good-looking gel in any light," the duchess said impassively. "But I'll bet you've been told that by the gentlemen before."

"No, of course not," Catherine protested, totally at sea, and wondering if the duchess were in fact, a little deranged.

"Haw. You're a good little actress. Sit down," the duchess said, "and I'll put the proposition to you. You can let down your hair now and be frank. Your job would be to travel with me and to accompany me on my rounds. And to make sure I'm comfortable. I have a lot of friends. A lot of gentlemen friends, and I'd expect you to make them comfortable too, in a different way. You get my meaning?"

Catherine didn't at first. The first meaning she thought of was clearly preposterous and she was ashamed of herself for even thinking it. But she certainly was conversable and tactful enough to chat up any old gentlemen the duchess entertained to put them at their ease. So she nodded, so many thoughts crossing her mind that she was momentarily speechless.

"Good." The duchess sighed. "I thought I was right about you. My usual companion, Rose, the lazy slut, has gone off and left me. And Violet, who sometimes travels with me, has gone and got herself another position. So I'm left in the lurch and I'm off to Paris in a month and demned if I'll go alone or with any of those old crows out there. So, gel, you understand?"

"Paris?" breathed Catherine, unable to take in her good luck. Was she being offered the position, in Paris?

"But let us get it clear. I travel in a fast set. You are very young. Perhaps you haven't understood. Are you worried about what people will say of your reputation?"

Catherine had the giddy instant thought of a group of old gentlemen and ladies being pushed rapidly in their invalid chairs or gambling wildly in their nightcaps while their attendants and nurses stood waiting to take them home to bed.

"My reputation?" Catherine thought quickly, searching for a precise answer that would satisfy the duchess as to her maturity and independence and put an end to this odd interview and perhaps win her the position she so desperately wanted. "My reputation," she said loftily, "is my own concern."

Seeing the wide grin on the duchess's face, she hastily added, "That is to say, it is excellent. It is widely known."

"All the better." The duchess beamed. "Fine then, gel, you've got the position."

Catherine was so dizzy with happiness that she could only sit and stare at the duchess, who was smiling at her in the most conspiratorial, friendly way possible.

*   *   *

In a study very similar to the one that Catherine and the duchess sat in, one, moreover, only three doors down the street, two gentlemen sat in front of a cozy fire and smiled at each other in a conspiratorial, friendly way.

"Sinjun," cried the younger one, waving a brimful brandy snifter at his friend, "a toast to the luckiest of chaps. I swear you are. Did you see the eyes on that filly? Blue as a summer sky. And moving in here right under your nose. All I have on my street are retired army gentlemen, and Sir Howard with two of the ugliest daughters known to mankind. And you've got the dowager and her lovelies right on your doorstep."

"I've also," drawled the taller man, putting down the papers he held, "got all this work you've brought me. And if I've read it right, it means I have some traveling to do."

"But not immediately, dear fellow. You've time to set things up. We don't expect you to hop off immediately. And in the meantime, what a lovely diversion you've got right here. 'Is this the Duchess of Crewe's address?' she says. Why, that means she's practically under your roof already. You just have to nip down the street and collect her."

"I don't," the taller man said, stretching out his long legs, "traffic with the duchess's companions."

"But in her case, you could make an exception, Sinjun. She's a stunner, and new on the town too."

"If she's in the duchess's employ, I doubt it. At any rate, Cyril, I seldom pay for what should be free."

"Oh, I didn't know you were purse pinched," the younger man laughed. "That'll be news to La Starr. How did you acquire that new bracelet she was sporting last week, for nothing?"

"I don't pay cash on the line." The taller man smiled. "Because I don't like to stand in line, and the dowager's doxies traffic in volume, as you know."

"What a lost opportunity for you then," Cyril mourned. "Still, a toast! To the fairest wenches in London, to the dowager's doxies."

"I think not," his companion demurred.

"Then one to the old lady herself: to the dirty dowager."

"No," his friend said gently.

"Then curse it, Sinjun, you propose a toast. I'm desperate for a sip of this '94."

"Very well." The taller man took his glass in hand and intoned, "A toast: to work." And he handed the papers to his friend. Cyril groaned. "To work," he sighed, and dashing down the drink, he bent over the papers.

Chapter II

The Dowager Duchess of Crewe sat back in her late husband's favorite chair and waved her butler away. She lifted the glass of port that he had brought her and raised it in a silent salute before she allowed herself a sip of it. And then, alone in the study, she leaned back in her chair and sat, eyes closed, smiling to herself. Even in repose she retained her air of dignity and power. Even while relaxing she maintained her rigidly imposing countenance. With her gleaming white hair pulled back to show her strong features, seated behind the massive gleaming desk, she presented the perfect picture of a woman of consequence, a rich stone in an exquisite setting. She was a fine figure of a woman. It had not always been so.

For all women, and men as well, there is one point in life when they are beautiful, truly beautiful. There are some rare fortunate few who retain beauty all through life. But for most, they must make do with that one moment of physical beauty. And no matter how ill favored, every person experiences that moment. Nature is kind in that fashion, but she is unpredictable.

Thus, when the midwife cries in delight, "It is a girl, and a perfect, beautiful girl!" there are times when that is strictly true. At that moment, never to be repeated, the baby is indeed one of the most beautiful infants ever seen. For others, their summit of physical perfection comes in the toddler years. Still others are graceful, beautiful children and visitors will often comment, "She is a beautiful child; she'll be a real heartbreaker when she's grown." Alas, that is often not true. For that particular child the epitome of beauty may exist only in that one afternoon of childhood. Later the snub nose may lengthen, the plump jaw grow rather like a lantern, the bright hair dim, and the glowing promise never be realized. For her, the moment came and passed in early childhood.

Still others are the envy of all their acquaintances in the years of early youth. For one brief incandescent time, the girl is lovely. But it is only for that time, never to be repeated. Others do make beautiful brides and the assembled wedding guests may swear they have never seen a lovelier bride and not perjure themselves. Yet, let as little as a few weeks go by and the vision is gone. Some are beautiful in the months of impending maternity, some as young mothers have an unearthly radiance that rivals religious paintings, some reach a glowing peak of ripened beauty in their middle years. For all, if they but live long enough, the moment will surely come. But it did not come for the Duchess of Crewe for almost seventy long and barren years.

Born as a simple "Mary," fifth child and second daughter of the Earl of Appleby, she was a thin and red-eyed infant. Raised in the shadow of three hearty, boisterous brothers and a jolly older sister, little Mary looked rather like a shadow as a child. She was thin and pale with mouse-hued hair, and where the Appleby nose sat well on her father and brothers' faces, it overshadowed all else on her lean countenance. Sister Belle had mother's impudent nose, and grew to be a buxom, dashing sort of girl. Mary remained thin and gray-faced, although she elongated considerably as she grew and soon towered over both her mother, elder sister, and one of her brothers.

Nature, having given an impeccable lineage, an earl's castle to live in, and an impressive dowry to lure suitors with, did not see fit to overendow her with intelligence, beauty, or personality. Hers was a lonely childhood, but she did not seek refuge in books, as they were too difficult to read, or fantasy, as it was too much trouble to invent, or friendships, as there were too few children up to her weight in status or fortune.

When she reached the age of twenty-four, her father was reminded that he still had one great hulking girl at home who had received no offers even though she had been dutifully togged out and brought to London each season. He was a forthright man and it was a simple matter to remedy. After a hard day's hunting with his old school friend, Algie, Duke of Crewe, it was discovered that Algie had a son who was ready to be shackled into matrimony. At twenty and seven, George was a very eligible parti. He was no vision to set a maiden's heart thumping, being rather squat and square. He had not done too well at school, and his conversation consisted solely of horses and hunting, but he had the right breeding, fortune, and when his father quit this world he would be a duke. At dinner that night, between the buttered crabs and the haunch of venison, the matter was settled to all concerned parties' satisfaction.

At the wedding, the bride was not beautiful. Impending maternity only made the prospective mother ungainly and uncomfortable, and when her first child was born, no unearthly radiance transformed the new mother's face. Nor did it for the second, third, or fourth child. After the fourth heir arrived, duty done to king and country, George, now Duke of Crewe, devoted his amatory attentions solely to his amiable mistress in town, to his own, and his wife's, great relief.

Mary, Duchess of Crewe, had led a long good life. But something was missing. Some small niggling worm in the apple troubled the Duchess of Crewe obliquely during all those long privileged years. Not being a clever or introspective female, she never examined the problem too closely. But it was there, and it grew as the years went on.

For with all that she had had, she had never had attention, or at least any she had not paid for. No heads ever turned when she entered the room, as they had for jolly Belle. No one ever cried, "We must have Mary to our masquerade, she is such fun!" Rather they remembered that the Duchess of Crewe should be invited. George, while he lived, accepted that she was his wife as he accepted the fact that the title was his from the moment he could toddle. Her children knew that she was Mama, and that she must be visited every day for an hour when Nanny brought them to her. The world knew the Duchess of Crewe, but she was not in demand. For such a large female, she was, withal, seldom noticed.

In the natural way of things, if the duchess had succumbed to a chill in her sixth decade, she would have passed an unexceptional sort of life. The world would have briefly noted her passing and gone on smoothly. But her health was vigorous and two great events changed the course of her life forever when she contemplated her seventh decade.

First, George died, and she noted his absence more than she had ever noted his presence. And secondly, nature at last blessed her with beauty. It was nothing short of miraculous, almost like the transformation of a plain window pane after frost has touched it in the night. For age came to the Duchess of Crewe and brought a great transformation overnight.

It turned her gray-speckled mouse hair to the color of silver. It hollowed her cheeks, turning mere leanness to high imperious cheekbones. At last, her unfortunate nose found a face that it fitted, and, thinned down, it stood high and hawklike, a perfect object for two glittering myopic eyes to peer down over. Her rigid, angular body suited an old woman to perfection: In youth it had been awkward, in her dotage it was imperial. Her height was no longer uncomfortable; it became regal. She had been an unobtrusive woman; she was now an imperial old woman. Nature kept its promise at last.

For the first time, Mary, Duchess of Crewe, excited attention and admiration when she entered a salon. Strangers in the street glanced at her. She was an ornament at the theater. No one ever again forgot her after an introduction. When she appeared, heads turned, and the gentlemen showed her every courtesy. Even the greatest arbiters, the other society matrons, deferred to her. At a great age, the duchess suddenly discovered all the unfair advantages of physical beauty. But equally suddenly, it was not enough.

Much as a born actor after his first taste of applause, the duchess discovered the one ingredient that had been missing in her flavorless life: attention. And as much as she received, it was not enough.

It was only an unsatisfactory brief shower, falling after a long parched life. She wanted more than a taste of it. Now, at a time when many of her contemporaries were content to settle back and watch others live their lives, she wanted to begin hers. She wanted to bask in that rare and lucent light that had always eluded her, the full glare of public attention. But there were impediments.

She was aged, she was female, and she was alone. Her children had all grown, married, and presented her with batches of uninteresting descendants. She could not look to them. She had few friends, and no close ones. And none of them could have given her what she wanted.

She was done with tea parties and tame entertainments. She sought glory. It hardly seemed fair or just that now that she had been presented with a new face and a new aspect, she should languish in obscurity. She felt as a young girl might when her body ripened to a woman's, that there was an attractive stranger within her that she must introduce to the world.

She had heard of the sort of life one could lead if one were wealthy, titled, and attractive. She had heard of, but never seen, the gambling establishments, the fast parties, the masquerades and travel adventures of those select few who cared for nought but pleasure and excitement. And knew that as a duchess she could have entrée to any of them, once. But that there would have to be something special about her to permit her constant presence.

It was a set, she had heard, made up of the cream of the gifted: the poets, the musicians, the authors, the intellectual, the beautiful, and the amusing wealthy eccentrics. She had now presence, beauty of a sort, and wealth. She would have to see to the rest.

Her first companion was a Lady Wiggins, a noble woman who had fallen upon hard times. Together they had traveled to Bath and to Brighton and had received an invitation to a house party at the country seat of a notoriously rakehell lord. All that she had heard was true. She found excitement, gaiety, amusing company, and a sense of privilege. She was accepted, admired, but then, ultimately ignored. For she had no special cachet, no entertaining conversation, no wit, nor even scandalous history.

Her next season, she traveled with Mrs. Coalhouse, a younger woman with pleasant looks and a genteel manner. And although the duchess now cultivated the affectation of taking snuff, and had gone so far as to purchase outrageously expensive antique and imported snuff boxes, this eccentricity was only duly noted and not remarked upon. For in an age where the reigning eccentrics kept upward of a hundred dogs, or traveled without male companions to the Near East, or rode horses into drawing rooms, a handsome elderly female who took snuff was not much noticed. Even her newly emerged forceful personality was not enough.

The following season, in a sort of desperation, she combed carefully through all the applicants for the position of companion. She stopped checking their references and began to note only their physical persons and personalities. For if she could not develop her own startling personality, somewhere in the recesses of her mind she reasoned that she could buy the services of one. Her choice settled on one Miss Violet Peterson, who was nothing like any lady's companion the duchess had ever seen. She was, to the duchess's myopic eye, more like the sort of female who ran the gaming halls and parties she had lately been to.

Violet was young—still in her twenties, the duchess thought, although a clearer eye could have said thirties with more certainty. She was buxom, and red haired, and staggeringly attractive. Her dresses were all slightly too extravagant: a bit too low, a bit too colorful, a bit too embellished. But she was bright and alert and cheerful as a songbird. Men's heads swiveled when she flounced into the room. She was, the duchess thought, sometimes a bit too cheeky, but there was no harm in the girl, no harm at all. If it came to that, she was good company, even though it was not company the duchess was after, but the admiration of company.

It was during that first season with Violet, at the country home of a notoriously dissolute duke, that the first whispers about Violet came to the duchess's ears. The whispers grew louder at Brighton, and by the time they got to the scandalous Lady Chester's country retreat, they were a roar. One late evening at the faro table, a noted gossip, a beau of the ton, eyed Violet as she left the room a few moments after their hostess's husband had signaled to her and he leaned over to the duchess. "I say," he said in a loud stage whisper, "did you know that your companion has spent more time between our host's sheets than her own? And for a price higher than the stakes we're competing for?"

Two high red spots appeared on the duchess's cheekbones. All the others at the table were pointedly looking elsewhere, but all were listening. If her sensibilities were offended, the duchess knew it would be social death in this room to admit to it. She decided to brazen it out, and, in a somewhat confused state of agitation, referred instead to what she felt were Violet's good qualities.

"Let the gel be," she said in stentorian tones. "She gives good service. Worth every penny she asks."

The duchess was a raging success after that. She and Violet were welcome to every affair they wanted to attend. If they were not welcome at the sort of parties and houses that the duchess was used to frequent during her long years of social correctness, well, she had put all that behind her now anyway. Attention was paid to the pair of them wherever they went. The duchess, through no overt act of her own, was now considered an amusing, clever, and charming eccentric. She even had the felicity to overhear society's pet bad girl of the season whisper to her cicisbeo, "There goes the Duchess of Crewe. Isn't she delicious? So dignified, so correct, such presence, such wit, to have a common trollop as companion. Plying her trade in the best houses. Oh, it's such a clever comment on society."

So the duchess turned a deaf ear to propriety, and only cautioned Violet not to get above herself or to involve her employer in any of her doings, and to fulfill her duties as companion before she set off on any "larks" of her own. And Violet, who had been, in her turn, actress, opera dancer, kept woman, and then, only in dire financial trouble and fear of turning to the streets, desperate enough to try for the position of lady's companion, was all too eager to agree.

After another season with Violet in tow, Rose came along. Claiming long friendship with Violet, Rose begged for any position in the duchess's household. The bailiffs were at her door, Lord Lawrence had withdrawn his protection, and she, at thirty-three, was too long in the tooth for any more ingenue roles in the theater. Rose was blond and billowy and friendly, and within months the duchess had two female companions in tow. And her reputation was assured.

Polite society might shun her, her children might plead impotently, but she had a title of her own, and money of her own, and a tenacity of character that only the none too intelligent might claim. It was possible, her children's lawyer said patiently, that they might, after a scandalous, arduous court battle, proclaim her incompetent, but again, it was possible that they might not. The dowager went her way unmolested to all the resorts and masquerades and parties she desired, and she desired them all for all the attention she had starved for all those unawakened years.

And if she heard the whispers about "the duchess's doxies," as the satirists were quick to dub her companions, she pretended not to hear. The contrast between her rigid aspect and her companions' life-styles tickled those she sought to impress all the more. And if she saw the caricatures in the shop windows of "the dirty duchess," she was careful not to recognize their subject. Her dignity in the face of such vilification was an exquisite delight to her champions. Yet, all the while, in some recess of her mind, she took it as tribute. There was the distinct possibility that if her children had not been so browbeaten and afraid of scandal, they might have won their case.

And now in this chill winter of 1814, she had narrowly escaped missing another promised treat. For Violet, that wench, had only just sent notice she wasn't coming to Paris as she had netted the Marquis of Wolverton's protection. And Rose, that simple ingrate, had come and prated on about true love and the reformed gambler with whom she was going to settle down.

Even the Duchess of Crewe could not advertise for a trollop. And she had no notion of how to go about acquiring one as companion. One couldn't just pick a girl off the streets. And she could not very easily ask her butler or a footman to frequent a house of ill repute and choose any stray female. And she certainly could not be seen going to one herself. She never chose to think of exactly how her companions earned their extra keep. The whole thought of what transpired at those houses made her ill. So she had cast her net again, asking employment bureaus for a companion and hoping to luck upon, by accident, another woman like Violet, in the same way that she had gotten Violet, through the applicant's own bold deceit.

For three days she had interviewed women of all classes and sizes and condition. To some that she had felt were marginally suitable she had hinted at her purpose and their duties. Those who had understood had left in a huff, or stared at her blankly, apologized, and left. But then this lovely little wench, Catherine, had appeared. As pretty as, or prettier than, the selfish ungrateful Rose and Violet, and not so long in the tooth either, the duchess thought. And she seemed ready for any rig that might be running. The duchess finished off her port and rose to stare out the window. There was a great deal to get done. Travel arrangements to make, dresses to buy, reservations to plan ahead. But her major concern was settled. She had another companion. One who would really make them stare in Paris. And give her employer an international reputation.

After the coach had left them at the hotel, Catherine and Arthur spent the next two hours in a corner of the lobby, in hot debate. She was weary and excited, and would have loved to have been somewhere more private and comfortable. But Arthur was shocked at the idea of discussing anything in their rooms. She might be his sister-in-law, she might have lived in his house for almost four years, but she was a single woman. And he was a man not related by blood. Arthur had very exact notions of propriety.

He refused to postpone their discussion till dinner, for he knew that heated conversation was bad for the digestion. So they sat at a little corner table, beneath a very sick potted palm, and spoke in hushed, but agitated tones.

"She is a duchess, Arthur," Catherine insisted again, "and very dignified. And if she wants a young companion, I am sure that it is so that she may be cheered up a bit."

"I still," he said, as he had said for the past hour, "do not think it a good idea. You do not know her, or her family, or the conditions under which you will be employed."

"Arthur," Catherine cried loudly, and then ducked down and flushed for she had not wanted to raise her voice, "you knew all that when I first went to apply for the post. And yet you took me anyhow."

Arthur flushed a little himself and, because he was by nature not a devious man, admitted, "I just thought that it would help you get the whole mad notion out of your system."

"You didn't expect me to get the post!" Catherine accused.

"No, I didn't, and to tell the entire truth I still don't know why you did. One"—and here Arthur raised his plump fingers—"you haven't the experience. Two: You are far too young to companion a dowager in her dotage. Three: No matter how well born you are, you have never had traffic with the nobility. Why hasn't a duchess a whole slew of acquaintances and relatives who could recommend a companion to her?"

Seeing the momentary hit he had made, Arthur went on, "Four: You don't know London. And Five: It is dangerous to travel abroad to Paris, even if Napoleon is mewed up on Elba now and the hostilities have ceased, with a female whom you and your family do not know."

"One," said Catherine in a hot whisper, "she doesn't care about work experience. Two: I am twenty-one, old enough to be able to be good company for any female. Three—oh, dash it, Arthur, I do want this post. She is a duchess and wealthy so I won't suffer any privation; truly, I can't see how I would. And perhaps it is just that she is lonely. And, after all, dear Arthur, it won't be forever. She said just for the season, to see how we will suit. It is October now; by summer I should be home again. And if I am not happy with her, I shall come home to you and Jane and the baby, and be a good devoted auntie and never stray again. Only I'll have earned the wages to buy the baby a present all on my own, at last. That is, if you will have me back?"

Arthur patted her hand in embarrassment. She looked so woebegone. Her bright blue eyes were brighter with unshed tears, and a little crease had appeared on her white forehead. He felt like a beast.

"Of course, we'll have you back. We want you back so much we don't want to see you go." He laughed, and she laughed with him at his unfamiliar excursion into humor.

"But I do worry about you. You are such a bright girl, Catherine, but you haven't any experience of the world. I worry about you over there across the channel with a strange female in charge of your destiny."

"Oh I make no doubt," Catherine laughed, "that she will sell me into bondage, and have me locked into a dank rat-ridden cell if I don't do her bidding. Arthur, do understand, it's not that I love you and Jane less that I wish to be independent; it's that I love you the more."

"But if you feel that way, no matter what we say, why come so far, to London, to be a menial? Why not contemplate marriage? You are a fine-looking girl, Catherine." Arthur was a little shocked by his presumption, but he was earnestly trying to counsel her, and was casting all inhibition to the winds.

"Oh, I do contemplate it," Catherine said ruefully, creasing her gamine face into a parody of sorrow and causing Arthur to chuckle. "But who is there to contemplate me? With all of two shillings as dowry. Arthur, there is no one for me at home. Perhaps there might be someone for me in London, or Paris."

"Your head's been turned by those two dandies I saw you asking the duchess's direction of when you got out of the coach," Arthur accused.

"No," she said, "they were way above my touch. And one doesn't meet one's future husband in the street."

She rose and shook out her skirt.

"Now, Arthur, shall we cry off this battle? You know, and I know, that the thing is done. Or are you trying to starve me into submission? I haven't eaten in so long, I shall forget whether to use a fork or my fingers. Come, let's have a lovely reconciliation over dinner."

Arthur sighed and rose, conceding defeat, and heeding the insistent clamor his stomach had been setting up for past hours.

They sat in the hotel's dining area and chatted amiably through all the courses. And by the time evening came Arthur bade Catherine good night at her door without one further premonition of doom about her future employment.

In the morning they breakfasted in solemn silence, and then

Arthur collected his bags and Catherine's. She wanted to accompany him to the stage to say good-bye, but he insisted on loading her case into the hackney to drop her off first. "You must never go unaccompanied, Catherine," he said sternly. "You must write us your address in Paris," he cautioned, "and be quick to come home immediately if anything goes awry."

It was a bright morning, and the hackney found the duchess's house with no trouble. As Catherine made to leave, Arthur stayed her. "Here," he said gruffly, reaching into his pocket, "no young woman should go without funds," and he pressed a small purse filled with coins into her hand.

"But I shall be earning money," she said, returning the purse. Then she bent swiftly and pressed a quick kiss on Arthur's cheek, which made him color up. "I do love you and Jane," she said in a shaky voice. "And I do thank you for all your concern."

And then quickly, before she should embarrass herself and Arthur again, she stepped out of the coach. Her trunk was handed down to her, and she stood on the curb, in front of her new home, and waved farewell to Arthur. The last look she had of him was of his worried face at the window.

Then she turned and went to mount the stairs to the Duchess of Crewe's house. There was no fog this morning and no mysterious gentlemen to unsettle her by saying that it was exactly the right place for her. But it was, and she went up the stairs.

Chapter III

As soon as the maid had left her, Catherine went to the window of her new room. And when she saw that she was safely two floors above the street level, and that there was no way any eyes but pigeons' could peer into her room, she turned and went directly to her bed. And sat there, bouncing up and down, giggling softly to herself just like a child. For if this is what Miss Parkinson had meant about a companion's life being a difficult one, she did not think she could have borne an easy one. The luxury would have flattened her completely.

She had, late in the night, when all of London had lain sleeping, been too afraid and too apprehensive to sleep. For once she had realized the position was indeed truly hers, she had at last the leisure to be anxious about her future and the opportunity to have all the second thoughts Arthur would have wished her to have. It had taken all her courage to be confident and light-hearted when she had taken leave of Arthur.

But once she had presented herself at the door, the butler had signaled to a footman, who invisibly signaled to a maid, and she had been, with no further comment, taken to her new room. And such a room! Catherine thought that no cosseted daughter of an earl could have been housed so extravagantly.

The room was large and airy, with windows overlooking the street. It was furnished with graceful taste in hues of green and white, picked out with pale yellow. After a few minutes of dazed delight, Catherine shook herself mentally and went to the wash pitcher. After only a few seconds of admiring its graceful gold trimmings, she poured water into a bowl and resolutely scrubbed her face and hands. It was time for work. Later she might have

31

earned the leisure to simply sit and admire her room. She braced herself and went downstairs to begin her duties as companion to the Dowager Duchess of Crewe.

All her fine resolve was wasted. The butler informed her impassively that Her Grace was still abed, and, further, that she had left no message for her new companion. So Catherine spent her first full day of gainful employment too wrought up to properly luxuriate in her new quarters. Instead, she paced the room awaiting her employer's summons.

It did not come that day, nor the next, nor even the next. Catherine had time and to spare to memorize every detail of her delightful room. She was informed, each time she asked, that the duchess was variously occupied: at her mantua maker's, with her man of business, or dining out with friends. And, no, she was answered blightingly each time she inquired, there were no shawls to be mended, nor was there any knitting to unravel, nor even letters to copy out. In short, there was nothing for her to do but to wait upon Her Grace's pleasure. The members of the duchess's staff were uniformly polite to Catherine, but all those she encountered as she drifted through the house in search of occupation seemed in some indefinable fashion to look down upon the new female in their midst. Contemptuous, and rightly so, Catherine felt, of a female who was clearly not earning her way.

As the week wore on, Catherine began to wonder why the duchess had bothered to employ a companion at all. And once, in a small hour of the night, she sat straight up in bed in horrified alarm as she wondered whether the duchess was so advanced in years as to have forgotten the existence of her new companion altogether.

However, in the sixth day of her employment, while she was reading through a volume of poetry, Catherine received a summons to be present at her employer's side. She put down the volume with slightly trembling hands, smoothed down her wayward hair, and pinned a smile to her lips. At last, she would begin.

The duchess was sitting up in bed when Catherine was shown into her chamber. Even in bedclothes, she looked imperious and dramatic. She squinted up at Catherine and then motioned her to sit down. She seemed to be consulting a list she had on her lap, along with the dregs of her morning chocolate.

"There you are. Been settling yourself in, gel?" she boomed at Catherine.

"Yes, Your Grace. I have been waiting for your summons, and ready to be of whatever assistance you require."

"Why would I require your assistance here, in my own house?" the duchess asked with amazement. "I have everything I need here. Got Gracie—she's a lady's maid who knows her business." And here Gracie, who'd been picking up about the room, sniffed disdainfully, met Catherine's eye for one bleak moment, and then went back to work. "And that old stick of a butler, Griddon, to see to the running of things, and Mrs. Johnson to order up the house. No, I don't need you yet, gel. Can't keep calling you gel, neither; Robin's the name, ain't it?"

"No, Your Grace. It's Catherine."

"Catherine then. I'm getting all my plans in train for our little jaunt. Paris! It's been years, and now we can go again. Parties and folderol, and good fun. I can't wait. I called you here to see if you're ready."

"I'll be ready to leave whenever you are, ma'am," Catherine said. "At a day's notice."

"A day's notice." The older woman guffawed. "Not likely. Not with what all I've got to get readied. What are you wearing?" she demanded suddenly, staring at Catherine fixedly.

Catherine glimpsed down at herself in horror, wondering whether she'd spilt something on her gown. But no, it was the neat pristine gray one she'd worn the first morning. It had been nearly a week since she'd arrived and she'd worn each of her gowns in succession, so if it was Thursday, it would have to have been her gray.

"It's ghastly," the duchess went on. "Ain't you got something livelier?"

"I do have one gayer frock," Catherine heard herself say, thinking of her simple sprigged tea gown, the prize of her wardrobe, that she kept for visiting at home, and that she had worn to a house party with much favorable comment.

"It won't do. I don't know what your game is, and I don't care. Maybe there's some that like a gel that looks like a nun, maybe there's a few that will find it amusing, but it won't do. You've got to dress with some dash. I can't have a little mouse, no matter how saucy a mouse, trailing through Europe with me. You've got to be togged out right."

Catherine thought with panic of how she could dress up her meager wardrobe with dash, for in truth, she realized, a companion couldn't look shabby. Although her dress was considered proper by Kendal standards, this was, after all, London.

"Good thing I took a good look," the dowager grumbled. "Get me my paper, and some ink, and a pen, gel."

Catherine hastened to obey the duchess's command, and brought her writing implements from her inlaid desk. The dowager mumbled to herself as she scrawled a note, pushing aside coffee cups and napery as she did so.

"There, good as gold. Go to Madame Bertrand, she's the one Violet used to go to, and she looked fine as fivepence. Even Rose gave up her modiste when she saw what an eyeful Violet looked when Madame Bertrand got through with her. She'll set you up."

"But," Catherine protested, accepting the note the dowager thrust at her, "I haven't received wages as yet, and I don't think I can order a new gown as yet."

"I'll stand the nonsense, gel, and I don't want you ordering one gown. Give me that note back. I thought you was up to the mark. Why did that demned Rose have to go and get herself tied up?" the duchess complained as she scrawled another line on the bottom of her note. "Go out today and get yourself suited up in style. Got looks, but no style."

The maid who suffered to accompany Catherine to Madame Bertrand's sat opposite her and looked everywhere but at her. She was a plump downstairs maid, and found getting into the carriage a treat, and had even vouchsafed as much to Catherine. But when Catherine had agreed eagerly, and tried to begin a lively conversation, the girl had recalled herself and shrunk back into silence. The duchess, Catherine thought, must be a high stickler for the social order of her servants.

They rode in stately silence through the streets of town till the coach stopped in front of a plain shop window on one of the busier business streets. One dress was artfully arranged in the window, and a great deal of drapery covered up the rest of it. But as there was no name or even number visible, Catherine hesitated to alight. The coachman, a jolly-looking young freckled fellow, held the horses and sent a footman to lower the steps.

"You're here," he said, leaning down and looking into the coach, and giving the downstairs maid a ferocious wink. She colored up and pursed her lips and looked expectantly at Catherine, so that Catherine had no choice but to dismount.

Opening the door to the modiste's establishment was like

opening the door onto a new reality. Whereas the outside of the shop might have been discreet to the point of plainness, the interior reminded Catherine of what she had always imagined a harem to look like. There was a quantity of rich fabric tossed about a large carpeted room. Several couches and divans and chairs stood at odd angles everywhere. Bolts of scarlet velvet, royal blue gossamer, and shining emerald silks lay opened and half opened, spread out for display over all unoccupied surfaces.

There were a few women dressed in dazzling style peering at the bolts of fabric, and, to Catherine's surprise, there were also a few fashionably dressed men lounging or sitting and gazing at the women and each other through quizzing glasses. There was a low babble of talk as she entered, and, to her chagrin, the conversation seemed to come to an abrupt stop as she stepped into the shop. Both the women and the men, Catherine realized, were staring at her with undisguised curiosity.

She held her head high and motioned the maid to sit, and when a small black-eyed woman approached, wearing a quantity of measuring tapes about her neck, as if they were a priceless necklace, Catherine held out the duchess's note.

"I am Catherine Robins, the Duchess of Crewe's companion. She sent me here to purchase some gowns."

There was stifled laughter from somewhere to Catherine's left, and the other occupants of the room began talking again, some, however, still staring at her fixedly.

"Right," said the little woman smartly. "She says you're going to Paris. You're dressed for a convent now. Come along, I'll take things in hand."

She led Catherine, who was trying to hold her head high and ignore the attention she had caused, to the back of her shop. There, in another room, were several tables, each with a row of girls stitching. She walked past them and took Catherine to one of a few curtained partitioned stalls. As Catherine stood undecided as to what she should do next, one of the curtains billowed and a ravishing-looking woman stepped forth. She was tall and statuesque. Her hair, great golden masses of it, had come loose with her dressing, and she swung her hips slowly as she stepped up on a little dais in front of a mirror in the center of the room. Her heavily lidded eyes lit up with satisfaction as she caught her reflection.

"Perfect," she breathed.

Catherine stood transfixed. She had never seen a gown so low

in the front that most of its occupant's person seemed to threaten
to spill out at any moment. The fabric above the high waist
seemed sufficient for a waistband, and the magnificent creature
in the gown surely needed three times that much before she
could go out in public. Still, she had to admit that the startling
vibrant blue color and the extreme cut of the gown made the
woman in it an unforgettably vivid picture.

"He'll be pleased," the woman said and smiled at herself in
the mirror. "But I want him to see me in the amber, so he'll
come across for that one." And, without further ado, the
sensational-looking female reached behind her, unbuttoned a few
buttons, and quickly slipped out a few pins. Then with a shrug,
she stepped out of the gown, leaving her entire person, Catherine
noted with shock, nude from the waistline up, and only wearing
a gossamer-thin demi-train below.

Catherine gaped. She had seen her sister nude, of course, on
rare occasions when they were growing up. And seen herself,
when she was undressing. But this female was as unaware of her
nudity in front of strangers, even though they were all female, as
a child might be. Although, she thought quickly, as she watched
the woman's eyes linger lovingly on her own reflection, she was
not quite unaware of herself after all. And there was nothing
childish in her expression of self-satisfaction. She swept past
Catherine into her cubicle agian. "Bring the amber one quickly,"
she ordered. "He grows bored quickly."

The middle-aged woman looked at Catherine impatiently.
"Come along," she said. "Let's have a look at you without that
nun's habit on. Come along, strip it off and I'll be back to have a
look-see. La Starr's in a taking, and I have to get her amber
gown sent to if she's to get it from her gentleman today."

Left alone, Catherine hurriedly removed her dress. She held
her discarded gown in front of her chest as she waited, chilled,
for the dressmaker to return. There was a small mirror in the
little alcove, she noted, and she realized that the other female
could just as easily have seen herself there in privacy, without
swaggering out to display herself in front of strangers.

As she waited she could hear the voices of a few other women
admiring their gowns or calling for changes in them. None spoke
in the accents she thought acceptable for a lady. Bored, and
feeling cold, she watched her reflection in the mirror. Her black
hair had come loose from its pins again, and there was a high
flush along her cheekbones. On an impulse, seeing her reflection

clutching her gray gown in front of her, and hearing no one approaching, she lowered the gown from in front of herself. She gazed at the reflection guiltily. Hers, she thought aimlessly, were higher and a better shape than the other females'. And then, scandalized by her train of thought, she whipped the gown in front of her again and held it in a death grip.

"Let's have a look," the dressmaker said, bustling into the alcove with her. "Take that gray rag away; I can't see through it."

Catherine lowered the gown again, shrinking with embarrassment.

"Right," the little woman said briskly. "You're a knockout all right. The dowager's grown some taste, leave it to her. I know just the things that'll do. Almost the lady, that's the ticket," she muttered to herself, and left again.

"I can't," Catherine cried out, fifteen minutes later, as the dressmaker told her to turn around. "I can't possibly appear like this in public. I am a companion, not an actress. This gown is lovely, but it is not seemly." She had been resigned to the duchess providing her with a new wardrobe; after all, one's employer had the right to dictate in matters of an employee's garb. But this gown and the others that the dressmaker had shown her were out of the question. At the dressmaker's brisk insistence, she had allowed herself to be pinned into it, but she knew it was entirely unsuitable in the dressing room, and now, in front of the mirror, in front of the other girls at their sewing, she knew it was impossible.

It was of a rich and ruby red, and it was so low in front that even her spanned hand could not cover the naked expanse it showed. Looking down, she could clearly see her breasts as they appeared to her when she was in her bath. The reflection showed little less. The waist was high and its folds clung and draped about her lower person so that she seemed to have been mired in some rich red sea kelp that outlined all her lower body. Her hair, untidy from changing so often, had loosened and curled. The whole effect was that of a wanton.

"No," she said desperately, "I know the duchess would never approve."

The dressmaker snorted.

"In a pig's eye, my girl. Didn't I have the entire dressing of Violet? And then Rose? Never fear, the duchess will approve. Come," she said, more kindly, "it's the very thing. It's all the rage. You're going to Paris, my lady, and anything else would make you a dowd. And the duchess can't abide dowds.''

Seeing the indecision on Catherine's face, the dressmaker began to chuckle, as if struck by a new idea.

''Come, let your maid see it. She'll tell you what all the fine ladies wear, and what the duchess likes. Come along, come with me.'' And taking Catherine by one cold hand, she pulled her into the outer room.

Catherine allowed herself to be tugged forward by this intractable little woman and before she had time to think of the audience that lay outside the door, she found herself the center of their attention.

She stood, cheeks high in color, eyes wide and expectant, in her incredibly indecent gown, in the midst of all the strangers waiting in the front room. There was a sudden quiet as she entered. Conversation ceased as they caught sight of the lovely young woman before them. Catherine held her head high and wished to disappear into the ether as she heard the dressmaker, through the pounding in her ears, ask the little maid what she thought the duchess would say. But curiously, the dressmaker's eyes were not on the little maid, but rather watching the tall blond-haired female she called ''La Starr'' in the bright amber dress. The blond woman had been posing and turning and posturing in it, showing it off to a gentleman, before Catherine appeared. And the moment that Catherine appeared in the doorway, the gentleman's eyes left her and did not return to her. She stared angrily at Catherine.

Catherine looked over in their direction and saw the amused gray eyes staring at her insolently. It was incredible how she had not forgotten a detail of his face since that morning in the fog. He stood leaning against a mantel, his long athletic form impeccably clothed in gray again. His face resembled, Catherine thought, a picture she had seen of a red Indian, with his cool angular good looks, high cheekbones, and black hair. But his look held mockery and disdain and an infuriatingly belittling humor.

He glanced over at the dressmaker. ''I applaud you, madame,'' he drawled, ''as I am certain the duchess will. You have turned a little country mouse into a dazzler. Congratulations.''

He walked slowly over to where Catherine stood poised for retreat, although perversely refusing to flee in the face of his impudence.

''I see you found the right place, little one.'' He smiled with

what was not at all a smile. His eyes lingered at her breasts, and
while her hands itched to fly up and cover herself, she only stood
stock still and tried to return his stare with all the dignity she
could muster. "See if you can make my little Starr something on
this order," he said over his shoulder. "It is a most impressive
display of . . . taste." And then, with a careless shrug, he turned
and went back to the blond female, who was darting glances of
the purest dislike at Catherine.

"Who," Catherine panted, stripping herself out of the hated
dress with fever in the curtained alcove, "was that insolent man?
That popinjay, that man who spoke to me?"

The dressmaker spoke through a mouthful of pins.

"Who?" Catherine insisted, buttoning herself all wrong in her
haste to get back into her good, decent little gray dress again.

"He is the Marquis of Bessacarr," the dressmaker said placidly.
"A neighbor of the duchess's. I expect that's how he knows
you. And you should be flattered that he did. He doesn't acknowledge everyone, you know."

"He need not acknowledge me," Catherine insisted, setting
herself aright again. "He need not ever acknowledge me
again."

Catherine left, with her maid in tow, carrying the few parcels
the dressmaker had readied for her. The rest, she promised
would be delivered as soon as might be. She had turned a deaf
ear to all of Catherine's protests, telling her she knew well
enough what would be a suitable wardrobe for the duchess's
companion.

Catherine swore to herself, on the way home in the carriage
with the stony-faced maid, that she would sit up nights if need
be, adding on fabric to those indecent bodices. Style or no, she
was never again to be ogled in that fashion.

Madame Bertrand sipped her tea and chuckled at her work
table. It had been worth it, even though it had cost her some
trade, just to see the look on La Starr's face. Brazen little hussy,
going to her competitor for her dressing when she was in funds,
and coming back to her dear Madame Bertrand when she was
sailing the River Tick. Madame Bertrand knew her clientele
well—they were the cream of the demimonde. And she had
discovered that La Starr was going to a society modiste when she
was in clover. But now, when her protector, the marquis, was
growing bored with her, she had entreated her old friend to let

her pose in a few gowns to see if he would bite and purchase them for her. But he had paid for only the blue one, after all. And after seeing that black-haired new beauty, he might not buy her any others either. Well, Madame Bertrand thought, there were plenty more where La Starr came from, both for herself and for the marquis.

"Sinjun," the blond woman cooed at her companion as they walked down the street, "did you not like that amber gown? I swear I thought it would suit you down to the ground."

"It would hardly suit me, my dear. Amber is not my color," he said in a low amused voice, "and it did not suit you so well either. But that is not strictly true. Truly, I grow weary of clothes shopping with you. I think in future you should go yourself. I will draft you a check, my dear, to better enable you to do so. Oh, don't look crushed. It will be a very substantial amount—just recompense for the delightful time we have spent together. But I think the exclusive nature of our acquaintance is over. After all, I plan to be traveling again soon, and it would not be fair to tie you to one companion now."

"Travel to Paris, for example," she said spitefully, "where the duchess might have a companion to compensate your idle hours?"

"Hardly," he said, with real amusement. "Her companions are not so exclusive, you know. And it was the exclusivity of our relationship that I valued. As well as your own delightful self. One may admire a thing without wanting it," he said slowly, "much as one may admire a public prospect, such as this pleasant well-worn thoroughfare, without wanting to spend all one's time on it. It is too public a place, after all. Private places bring more pleasure."

Mollified, she sauntered along with him.

"Sinjun," she asked sweetly, "shall we have a farewell party exclusively and privately together tonight? At my expense?"

He smiled down at her.

"You do me honor," he replied.

"You will have to do me a great deal better," she said roguishly.

And, laughing, they went on, in total understanding and accord.

The gentleman was not laughing a few short hours later. In fact, St. John Basil St. Charles, Marquis of Bessacarr, paced the floor of his study in a singularly humorless state.

"Damn it, Cyril," he swore, with unaccustomed vehemence, "I thought it was to be Vienna. That is where all the business is going on. Why in heaven's name did he decide upon Paris? It is over and done with there. What earthly good can I do for you there?"

His friend sat and watched the marquis in his travels around the carpet.

"Sinjun, the old chap is never wrong, you know. I thought it was to be Vienna too. But he said that he had enough of his fellows there. What he needs, he says, is a good ear in an unexpected place. Paris, he said, and it is Paris he meant. You will be seeing him soon yourself, and doubtless he can explain it better than I can. But he fears treachery on all sides, and his man in Paris is a looby, he says. 'Sinjun's the chap for it,' he says. Everyone will accept you as just another merrymaker, and you can find out whose loyalties belong to whom. It's a hotbed over there now, he said, with some supporting the old Bourbon and some still working for Bonaparte. He won't be easy in his mind about Bonaparte till he's two years dead, you know."

"And that I can't blame him for," the marquis said, sinking at last into a chair. "But I had felt that I could do more good in Vienna. I have done before, unless he's come to doubting me now?"

"Nothing like it," his friend assured him. "He still thinks you one of the best agents he has. But you're well known in Vienna now, for all your subterfuge. You've practically got the stamp of the foreign office upon your forehead, he says. And you can't work well unless there's *some* doubt as to your aims, you know."

"It's not so bad as that." The taller man grinned. "But I'll grant that there may be a suspicion there that I'm not just another disinterested tourist. But Paris just now is filled with fools, with empty-headed nits who've gone for the fun and games of it. And I suppose I'm to be just another one of them?"

His friend nodded with a sympathetic smile.

"Ahh, my reputation," the marquis sighed, passing a hand over his forehead. "My lamentable reputation."

Cyril laughed aloud at that. For the marquis had posed as many things, many times, in his jobs for the foreign office. Aside from that, if there was ever a man who cared less for his reputation in the ton, Cyril did not know of him. The marquis had never cared for what any other soul in the kingdom thought

of him, or any other soul in Spain, or France, or Italy, or any of
the places to which he had traveled since he had enlisted his
services in the war against Bonaparte. It was that, the old chap
said, coupled with his winning manner and his natural intelligence,
that had made him such an invaluable asset to their operations.

"Paris it is, then," the marquis said derisively. "I will have
to pack my dancing slippers."

Cyril rose to go and stretched himself.

"I suppose," he yawned, "that you'll be taking Jenkins?
Where is he, by the by? I haven't set eyes on him in some
time."

"Down at Fairleigh, taking care of estate business. He's very
good at that too, you know. But he'll be here like a shot when he
gets my message. He's like an old gun dog—one sniff of powder
and all else flees from his mind."

"Just like his master, eh?"

"Don't let him hear you say that; Jenkins has no master. He
chooses to stay on with me and work for me. We have no title
for his duties as yet, not even after all these years. He is estate
manager, overseer, accountant, and, most of all, friend. As it is,
I'm delighted to just be his friend and be able to employ him.
He's the one man I trust in this whole weary world."

Cyril turned back at the door and pulled a hurt face.

"Oh, you don't trust me, Sinjun?"

"Not so far as I could toss you, old dear." The marquis
smiled slowly. "For if the old chap told you to place a knife in
my ribs, you'd do it without a backward glance."

"I'm hurt, old fellow, wounded to the quick. For I would give
a backward glance, you know. To see if Jenkins was after me
with another knife."

They laughed and parted with a handshake.

The marquis went to his desk to write a note to his estate
manager, valet, traveling companion, assistant, and friend, Jenkins.
He smiled to himself and was actually laughing softly as he
added a last flourish to the note. That would get the old boy
running, he thought. A hint of subterfuge, spying, lying, and the
possibility of mayhem, and Jenkins would drop anything he was
doing to come along. Cyril was right, he thought, Jenkins was
just like him. When they had met those years ago in Spain, they
had each recognized it. The marquis had been on the crown's
business, and Jenkins a batman who had just lost his officer.
Exactly who had saved the other's life when they had met they

had never resolved, but each had instantly appreciated the other. Regardless of class distinctions, education, and lineage, they had banded together, recognizing their common bond.

There was a time, the marquis thought, the smile fading from his lips, when style and reputation had meant everything to him. More than honor or love or duty. And only now could he jest about it, only now could he remember it without shrinking, as though remembering a thing he had read once in an old book rather than lived himself.

For he had been born to a title, and born to a dignity. Yet before he had reached his majority, his father had gambled it all away, as well as his mother's health and life, all save his title. And he had inherited nothing but the title and a mountain of debts. And a handsome visage and a strong body and agile mind. He had gone out and earned his money, at tasks and trades he chose not to mention to the world, and invested the proceeds wisely and husbanded them well, and not only rebuilt his father's lost fortune but added to it as well. But all the while he had worried about his dignity and his reputation. And what would become of him if people knew his methods.

He had done all so that he could present an unblemished name to the world. He had cared about his world and what it thought of him. And all that he did that enriched or amused him—all the trafficking in trade, all the consorting with women of the demimonde, all the gaming and the pleasures—he had tried to hide from the world.

"Ah," he thought, scowling, it pained him to think of it even now. He had been such a callow fellow. And it had, in the end, cost him dearly. The one woman whose mind he admired the most, whose temperament most neatly matched his own, he dallied with and then dropped, because he had felt her face did not match the ideal of what the world would think his marchioness's face should be. And by the time he discovered how he missed her and how unimportant a face could be, only important if that certain face bore a smile for him alone, she was gone to another man wise enough to know the difference between a package and its wrappings.

And there had been another woman, whose face was so glorious that he forgot to look into her heart. And whose position and status were so low that he did not seriously think of her for his marchioness, for he thought the world would not either. So he only offered her a paid position as his mistress. But she too had found a wiser man, who had looked beyond the surface and not thought of the world's opinion, and offered her his hand as well as his heart. And he, the marquis of impeccable birth and reputation, had been left with an impeccably empty heart.

Such memories were only cold ashes to rake over. Valuable only because he had learned from his mistakes, they had served their purpose well—let them lie at rest. He had found occupation in serving his country; spying suited his temperament. He no longer cared for appearances; he, of all men, knew what a sham reputation and titles could be. He had learned to look beyond the obvious, to seek the truth beneath the surface clutter. And so he no longer cared for his own name; his reputation was no longer of any importance to him.

And the cream of the jest was that once he had left off caring and dissembling and trying to impress the world with his purity, his popularity soared. And his reputation, which no longer interested him, was pronounced to be of the highest. He gamed openly—he was called a daring gentleman. He wenched openly —he was called a dashing ladies' man. His growing cynicism was thought to be wisdom; his rudeness, wit; his unapproachable air, dignity. He sought no wife and was deemed the most eligible of the ton.

Someday he would have to marry, he expected, but he would remain heart-whole. He could not see himself letting his estates go to his only sister's eldest, a spotty, disagreeable little boy who whined. But even though the marquis had reached the age of five and thirty, he was in no hurry to be bound in matrimony. He thought of marriage in much the same way that a sinner thinks of confession and redemption, as something to be done at the last moment, on the deathbed preferably.

For with all of his wide experience with women, the marquis did not trust his perceptions of them too far. He shied from involving himself with them seriously, as he had been wrong once too often. He was scrupulously honest, however, with them and about his expectations of them. He enjoyed them physically and had learned to give them pleasure as well, and asked no more of them than that, and promised them no more than that. This attitude caused him no impediments to his desires. There were too many females eager to accept him on his own terms.

And those few who tried to change the terms were soon brought to realize their folly.

The marquis glanced at the note in his hand and rang for a

footman to collect it from him. When the difficulties with France were finally irrevocably ended, he supposed he might find boredom at last. An emptiness might enter his life without occupation that did not offer such danger and interest. But he had learned to push such thoughts away. For now he was content to be a superior spy, and that was all that he cared to dwell upon.

St. John, Marquis of Bessacarr, darling of the ton, peer of the realm, patron of the frail sisterhood, social lion, and most superior spy, impatient with waiting for a footman to answer his summons, stepped out, on his way to a farewell dinner with his mistress, to send a message to his one true friend, his accomplice. And the message was to come to London instanter. For the assignment was at hand and they were off to Paris!

Chapter IV

The trunks began to pile up in the great hall, as their growing number had already outstripped the confines of the back pantries. The duchess did not like to travel with any discomfort. So there were innumerable indispensable things to pack.

The duchess's modiste, a staple of the ton who would be horrified if her name were mentioned in the same breath as Madame Bertrand's, was giddy with ecstasy over the amount of clothing she was flogging her girls to turn out in time for the duchess's departure. Catherine no longer measured the time till their going by the calendar, but rather watched the trunks slowly take over the hall. By the time, she reasoned, that Griddon could no longer pick his way to the front door, the time of their departure would be at hand.

No one could have awaited their departure more eagerly than Catherine. Despite all the splendors of the duchess's accommodations, it had been a lonely time for her. Not even the lowest servant in the house had ever had the inclination or the time to chat with her. Thus she had passed her days in sewing or reading or gazing out the window at those more fortunately occupied, afraid to leave the house lest a summons from the duchess come while she was out. Only a few times had she dared hasty trips to the shops, and those only when there was a purchase she must make. On those rare occasions, it was a treat to be able to converse with the tradespeople she transacted her business with. There were times when the purchase of a spool of red thread had been the highest point of Catherine's day.

The only person she ever encountered in the street whom she knew, and he only by accident, was the duchess's near neighbor, the lofty Marquis of Bessacarr. When their paths crossed, he invariably would take note of her, to her distress. For he took special care to say something cryptic to her in passing. "It's a good life, isn't it, little one?" he said once, smiling, and, "My regards to your employer. Why does she still keep you under wraps?" he greeted her another time. Each time she steadfastly and properly ignored him. And each time he said a thing which seemed to amuse him, and which perversely always troubled her far into the night.

But today she was to have conversation. She stood in the duchess's bedchamber again, waiting to be noticed. For today she had come at her own request.

When finally the duchess had given Gracie instructions for the securing of yet another new trunk, this one for bonnets alone, she had time to look up at Catherine.

"How are you going, gel?" she asked pleasantly enough. "All packed and ready to scoot with me? Did Bertrand deliver as promised?"

"Oh yes, ma'am," Catherine breathed, still embarrassed about the amount of clothing the duchess had thought necessary for her companion to have. Her fingers still ached from all the midnight sewing she had done to tame some of Madame Bertrand's more outrageous creations, and her conscience still pricked about the secretiveness of her stitchery.

"But there is a thing that I have to discuss with you." She hesitated. This was difficult, although she had spent the better part of yesterday preparing herself for the interview.

"You see, Your Grace, there is the matter of my"—Catherine swallowed—"wages."

It did not sound so terrible once it was out, so Catherine rushed on, "I have been with you since October, and there have been certain expenses I have been forced to make. Expenses of a personal nature," she hurried on, so as not to seem grasping or ungrateful for her food and pleasant housing, and not wishing to go into particulars, since most of her money had gone to laces and trimmings to alter her wardrobe.

"And as this is my first position, I did not think to ask originally as to when I would be paid. I do," she went on with painful honesty, "realize that Your Grace has seen to my every comfort here, but Christmas is upon us, and so I wondered if I could ask that the wages I have already earned, only those, be given to me so that I might send a few things home before I depart.''

It was so difficult, Catherine thought, to talk about money. And so very foolish to feel like a greedy, grasping creature when one was only asking for what one had earned. But there it was, it was unseemly for a female to discuss money. Perhaps that was why it was so unseemly for a female to be actually employed.

The duchess looked hard at her for a moment, squinting her eyes to get a better look, which was something she seldom did, preferring on the whole to see the world in her usual pleasant myopic blurred focus.

"I usually pay my companions quarterly," the duchess intoned, suddenly on her high ropes, and making Catherine quake at her own stupidity in not having discussed the matter on her initial interview to save herself this present embarrassment.

"But," the duchess said, with a sly little grin, "I understand your predicament. You're probably used to much more ready in your pocket. I have kept your wings clipped since you came here, haven't I? But that's only because I wanted to spring you as a surprise when we got to France. Watch their eyes bug out when they saw you. No use to having rumors spoil the treat beforehand. So you're feeling pinched because I've kept you from your usual source of income, eh?"

Catherine had not a clue as what the duchess was getting at, but then suddenly realized that she must mean that Arthur and Jane weren't there to provide for her as they usually did. Since that was true enough, too humiliatingly true, Catherine felt her face flush in embarrassment.

"Well, don't fret. You've been a good gel, and there's a treat for you. I'll give you the first two months' wages now and you can go on a spree with them. But once we get to France, that won't be a problem, will it?"

Catherine could think of no heavy expenses she could incur when she began her travels. Pourboires for servants could be taken from her pocket with no stress, since she didn't intend to spend every penny the duchess gave her now. So she nodded in happy agreement.

"Thought not," the duchess answered. "But mind, I told Rose and I told Violet. I don't want to know about it. Do your duty to me first and be discreet about the rest, and we'll rub on well enough."

There was no reason, certainly, Catherine thought, to bother the duchess with the small matters of tipping foreign servants, so she agreed again.

"We'll get you your wages now," the duchess said, ringing for Gracie to get her her cash box, "and I suppose you'll want the same arrangements Rose and Violet did. I'll be your banker on our trip, and when it's over I'll hand it all over to you in a lump sum, or you can have it quarterly. It'll be like an extra cash bonus whenever you get it." The duchess chuckled. "Money in the bank."

Catherine took the money that the duchess handed to her, too grateful to count it. It seemed like a great deal, and even more, as it was the first money she ever earned by herself. And as far as the total sum of money being an extra bonus, it would be far, far more than that to her. The duchess, she thought gratefully, could have no idea of how penny pinched she really was. At the thought of the independence of spirit that the lump sum would buy her—the freedom to choose whether to work again for some other woman, or to take her earnings and pay Arthur and Jane back some small portion of what they had given her so that she could live with them again with ease and spirit—Catherine smiled with pure joy.

"Money's a great thing. Ain't it?" the duchess crowed, seeing the girl's rapturous face.

"It is, ma'am," Catherine sighed. "It is indeed."

"Get on with it, then," the duchess said, at first amused, but now bored with the chit's obvious greed. She immediately went back to chivying Gracie again about the whereabouts of her favorite feathered bonnet.

Catherine was as careful as a new mother with her firstborn child as she decided how to spend her wages. This time she had drawn Annie, a sharp little kitchen maid, as female escort. Annie was as distant and silent with Catherine as the others of her position. But Catherine had gotten used to the peculiar notions of status that prevailed in the duchess's household.

After hours of searching in the shops as carefully as a master chef searching for a perfect cut of meat, Catherine selected a warm but exquisitely made colorful shawl for Jane and a set of six beautiful enameled buttons for Arthur. Both presents were practical enough to please their sense of propriety, but extravagantly styled enough to be kept as personal treasures. And, best of all, both were small enough to be sent without incurring the world's expense on her shoulders. She was sure that Griddon could be asked to parcel them up for her, and that he would know how to go about posting them safely. For Catherine had never had to send a package to anyone before, never being far enough from home or knowing anyone far enough away.

To be sure, she thought, frowning slightly as she made her way back home, setting Annie to wonder if Her Grace's fine trollop had seen her wink at the butcher's boy, Jane's papa had lived far away and traveled further. But there was never any question of anyone posting anything to him, as he had never left a forwarding address.

Her own father, that dimly remembered handsome blue-eyed dark-haired man, had died when she was six. Mama had gone on alone, till she had met Jane's papa. He had been a slight, blond, elegant, and altogether charming widower. And Mama's heart had gone out to the outwardly blithe man with his little motherless, sober blond girl, only twelve to her own orphan's seven years. And if it had not, Catherine thought wryly, he would have pirated it anyway. For he was a persuasive man. Merry and laughing, charming and light spirited, he had invaded their house and swept Mama away with him. But only so far as the vicar's.

For after they were married, he had soon grown bored with Mama and two little girls, as he had grown bored with everything that he had encountered in his life. Soon he was charming and delightful only to his drinking cronies, and soon after that, having found a safe harbor for his little girl—say that much at least for him—he was gone altogether, off on his own journeys. In search, he had said, of his fortune.

And he had left Mama with Jane and Catherine both to raise as best she could on what little her first husband had left her. When they had heard of his own death a few years ago, somewhere in Ireland, his own daughter had not even shed a tear. Small wonder, then, that Jane had not looked for a handsome, dashing stranger to carry her off, after a childhood full of a handsome dashing father who had carried her everywhere and then abandoned her. When prim and proper Arthur had stepped out from behind the counter at his shop to ask to keep company with her, she had accepted with alacrity. And though Catherine had not known Jane's father too long or too well, she too was wary of gentlemen with easy smiles and pleasing graces. Not, she reminded herself, that she was much in the way of meeting such gentlemen, or any gentlemen at all, these days.

Catherine quickened her pace, as the wind was beginning to

bite fiercely, and the pavements at last communicated their chill through the bottom of her handsome kid slippers. She had been out shopping far longer than she had ever planned, and she was anxious to get back and get her parcels seen to, so that she could dream of Jane and Arthur's pleased expressions when they saw the bounty she had sent.

She was so intent upon her thoughts that she did not see him till he was almost abreast of her, although Annie had seen him coming from far down the street.

He tipped his hat, which he wore at a rakish angle, to Annie, and as she tittered, he swept it off altogether with a flourish as Catherine raised her eyes to him.

"Good day to you, little one," he said pleasantly enough.

Although she had never acknowledged his greetings before, Catherine knew it would be quite rude to simply pass him by and cut him dead. He was a neighbor to the duchess, and the duchess seemed to hold him in some awe. So Catherine reluctantly inclined her head in greeting. His words had been innocuous enough, but she had seen the same amused gleam in his eyes.

"All ready for your little trip?" he inquired politely.

"Yes. Thank you. Quite ready," Catherine answered, wishing he would end this interview, for she was not at all sure, all things considered, that it was proper for her to be speaking with him.

"Yes," he drawled, seeing her impatience and hesitation, "you'd best be hurrying home, little ladybird. Your house may well be afire. Reinforcements have arrived."

At Catherine's puzzled glance upward at him, something in his aspect changed, and he reluctantly withdrew his gaze from her clear blue eyes.

He replaced his hat jauntily and added, "You'd best see to your bonnets, child. The competition bids to be fierce this year." And again he nodded and went on down the street, leaving Catherine with the usual mixture of feelings of chagrin and confusion, and Annie pink with pleasure at having been noticed by such a fine gentleman.

Catherine gave her coat to the footman and saw Griddon coming toward her. She began to explain about her parcels and how she wanted them sent, when he cut her off gently, "Her Grace has been asking for you. She's in the study. With a visitor."

Catherine flushed with guilt, thinking of how on the one day that she was wanted, she was out. She reached the door and tapped lightly upon it.

"Come in," the duchess called.

There was a woman sitting at the desk opposite the duchess. A magnificent woman. Her red hair was a tumble of curls, pulled back with a simple green ribbon. Her figure was full and imposing and her green walking dress was afroth with lace and frogs and knots. Her eyes were large and brown, with the darkest, longest lashes Catherine had ever seen. Her lips were full and very red and pouting, and she had, as she looked at Catherine, something of the imperious expression the duchess herself affected.

"Look who's here," the duchess said wryly. "Look who the cat's brought back. It's dear Violet. And she's consented to come with me on my little jaunterings."

"Go now." The duchess waved at Catherine. "I just wanted dear Violet to get an eyeful of you and see how indispensable her services were. She and I have some business to iron out. I'll call you later. Go now." She waved again, as Catherine stood there, staring like a ninny at the magnificent lady who made her feel all of two years old.

At last Catherine nodded and fled up the stairs.

Once in her room, she shut the door quickly, laid down her parcels with unsteady hands, and pulled the curtains closed. She was reacting, she told herself a few moments later, when she got her thoughts under control, just like a two-year-old who has seen a stranger who's frightened her. Why don't you, she scourged herself, go and creep under the bed while you're at it, to make the picture complete?

After a few moments, she had herself adequately under control again, and her face was very sad when she at last met her eyes in the mirror. "So be it," she thought resignedly. "You cannot really lose something you have not had." And, in all honesty, she had not been the duchess's companion yet, and she had not, she reasoned, lost a position she had never actually filled. "At least," she told herself, with a little of her usual good humor, "there's very little packing to do," as she saw all her new suitcases neatly arow in the corner of the room, ready for departure.

"So," the duchess said, smiling hugely, "what do you think of your little replacement, Violet?"

"Quite the ingenue," Violet answered in her high reedy voice, "but I don't think she's up to snuff."

"She's a stunning little baggage and you know it," the duchess went on, quite pleased with the agitation in her erstwhile companion's face.

"I should think you'd want to travel with a female that knows her way about. A responsible sort of companion. That little tart looks like she's still on mother's milk. She'll land herself in the suds before you know it, or pack it all in for some layabout's promises before you even reach Paris," Violet said in the thin little voice that had been her downfall in the theater. For although the gentlemen had cheered every time she swept across the stage, no one past the middle rows had ever heard a line.

The duchess acknowledged the hit with a shrug. "Perhaps, but you'd be there to show her the ropes, wouldn't you, dear Violet?"

The magnificent female in the green walking dress relaxed the tight set of her shoulders. Up to this point she had not known if the old dragon was actually going to take her on again. She'd had to do some fast and glib talking, and then when the young smashing-looking girl had appeared in the doorway, she had thought that all was lost. But resiliency was her best asset, so she masked her surprise and said laconically, "Oh, I'll see to it that she doesn't embarrass you. I know what I'm about."

"All because you're anxious to see Paris, eh?" the duchess prodded. "I'm pleased that you have acquired this sudden bent for travel. But of course, since Wolverton came down so handsomely with you, you wouldn't require any help from me with your wardrobe this time."

Violet saw the old woman's eyes mocking her, so she gave in at last, feeling that a half a loaf was better than none.

"No, he didn't. He made up some wild story about me sneaking about with an actor on the sly, and used that as an excuse to simply pull out, without leaving me a farthing. As if," she added, her bosom swelling, "I would sneak about with an actor, of all things, without a penny in his pockets and nothing but a handsome face to recommend him, and risk Wolverton's finding out."

The duchess nodded sympathetically, knowing that was just what Violet would do.

"And dear Rose, have you heard from her?"

"Haven't seen hide nor hair of her, and that's the honest truth. Last I heard, she was off on the road with that new love of hers. He'll drink her out of house and home before she knows it unless I miss my guess."

"This is all quite sordid." The duchess sighed, ringing for Griddon. "And I don't think I care to hear about any more of it. I'll take you on again, Violet, although I was most displeased about the way you were so ready to leave me in the lurch. But I do have a reputation to uphold, and traveling with two companions is what my set is used to see me doing. But I won't hear of you changing your mind again. Do your duties, keep the new girl in line, and you will find I will be pleased."

When Griddon appeared, the duchess asked him to call Miss Robins down again.

"Catherine," the duchess said as Catherine, white-faced and subdued, came to the door, "this is Violet Peterson. I have spoken about her. She finds herself suddenly able to join me again and will be going to Paris with us."

"I understand, ma'am," Catherine said in a small voice. "And when do you wish me to leave?"

"Why, next week," the duchess said, "when I do, of course—don't be such a gudgeon."

"I shall have to see to the stage schedules," Catherine said quietly. "Would you be so kind as to write me a recommendation so that I can secure future employment?"

Violet stiffened and gave Catherine a look of offended shock.

"Your new little miss don't think I'm a fit companion to travel with," she shrilled.

"Violet don't fit your nice notions of propriety?" the duchess growled, in her iciest dignity.

"Oh no, that is not it," Catherine foundered, "but I thought, when you said that she was coming with you, I thought you no longer required my services. That is to say, now that you have your original companion back, I did not see what need you would have of me."

Catherine had researched the duties of a companion as best she could before even coming to London. But some things were basic, even back in Kendal. An elderly female, or an incapacitated one, or even a healthy able young woman of means could not live in society without proper female companionship. If there were no female relations in the home, and no indigent women in some branch of the family who would be glad of a home to be pressed into service, a companion was hired. A companion served as aide, or as company, sometimes as nurse, and most often just as figurehead for propriety's sake. But she had never heard of any woman requiring two paid companions. And that seemed to be just what the duchess was now implying. Perhaps, Catherine thought, with an amazed sense of guilt, she had not looked into the social habits that prevailed in the higher echelons of society as well as she should have. And now she had unwittingly offended Violet.

"I have often told you about Violet and Rose. I frequently travel with two companions. I have a position to uphold," the duchess said, at her iciest, feeling obliquely accused by the mock innocence of this young upstart of a girl.

"Then I am sorry for the misunderstanding," Catherine said gladly. "I should be delighted to travel with Miss Peterson, really I shall," she said, looking beseechingly at the rigid Violet, and feeling a surge of delight at the thought of having someone to talk to at last nearer to her own age. "And I am relieved to find that you still want me."

"Go, then," the duchess said with unexpected relief. "Go and get acquainted. You'll be seeing a lot of each other, and I like my staff to be in harmony."

"So you've got the green room," Violet commented as she and Catherine made their way upstairs to Violet's room. "Rose, she used to have that one. What did you do before the old lady hired you on?" she asked disinterestedly as she walked unerringly into the room adjoining Catherine's.

Catherine, a little shocked at the familiarity with which Violet spoke of her employer, but not wanting to appear to be a prig and start the relationship off on the wrong foot, let the remark pass and merely said, "I lived with my brother-in-law and stepsister."

"And I lived with the pixies at the foot of the garden," Violet mocked, sweeping into her room and going straight to her looking glass.

Catherine looked nonplussed as Violet stripped the ribbon from her hair and examined her face in the mirror.

"Oh, all right, I'll play the game too," Violet said wearily. "You lived with your brother-in-law and stepsister. Is it your first time in London then, s'truth?"

"Yes, and it's all been so strange to me."

"Lord," Violet sighed, "I'm going to be going across the face of Europe with Juliet. Well, you really landed in gravy hiring on with the dowager. She's a right old sort once you learn her ins and outs. Just watch your step with her, though. She's half tiddly, but the other half comes up when you least expect it.

I remember once when Rose snuck out with that wild major before the duchess was ready to call it a night. Wasn't there an uproar about that, though? I thought old Rose was going to be chucked out in no time flat. But all was rosy again in the morning. Rose could never pick them. All for love, that's Rose. And not a penny in her pocket now to show for it. Not that I'm in clover either now, but after this jaunt I expect to have a few guineas put away, and you never know what gravy boats there are in Paris, do you?''

Catherine didn't know what to answer. Evidently Violet and Rose had both been up to some larks when the duchess's back was turned, and she supposed that the tedium of working for the duchess had to be relieved by some shows of spirit, but she honestly had no similar experiences to relate. So she simply smiled in a hopeful, friendly way at Violet.

Violet caught Catherine's expression in the reflection of her mirror. She stared thoughtfully. So the little miss was going to play it all airs and graces and not let her hair down? So be it, it takes all kinds, she thought. Rose had been more forthcoming, a right sort of girl. If this little chit wanted to play at being a society debutante, it was her business. And her dark hair and gamine looks and air of innocence might be a good contrast to Violet's own more spectacular looks. Just as Rose's blond buxom placidity had been a good foil for her own Titian vivacity.

But then, just for one moment, Violet caught one clear look of both their faces reflected in the oval of the mirror. Catherine's pure fine-grained white skin contrasted with her own powdered complexion; Catherine's clear startling blue eyes, with her translucent skin that allowed a faint blue tracery of veins to color her lids, contrasted with her own heavily soot-darkened lids and lashes; and the younger girl's faint blush of color above her cheekbones contrasted with her own heavily rouged cheeks. Then there was the chit's plump and dusky lips as opposed to her own richly red salved mouth, and, most damningly, the faint web of lines at the corners of Violet's eyes were not echoed on the girl's smooth face. No, Violet decided, only from across a room could the contrast between them be to her own benefit. She knew her assets as well as any banker knew his financial situation. Her own full figure and brazen coloring would catch the gentlemen's eyes long before they noticed the quiet beauty of this little miss. But standing side by side, Violet could only suffer by comparison. Her decision was made unerringly and irrevocably—she would stay away from Miss Innocence, stay far away in public, for her own good. And as far as when they were alone, time would tell if the chit would drop her air of sanctity.

"I'm for a quick kip," Violet yawned, and, without further comment, she began to unbutton the bodice of her gown. She stripped down her clothes, as though she were alone in the room. Catherine hastily retreated, calling a good-bye that was only acknowledged by a nod and another huge yawn.

Really, Catherine thought, seeking the refuge of her own room, the women of London thought no more of nudity before other females than they did of nudity before a cake of soap. She wondered if she should write of the phenomenon to Jane in her letter next week.

But when she wrote her next letter to Jane, she mentioned not a word of it. For Arthur, she remembered, would most likely be reading Jane's letter over her shoulder. She wrote instead of the quiet Christmas she had spent, and the expectations she had of her journey. She closed by inquiring after their health and wished them all the joys of a new year. She sealed the letter and blew out her light. Then she went to her window to gaze at the moonlit streets of London for a while. She watched some stray merrymakers reel past her observation post at the window seat and then she crept into her bed. She fell asleep as the bells rang out, and so celebrated the first moments of the new year of 1815 with quiet blameless sleep.

Chapter V

The deck of the packet to France was thronged with the fashionable of England and the Continent. Catherine tried not to goggle. There were gentlemen in the first and last cry of fashion, their capes billowing out in the wind, their hats defying every gust. The ladies wore rich garments and trailed retinues of more plainly dressed servants. Everyone boarding seemed to know each other, and the duchess nodded and smiled her tight little smile at gentlemen who bowed and ladies who stared. Gracie, like so many of the other servants who scuttled mutely and inconspicuously after their employers, only kept her attention on her mistress. But Violet, Catherine noted, behaved exactly as the duchess did, nodding and acknowledging old acquaintances. Evidently, Catherine thought, the companions of great ladies were treated exactly as their mistresses were, even though they were, in effect, no more than servants just like Gracie.

The duchess's retinue made their way to their berths. The duchess paused at the door of her cabin and looked at Violet.

"I shall rest. You know I cannot abide the sea. The mere sight of it makes me ill. But Gracie here knows what to do for me. I suppose you don't want to just languish in your cabin, eh? You'll want to see how the land lies. Well, get on with it. Let me know who's here and who's going where. But mind your manners. And take her with you," she added, pointing to Catherine. "Let them get a look at her before we sail. That'll tickle them right enough."

Violet looked as though she would balk at the suggestion, making Catherine feel like an ill-bred little sister who has insisted upon coming along with the grown-ups and so is hardly tolerated. But then Violet sniffed, "She's free to walk the decks, I'm sure."

Violet was dressed, Catherine thought, as they turned from Her Grace's room, as though she were going to a high tea rather than sailing across the channel. She wore a bright burnt orange ensemble, and from the way she held her head as her fellow passengers turned to stare at her in the corridor, she acted as though she were the hostess of a large seagoing fete. Catherine felt mousy in her own rich, warm blue velvet cloak beside the glowing Violet.

As they were going out into the fresh cold sea air of the deck, Catherine noticed a small altercation taking place between the captain and a stunning attractive blond female. Although she too was dressed in the height of fashion, and was almost as theatrically brilliant as Violet, she wore an expression of consternation and seemed to be arguing with the captain. As they approached, Catherine heard Violet give out a low startled exclamation.

"Coo, now here's a turn. Look who's landed on us."

"There," the blonde cried, noticing Violet as she drew closer, "just ask her. That's the duchess's companion. She will tell you."

"Excuse me, miss," the captain said, wiping his brow, "but this lady says that the Duchess of Crewe is expecting her. She does not have her ticket, however, and I do not like to disturb Her Grace, and so perhaps you . . ."

He trailed off, looking perturbed.

"Hello, Rose, old thing," Violet said, with a slightly twisted smile. "Allow me to present Miss Catherine Robins, Her Grace's new companion."

The blond woman looked stricken, but recovered quickly to say, "There, you see, the duchess's companion knows me. I'm sure Her Grace won't be angry if you take me to her. In fact, she might be very angry if you do not."

"It's true that the duchess knows Miss Tomkins," Violet said loftily, to the blond woman's evident relief. "I'm most surprised to see you here, Rose, and I'm sure Her Grace will be curious about your presence as well."

Rose turned to the captain triumphantly. "There, did you hear that?"

The captain shrugged, content to have the burden of decision taken from him. "Very well," he said, "but we sail in an hour."

Rose turned to go below deck and gave Violet a radiant smile. "You're a good old thing, Vi," she whispered, "and I'm not forgetting."

"Is that," Catherine whispered to Violet as they strolled on, "Her Grace's old companion Rose?"

"Don't let her catch you saying 'old,' " Violet smiled.

"Whatever is she doing here?"

"With Rose one hardly knows," Violet said disinterestedly. "Perhaps she's companioning someone else. Perhaps she's short of the ready and wants to touch the old girl's heart before she sails for a guinea or two. Time will tell."

Violet spotted someone she knew in a clutch of travelers who were standing and joshing with each other by the rail, surveying late arrivals as they hurried up the gangplank. She turned and eyed Catherine obliquely. The wind had whipped color into the girl's cheeks, she noted. And her eyes gleamed bluer than the slate-blue sea beneath them. Her hair spilled out from the blue bonnet, tugged into curls by the sea winds' damp fingers. She looked as fresh and bonny as a young doe. Violet pursed her lips.

"I see some old acquaintances," she said quickly. "Do you continue on your walk. Once the boat begins to move, you may not feel like staying above deck. So here's your opportunity to catch the lay of the land. I'll see you later."

And, with a nod, she left Catherine's side and disappeared into a crowd of people.

Catherine walked on alone. She felt uneasy about walking by herself in a crowd of strangers, for she knew it was not the sort of thing a young female should do. At least, she ammended, not the sort of thing she should do in Kendal. But the duchess had told her to go for a stroll, and Violet seemed to find nothing amiss with it. It would seem, she thought, a poor-spirited thing to rush below decks now and huddle alone in the cabin when all the world was up here on the main deck. That had been just as she had been doing, she thought, since she came to London, huddling alone while the world went by her window. Well, now she was to be one of that world. It was certainly time, so she walked on, watching the others, observing the scene.

However, she did not observe much of it. She was so flustered when one young gentleman swept her a bow and gave a white-toothed smile, and so distracted when another elderly gentleman grinned most improperly at her, and, finally, so devastated when a trio of young women stared her up and down with cold disdainful eyes that she hardly had time to make the sort of observations she expected to. So she found herself a quiet corner of the rail and positioned herself there, staring pointedly out at the shore, so that anyone seeing her would think she was waiting for an escort to board the ship and come to her side. That, she felt, was a safer pose than merely perambulating the deck looking for insults. For it seemed, the fashionable world had the same opinion as regarded young females alone as did the world of Kendal.

It had been, she congratulated herself, a clever ploy, for no one bothered her now. However, she could see little of what was going on behind her and had to content herself with hearing bits of the conversation that flowed around her. Mostly, people were gossiping, she concluded. Talking about who was here and whom they expected to see. They spoke of "Lady This" and "Lord That." She heard them joke about someone's bonnet, and someone else who had put on a few stone since they were last seen. They spoke of nicknames such as "old Bertie" and "Sly Betty." All seemed to be code names, as when they giggled over "Viscount Viperous" or "the Dirty Duchess" and "the Deacon." It was odd, she thought, that no one seemed to be speaking of the trip that was to come but instead only gossiping about who was there. She could not know that in the duchess's world people traveled not to see new things, but to see who else was traveling with them and who they knew that would be at their destination upon their arrival.

And so she was almost relieved when she heard a familiar voice at her elbow address her. Although the same voice caused only consternation every time she had heard it, this time it was with almost a feeling of pleasure that she listened to its deep laconic tones. At least it was familiar and she felt no longer so alone.

"Well," he said, "and so the little country mouse takes to the sea at last. Are we to have the pleasure of your company all the way to Paris? Why, I suppose we shall," he smiled not waiting for her answer. "I had quite forgotten that the duchess was never one to miss a gay party. Ah, but my manners—allow me to introduce you, Jenkins, this is the Duchess of Crewe's latest companion, Miss . . . ah, my lamentable memory. Miss?"

"Catherine Robins, Your Lordship," Catherine said quickly, to avoid further embarrassment, worrying about whether it was proper to introduce herself, and then once she had, wishing to bite off her tongue for admitting she already knew his name and rank.

The gleam in his gray eyes showed her he well knew her predicament.

"Allow me to present Robert Jenkins, my friend and my traveling companion."

Catherine, turning and dipping a little curtsy, was further confused when she saw the gentleman she had been introduced to. For while the marquis, she noted, was dressed quietly but splendidly in dove gray and black in the peak of fashion, the shorter, muscular older man at his side was dressed as soberly and unobtrusively as any of the valets she had seen in the trail of their employers. Could it be that he was introducing her to his valet? Catherine hardly knew anymore what was proper in this strange milieu she had entered, and, throwing propriety to the winds she smiled up at Jenkins when she saw the sympathetic look on his grizzled homely square face.

"How do you do," she said.

"Oh he'll do fine, now that he's met you," the marquis went on. "As who wouldn't? You glow, my dear, you positively glow. Life with the duchess seems to have suited you to a tee. Do you know, Jenkins, that when I first met Miss Robins, she did not even know a street address in London? In fact, I flatter myself that I was the first to meet her, when Her Grace was conducting interviews. Of course, I shall not be the last. But from the moment I saw her, I knew that she would put an end to the stream of elderly parties that were quite obstructing the street in their eagerness to find employment with the duchess. It was becoming difficult to go out of doors, with the roadways thronged with elderly indigent females. Rather like stepping out into a massive sewing circle every day. There were so many old dears littering the walkways, it was becoming a traffic hazard. But then, as I laid eyes on Miss Robins, I knew she would put an end to it. We owe her a debt, Jenkins, for clearing up the public thoroughfares."

Jenkins shot the marquis a look, Catherine thought, of censure.

"Delight to meet you, Miss Robins," he said in a gravelly voice, "but you must excuse me now. For I've things to see to."

He bowed and took his leave, but the marquis seemed content to lounge at Catherine's side. He leaned back against the rail.

"Quite a change for you, isn't it?" he said to Catherine, in the same light bored tone that he had used with Jenkins. Rather, she thought angrily, as if he were still talking to someone else, even though there were only the two of them there now.

"Here you are, in the cream of London society. But you don't know a soul and can't yet get a taste of it. Her Grace has kept you cloistered, hasn't she? Now that's at an end, and you're free, but there isn't a familiar face about. Except, of course, for Violet, but she's feathering her own nest already. I," he said, with mock bravado, "shall help you. For, God help me, I know every soul aboard this packet. There," he said, turning his eyes toward a red-faced gentleman with bulging eyes, "is Old Hightower. Buried two wives and looking for a third rich enough to make matrimony worthwhile again. He lives in high style, but don't be fooled. His estates are mortgaged to the hilt, so he'll need to be quick about finding someone who hasn't heard of his financial distress. That's why he's off to Paris. Don't waste a second on him, little one, regardless of the diamonds at his throat. And there's Prendergast. Comely enough—there, that sort of a willowy-looking chap. . . . Fancies himself a deep thinker, and he'll make up a poem for you the moment you flutter those incredible eyelashes at him! But that's all you'll get. He does have a fortune, and he'll likely keep it forever, for he doesn't spend a groat if he can help it. He's a perennial houseguest and as tight with a penny as a drum. And ah, there's Lord Hunt— pass him by, child, pass him by. Drinks, you know, and forgets all of his promises in the morning. But now there, by his elbow, there's Sir Lawrence. That's one to keep your eye on. Old, but not infirm yet, and a chap who comes down handsomely when he's pleased. And he's not hard to please. And yes, there's Richard Collier, quite a prize despite that weathered look. There's many a good year left in him, and there's not a party he's likely to miss."

Catherine drew breath in fury. She cut the marquis off just as he was gesturing toward the poor old gentleman being pushed aboard in his bath chair.

"I do not care about prizes and the personalities you have been so kindly explaining to me. My job is to be a companion. And whatever you may be thinking, please disabuse yourself of the

notion that I am looking for a husband. I am here to be Her
Grace's companion. To work, not to set my cap at anyone."

The marquis stopped and looked at her with an arrested expression
in his eyes. He stared down into her face, seeing the genuine
anger and disturbance there. His eyes lingered for a moment on
her lips, and she dropped her gaze, flustered both at her temerity
in scolding him and at his intent regard.

Then he gave a shout of laughter that caused others on the
deck to stare for a moment at them.

"Wonderful," he said. "The intonation, the indignation, the
heated countenance, all wonderful. Unless, it could be . . . No, I
am not so wet behind the ears. Still," he said, in a considering
way. "What do you think of dear Violet?"

"Why, she is a delightful companion," Catherine said stoutly.

"And what of the duchess's outline of duties?" he asked in a
warmer tone of voice.

"Unexceptional," she replied.

For once the marquis himself seemed puzzled. He gave her
one more lingering look and then straightened.

"We shall see," he said cryptically. "I hope you are a good
sailor, little mouse, for the wind is picking up. I shall see you
again, I am sure." And bowing, he left.

Everything proper, she thought, with chagrin, while being
everything improper.

Catherine watched him stroll away, stopping every few moments to bow or have a few words with other passengers. He
was, she thought, watching his tall straight figure, quite the
handsomest man aboard, but then she noted, watching the expressions of the females he greeted, she was not alone in thinking
that. If only he were not so familiar and so puzzling, she sighed
as she watched his slow progress across the deck.

And as she watched, he was stopped by Violet. Violet raised a
glowing face as she flirted up at the marquis, and soon the two
were deep in conversation. While Catherine stood watching
intently, the marquis caught her at it. He looked up at her with a
glance of rueful amusement as Violet motioned toward her. And
then, before she could turn her head away, he gave her a
curiously knowing smile. Then he linked Violet's arm in his and
the two strolled away.

Catherine quelled her momentary feeling of dismay and then
resolutely turned her face toward shore again. What was it that
Miss Parkinson had told her so gently?

"A female who is a companion, no matter her birth, must always remember that she is not the social equal of her employer or of her employer's friends. However elevated her birth, she is yet an employee, and she must never imagine otherwise or she will be laying herself open to insult."

Good advice, Catherine thought; perhaps I should work it in needlepoint and hang it above my bed, for I should not forget it for a moment. And neither, she told herself sharply, should I care about the marquis' choice of companions. And she stayed at the rail till they began to call ashore and the wind turned bitter enough to drive her below.

Once she reached her cabin again, Catherine opened the door without preamble and then stood motionless in the doorway. For there was Violet, her hat and slippers off, lying back against her bed pillows, talking animatedly with Rose. And Rose, the duchess's former companion, had made herself comfortable and sprawled out all over what Catherine had assumed to be her own bed.

When Catherine appeared, the two let off talking, and it was Rose who spoke up immediately, "There you are, Catherine. I'm happy to meet you. Seeing as how we're all going to be traveling together, I wanted to meet you. I was in such a state up there, I didn't have time for a word. But now, all's tight and we can have a nice coze."

Violet watched them with a highly amused expression as Catherine stammered, "Oh, then you're accompanying someone to Paris, as well?"

"Oh, Lord love you," Rose beamed, "I've gotten my old job back. But don't look so downcast. It'll be heaps of fun for us. Imagine, the duchess is going with three companions this time! She thought it was a right old joke too. I do confess, when I saw you with Vi here, I thought I was sunk, I did. But I got down on my knees to Her Grace and told her all my troubles. I groveled, I did. I was that afraid she'd pitch me out. It would serve me right, but then where would I be? She gave me a hard time, calling me all sorts of a fool, and what could I say when she was right? Giving up a soft berth with her to fly off with a gamester and letting the world go hang—it was madness. Yes, Vi, you were right. A leopard don't change his stripes. And he going off with another like that, leaving me high and dry without even fare to get back to London. But first thing I do back in town is to go haring back to Her Grace. And then I hear she's off to Paris! Think of it, me giving up Paris like that.''

Rose shook her head in distress at herself. She was beautiful, Catherine thought, in a very different manner from Violet. She was fair and blonde, with a full figure and a warm, comfortable manner. She had fine large brown eyes and a high bosom and a head of flaxen hair, and was fully as red of lips and dark of lashes as Violet. But she was not so elegantly stylish as Violet. Rather, she was comfortable and plushy looking, and as she prattled on in her soft voice, it was impossible not to warm to her.

"So I borrowed here and I borrowed there," she said, ignoring a trill of laughter from Violet, "and I hied myself to the docks just in time to catch Her Grace. And still, I don't think I turned the trick till I said to her, I said that everyone would be positively agog when they saw her with the three of us in tow. A redhead and a blonde and a brunette. I said, what could be more smashing? More eye-catching? More distinguished? And then I saw her thinking and I went on that she'd be the success of the Continent—her name would be on everyone's lips, I said. And she upped and said, 'Yes, I think you're right.' And so here's old Rose. Coming along to Paris with you. And you needn't worry, for I won't step on your toes at all. Vi here can tell you I'm very amiable, and I'll never stand in your light. I know I'm not terribly bright, like Vi here," she said, looking imploringly at Catherine, as though Catherine's opinion meant the entire world to her, "and neither am I so elegant as you. You look a treat, just like a young lady should. So I won't take the shine out of you. But I needed this job, truly I did, so say you'll be friends and we'll have a jolly time. For if I've gotten your nose out of joint, it will be rotten for us all, and I'll feel badly for having upset everyone."

"No," said Catherine, "I don't mind. Why should I? If that is what Her Grace wishes, why should I cavil? But I truly don't understand," Catherine said sadly, shaking her head and sitting down in one of the gilt chairs in the cabin, "why someone would need two companions, let alone three. Especially when she doesn't seem to even require one, what with her personal maid seeming to do all the work for her."

"You see?" Violet said in disgusted tones, lying back on the bed again, "it never stops, not even when we're alone together."

"I think that's horrid of you," Rose said indignantly to Violet.

"Live and let live, I say. She don't mean no harm by it. She's probably born to better things, like Henrietta was, back in Tunbridge Wells. Never you mind, Catherine," Rose said pleasantly. "You go on just as you want to. I just wanted to make sure you knew that I mean no harm. And that there's plenty to go round for all three of us, seeing as how the duchess means to hit all the high spots."

Catherine looked at Rose and felt a distinct frisson of unease starting somewhere in the region of her stomach that had nothing to do with the motion of the ship.

"Enough of what to go round?" she asked slowly.

"Oh, Lord," Violet groaned, and most inelegantly flopped over on her stomach and held a pillow over her head.

"Enough gentlemen, of course, dear," Rose said, with puzzlement. "Enough gentlemen for us all to go around. There's plenty of fish in this sea. And even though there'll be three of us, we're all so different, there'll be money enough for all of us to make. I'll never cut into your takings, dear," she said, eyeing Catherine's pale face with distress. "Never fear, we'll get on beautifully, like three sisters."

Chapter VI

Not many people were above deck now. The sky was lowering and the motion of the boat had already sorted out the good sailors from the bad, sending the latter below to suffer in privacy. And even those who did not mind the rolling sea, did not care to brave the chill winds and stayed below as well. Catherine had discovered that she was a good sailor, or perhaps it was just that she was so distressed that it would not matter to her if she were in the center of a tidal wave. Her own thoughts were in such turmoil that the motion of the ship could not match them for turbulence.

She stood at the deck and gripped the rail tightly with her mittened fingers. A great many things made sense to her now— from the duchess's servants' attitudes to the attitude of Madame Bertrand, to even the marquis' mocking comments. Her face flamed when she thought of him and what she now knew he had meant every time he spoke to her. But she was not a stupid girl, and the fact that she had seen nothing in her situation that was not glaringly out of line distressed her almost as much as the opinions of the marquis and everyone she had met in the duchess's service.

For there was no doubt in her mind now. The artless Rose had prattled on and on till she had erased all doubts. She had been hired on only because Rose and Violet were not available, and Rose and Violet had been beautiful women, and young, at least far younger than the general run of ladies' companions in the marketplace. But there was no doubt, as incredible as it seemed, Rose and Violet were women of low repute. Catherine thought of all the euphemisms she had ever heard. They were demireps, they were fancy pieces. Oh, Lord, she thought, have an end to it, they were women who catered to the darker needs of strange gentlemen, whatever you called them.

And here she was, Catherine Robins, unmarried daughter of a younger son related to the great house of the Earl of Dorset, brought up as properly and as poorly as a churchmouse, traveling companion to a duchess and two highly paid cyprians. And presently almost penniless and precisely in the midst of the English Channel. I truly am "at sea," Catherine grieved.

She tried to marshal her thoughts. For she had to decide on some plan of action immediately. Every moment brought her closer to France. The worst, she thought sadly, was done. She had hired on—she had been introduced into the household of the Duchess of Crewe. And all those that had seen or met her most probably thought her on a par with Rose and Violet. What is done is irremediable, she thought vehemently, in an effort to think clearly, pushing aside intrusive thoughts of the disdainful marquis. It was the future she had to think on.

Her first impulse was to cut and run. She felt sullied by her new knowledge and sick at heart at her new understanding of Rose and Violet. The best thing would be to turn and go at once. But then she did some sums rapidly in her head. She had spent a great deal of her money on those foolish lace and brocades she had bought to embellish and repair her gowns. And most of the remainder of her income had gone for Jane and Arthur's presents and gratuities to the servants in the duchess's London house when she had left. If she should decide to turn right back and go home on a return ship when they landed at Dieppe, she would have barely enough to reach her home shores. Then there would be the problem of how to obtain enough funds to pay the many stage fares to see her home to the north country.

How could she even think of borrowing from either Rose or Violet? She could not approach them and say, "I cannot travel with two females as low as you are. My sensibilities are wounded to be even considered in the same light as you. So please lend me enough money to go home." And if she shuddered to think of how respectable people thought of her, she now also had a few guilty feelings about Rose and Violet's opinions of her. For no sooner had Rose done with her long and artless talk than Catherine had stared at her and blurted, "I did not know! I had no idea," and had rushed, shocked and shamed, from the cabin.

That, she thought, furious with herself, had been unnecessary and cruel.

The major problem, she tried to think dispassionately, was the duchess. For she did not know her well enough to know what her true opinion of her companions was. The dowager was such a dignified, socially secure woman that Catherine found it hard to believe she knew the truth about her companions. She had always spoken of Rose and Violet's doings in terms of their "high jinks" and "larks" and "nonsense." It was, Catherine thought desperately, entirely possible that the old woman was naive enough to think they were just innocent romps. Or equally possible that the duchess's mind was turned with age, and that she truly did not notice such goings-on.

The duchess had made it clear that she would hold her wages till the trip was done, or pay quarterly, and, in truth, since paying a sum of money a few weeks past, she owed not a cent to Catherine. All of her wages were yet to be earned. Why should the dowager just hand over monies to a companion who quit her employ the moment they had begun their journey?

And, Catherine thought with a start, if the duchess's companions had such a reputation, how could Catherine ever find decent employment in London again? For the duchess would never write a reference if she quit so precipitously. But more, even if she did, such a reference would not be worth the paper it was written on.

After a half hour in the biting wind on the rolling deck, only two things were abundantly clear to Catherine. One was that she did not have enough resources to get safely home by herself. And two was that she did not have the resources to go safely on with the duchess. Yet every moment the ship bore her onward.

She bent with her head cradled in her arms, by the rail of the ship, cold within and without, until a light touch on her arm recalled her to herself.

"Why, Miss Robins, are you ill?" Jenkins' voice asked softly.

She looked up to see his concerned face close to hers. His was a lined and weathered visage. His hazel eyes looked as though they had squinted against many suns, and his short-cropped brown hair and neatness of person made him seem a comforting figure. He was old enough to be her father, and looked as though he might consider himself as such. She was tempted to blurt out her whole wretched story to him, stranger though he was. But then another familiar voice said, "The sea is not always kind to newcomers. Our little country mouse has strayed too far from her farmhouse.''

Catherine's head shot up and she looked with a mixture of embarrassment and defiance at the marquis. "I am not ill," she said. "I was only thinking about things. And I lost track of the hours."

She wondered suddenly if she could confide in him. He, alone of all the people on the ship was a familiar face. He would certainly have the resources not to miss advancing the small amount of money to see her safely home. If only she could strike the right conciliatory note, perhaps he could even give her some advice, for he was a worldly man. She hoped that he would unbend for a moment to give her the chance to speak freely. Jenkins, she saw, was watching her with a kind, concerned expression. She kept her gaze on the marquis as he stood and looked down at her with eyes as fathomless as the slate-gray sea they were crossing and she began to pluck up her courage.

Before she could speak again, he smiled, not at all kindly, and said in an explanatory fashion to Jenkins, "No, she's not a bit afflicted with mal de mer. So put away your vinaigrette, Jenkins. Rather, I think, Miss Robins is afflicted with a surfeit of companionship. Her cabin is literally bulging at the seams. The fair Rose has joined Violet, and now the duchess has a veritable bower of pretty flowers in her employ. Rose, Violet, and Catherine. That does not have the right ring to it. You ought to change your name, little one, to Forget-me-not, to ensure your standing with the duchess. And the gentlemen. Miss Robins is here, I think, Jenkins, because it is difficult for a little young country flower to keep her head high in the presence of two such spectacular blooms as Rose and Violet. But never fear,'' he said, laying one gray-gloved hand across her cheek to tuck back in an errant wind-whipped curl. "There are many gentlemen aboard who are weary of hothouse blossoms and who will welcome a fresh young English nosegay such as yourself."

All of Catherine's fears and shame coalesced into one direct and burning emotion of hatred toward the marquis. He stood there smiling, he who had been her one possible lifeline, and dashed all her nebulous hopes of escape to bits with his words. She had thought to confide in him, but before she had been able to breathe one word, he had begun a frontal attack upon her. She dashed his hand away and looked at him with brimming eyes.

"I find your humor ill bred," she said. "And your inferences

impertinent. Good day.'' And she turned on her heel and walked
off. After one moment's silence, she heard a laughing "Bravo!"
called in the distance behind her.

"Didn't she carry that off well?'' the marquis laughed. "Like
the dowager herself. She is a quick study, I'll be bound.''

"I think you're being a bit hard on her, lad,'' Jenkins said
reproachfully.

The marquis' face hardened and he turned to look out to sea.

"She's only a little artificial flower, after all, Jenkins. Don't
tell me you're touched and believe her role as ingenue?''

"As to that,'' Jenkins said, turning to face the sea as well, to
get a last glimpse of home, "I couldn't say. But no matter what
she is, she's only a girl. It's not like you to get so spiteful,
especially toward a woman. I saw you chatting up Violet as nice
as can be. And she's a right old tart.''

"But she's an honest old tart,'' the marquis answered slowly,
"with no dissembling. Our Miss Robins aspires to play the grand
lady; it's that, I think, that tickles me.''

"Don't seem to tickle you. Seems to gall you,'' Jenkins said.

"Perhaps. Perhaps it is just that I value honesty. And I might
like her very well if she would drop that facade of purity.''

"Well,'' said Jenkins at length, "facade's what it's all about,
isn't it? With all of them? Pretending to be attracted and then
pleasured, with a fellow pretending he don't notice the pretense.
That's all part of the trade.''

"And probably why I don't patronize such businesswomen,''
the marquis said loftily, till he caught Jenkins' eye and then
laughed lightly. "Or at least such obvious tradeswomen. You
old wretch, you make me admit my every pretense.''

"Seems you were interested enough in our bold little Violet,''
Jenkins ruminated.

"It always pays, Jenkins, to have the friendship of such
females. For there's a great many pillows that they have their
ears to, and a great deal of information they can, all unwittingly,
be privy to. So although I don't have any designs on Violet, and
well she knows it, it does pay to be in her good graces.''

"Then, why are you going out of your way to alienate the
little beauty?'' Jenkins asked innocently.

"Be damned to you,'' the marquis said pleasantly, and as he
cuffed Jenkins' shoulder, they both began to laugh.

"It's just that 'tis pity she's a whore,'' the marquis finally said,
when Jenkins thought he had forgotten the subject.

"You can't be sure of that, either," Jenkins finally replied.

"Oh yes, and Violet may be contemplating a life in the convent. Give over, old friend."

"Then meet her price and see."

"I'm not interested in the question," the marquis said, yawning.

And it's not often that you lie to me, Jenkins thought, looking at the marquis' profile, or to yourself.

"It's not such a bad crossing, for January," Jenkins said eventually, to dispel the marquis' frown.

"What? Oh no, it isn't," his companion replied, and they talked of ships and crossings till the wind blew them below to seek refuge as well.

Catherine went back to her cabin, because she had nowhere else to go. And because she wanted to make amends to Rose and Violet.

She had no idea, as she crept back in, of what a fight had been raging before her return. For Rose and Violet now sat calmly, looking through their belongings, not speaking a word to each other.

But the moment Catherine had risen, ashen-faced, and fled, they had both sat there in stunned silence.

"Oh Vi," Rose had wailed after a moment, "see how you've made a mull of it? You told me she was one of us, up to every trick, young as she was. And though when I first laid eyes on her I doubted it, really I doubted it, still you told me she was a deep one. And now, you see, you was wrong. She's just a little innocent and I've gone and shocked her to the bone. Oh I could bite out my tongue."

"Don't be a fool," Violet countered, sitting up and throwing away her pillow, with a look of furious dismay on her face. "It's all part of her game, I tell you. She never drops her guard, not for a moment. All meek and mild, and she'd stab you in the back in a minute. I know her kind."

"That you don't," Rose shouted with unaccustomed heat. "For where would you ever meet such a sweet young innocent?"

"Stupid cow," Violet charged back. "If she was such a sweet young innocent, what would she be doing signing on with the old torment for?"

"Well, that's it exactly," Rose sniffed, overtaken with remorse. "She'd hire on with Her Grace exactly because she didn't know what she was about. For we did leave the dowager in the lurch, and that you do know. And when she asked me for the name of a replacement, I didn't give her any, 'cause I wanted to leave the door open, in case things didn't work out. And it's a good job I did. But I'll wager you didn't give her a name neither. So she must have hired on this little pretty, just 'cause she's so pretty and young and know-nothing.'' And Rose dabbled at her eyes with the edge of the bed covers.

"I never thought you were such a flat, Rose," Violet sneered. "To be taken in so by an act of innocence.''

"Well, it's true that I've been taken in, many times, by the gentlemen," Rose said slowly, "for I don't understand them at all, I think. Or maybe it's just that I keep expecting things of them that just ain't there. But I do know women. And I'll stake my life on that little thing's honesty. For if she was up to snuff, why shouldn't she come clean with us? You've done a terrible wrong, Vi, that you have.''

Violet, assailed by self-doubt, struck back instantly. "Rose, I vow Carlton took half your brains with him when he took all your money. Do you think the old fiend would run the risk of hiring on a good girl of good birth and reputation?''

"And I think you've gotten hard as nails, Violet; of course, she would, seeing as how she's half turned in the head. And well you know it too. Didn't you just say on our last trip as to how it wouldn't be long before the old cow would be in Bedlam, and how we might never meet on another jaunt together again? Not that I ever approved of how you refer to Her Grace. Because dicked in the nob or not, she's still a duchess, mind. Mad as hatter though she may be. So, of course, she'd hire on some sweet young thing. And a sweet young thing she is. I've never seen her on the town, and you haven't neither. Oh I feel like a brute, Vi, really I do, and you would too, if you hadn't grown so hard.''

"Well, I haven't grown so hard as your head, Rose," Violet shrieked in a voice that would have stood her in good stead in her first chosen profession, the stage. "And don't you start blaming me—it was your babbling, your going on and on about your exploits that sent her flying, not mine. I was close mouthed as can be with her. So don't put the blame on me.''

"You've grown cruel, and hard, yes hard, Violet," Rose stated with ponderous calm. "And I'm sorry for it.''

The two fell silent, avoiding each other's eye. And they went about pointedly searching through their portmanteaus, deep in their own thoughts, in exaggerated silence, till Catherine tapped lightly and entered their cabin again, after her time thinking on the deck.

Catherine spoke very quietly.

"I am very sorry," she said, in the voice of a small child who has committed some grave misdemeanor and is determined to beg forgiveness as nicely as she is able, "about the way that I behaved. It was unconscionably rude on my part. Perhaps it was just that I was angry at myself for not seeing what was afoot. I quite deceived myself. And it was wrong in me to have given you the impression that I was disapproving or angry at you. For, you see, I was angry, but only at myself."

"Oh there, there, my dear," Rose cried, seeing the girl standing head bowed and alone in the center of their little room, "we didn't take anything amiss, did we, Vi? So you must not apologize, certainly not, right, Vi?"

"Right," Violet said, looking uncharacteristically conscious. "Not a thing to apologize for."

"That is very kind of you," Catherine said, and then, turning her large anxious eyes to both of them in turn, she asked, hesitantly, "But there is something I must ask you. And it is very difficult for me, so please bear with me for a moment, and pray do not take offense."

"Oh we shall not," Rose hastened to tell her, looking very anxious herself.

"It is just this," Catherine began. "Does Her Grace, that is to say, this is of primary importance to me, does the duchess know and condone your, ah, activities that go beyond companioning her?"

"As to that, you see, my dear, we really could not say," Rose said nervously. "Her Grace gives us free time once she is abed and no longer requires our presence. She is a very free, that is to say, a very—"

"Liberal," Violet put in quickly, seeing Rose stumble.

"Yes, an exceedingly liberal employer. And she does not care what we get up to when she is not abroad. That is, so long as we are discreet and do not embroil her in any of our activities."

"Then," Catherine ventured, raising her head, "you are not required to—to do," she stammered, "what you do?"

"Oh, Lord love you, no," Rose laughed in relief. "That is not the case at all. Why, just ask Vi, she traveled with Her Grace for a season before I signed on."

"Rose speaks no less than truth," Violet said hastily, "for the duchess hired me only as companion."

"Just so," said Rose in satisfaction.

"But I do not understand, surely she must have heard . . . she does not care, then, you say?"

"The duchess," Violet said quickly, "enjoys the attention we bring her. She enjoys the notice she receives when we are with her. As to what she may have heard, we cannot say."

"So, then," Catherine went on, thinking aloud, "she does not expect me to, she does not require me to . . ."

"Oh never, I'm sure," Rose said in horrified tones. "She never discusses such things with us."

"Then I can stay on," Catherine asked hopefully, "and only be a companion, and nothing else? No matter," she said, with a little shake of her head, "what anyone else thinks? I cannot see how I can turn and leave now. And once I return home to Kendal, I shall, in any event, hardly be running into anyone that I have met here. Kendal is such a long, long way from London and Paris in so many ways," Catherine thought aloud, "that it hardly matters what anyone in the duchess's set thinks of me. So, after this journey, I will retire and go to live out my life back home where no one has ever heard of the duchess to begin with. Not," she said, aghast at her ruminations, "that you would not be welcome in Kendal. Or that I think anything—"

Violet cut her off with a wry smile.

"Give over, Miss Catherine. If you are a nice little thing from the country, if you are well born, of course you're shocked to flinders to find yourself with us. We're hardly the sort of companions a well-bred miss hopes to find herself with. But that don't bother us. So you're staying on then?"

"If you think, and I truly ask you please to tell me the truth, that I can go forward with the duchess and not be expected by her to—to pursue another trade."

Violet gave out a little yip of laughter.

"Oh, that's a nice way of putting it. I suppose your pockets are to let, then?"

Catherine nodded sadly.

"Well, we can't help you out there neither. For we're both in the same case. But once we get ashore, we can remedy that, and if you want, we'll advance you the funds to skip out." Violet looked almost as shocked as Rose and Catherine did at her sudden burst of generosity.

"Oh no, no," Catherine protested immediately. "That wouldn't be right." Catherine thought suddenly of the names she could put to someone who profited from a cyprian's earnings and then blurted, afraid that her companions might know the nature of her thoughts from her horrified expression, "I would not ask you to be responsible for me. For if I can go on solely as a companion, as I was engaged to do, I can see the journey out and then take my earnings and go home."

"Of course you can go on with us. In fact, we can put the word about the gentlemen that you are not"—Rose paused—"of a sporting disposition."

Violet winced at Rose's effort to tidy up her speech, and then, considering the young miss so sadly lost in their midst, thought rapidly. For no doubt the little beauty would draw the gentlemen like flies to a picnic basket. And then she and Rose could only profit the more from the fact that she was unwilling to go off with them. She smiled with perfect charity at Catherine.

"Rose is right, we'll tell them, never fear. And there is no reason to concern yourself as to the duchess's caring one jot one way or the other. She'll be glad enough if you only play the companion well. All she wants is for heads to turn when she appears. She don't give a tinker's damn as to what you do to occupy your free time. Whether you sew a fine seam alone in your room or dance naked in a fountain, it's all the same to her. And that's the truth."

"Very true," seconded Rose.

"And," Violet said triumphantly, "you yourself said no one at home is likely to ever know what the duchess and her set is about. So cheer up. It will be a good journey. Rose and I will be amiable enough. And all the duchess wants of you is to keep by her side in good looks. You can just put all else out of your mind."

"You two must think me a fool," Catherine said sadly.

"Oh no," Rose protested. "We were all young once. Only, perhaps, not quite so young."

Catherine laughed. And then she looked at her two fellow companions.

"I think I shall grow up quite a bit on this journey."

"Travel is broadening," Rose agreed complacently, ignoring the weary look Violet shot her.

Chapter VII

The crossing, all agreed, was not so bad as it might have been. There were those, of course, who had been taken ill by the vessel's rocking over the January seas, and those who had been, as they expected, ill no matter what the conditions of the weather. But it might have been worse—there had been only the cutting wind and the winter's cold. Travelers who were more experienced with the vagaries of the channel's weather could only be grateful that there had been no pouring rains or wind-driven squalls of ice.

As the shores of France loomed in the distance, the passengers began to assemble themselves for departure. Catherine had spent the remainder of her journey hugging her newfound knowledge to herself and attempting to try on a new public face. For, knowing what she did, she reasoned there was no way she could delude herself into forgetting it for a moment. If she could not go homeward, she must go onward with a new attitude. But which one?

She could not appear to be constantly disapproving, because she felt that would make her a sanctimonious fool, to go on with people of whom she patently disapproved. The only hope for it, she thought sadly, was to maintain an air of irreproachable dignity. To carry on as though she well knew what people thought, but was too sophisticated to care. No, she thought, not sophisticated, for that she could not simulate as she was decidedly not a woman of the world. Rather, that she knew what was happening about her, but chose not to notice or care. That was, after all, just what she was doing. Her attitude must be then, she thought, much as her employer's was. Tolerant and uncaring.

And if she felt any squeamish qualms about having to affect any sort of attitude at all, and not simply give the whole matter up and fly off to try to get home in any manner that she could, she consoled herself by recalling that a young woman alone and without funds in the English countryside might be thought of as a great deal worse than one employed in the entourage of a duchess of the realm.

So Catherine stood, head high, surrounded by her trunks, on the deck of the packet and watched as the vessel began its docking procedures. And when the Marquis of Bessacarr strolled by with Jenkins at his shoulder, Catherine found her newly born affect of worldliness sufficient to allow her to acknowledge his presence with a smile and a nod in his direction.

He paused in his steps, for they both realized that it was the first time she had ever admitted his presence without his first having approached or accosted her. He smiled in his faint cynical manner and came to her side.

"So you have forgiven me my rash speculations? I am glad of it. I was, I fear, afflicted with the tediousness of the journey, and I let my tongue run away with me. How pleasant it is to see that you have compassion as well as beauty, little one," he said, bowing over her hand.

Catherine smiled politely at him and at Jenkins, and said, she noticed, without the usual fast beating of her heart or dryness in her mouth, "Certainly. There is nothing to apologize for."

It was amazing, she thought, now that she understood what all his sly references to her meant, her feelings of confusion in his presence had fled. It was as though she were a different person he was speaking to, and as though they both were part of an amusing play. Newly confident, she only smiled demurely when he gazed thoughtfully at her.

"I understand that we are both to be guests at Sir Sidney's little house party."

She knew nothing of the sort, but only said carelessly, "I am sure it will be most pleasant."

"Oh, delightful, I'm sure," he said, with a puzzled look at her. "And I shall be envied, for I think that Jenkins and I are the only gentlemen to have made your acquaintance as yet. For I see that you do not join your companions." He gestured toward Rose and Violet, who were chatting with a group of gentlemen.

"No," she said a little nervously, "but please excuse me, as I think the duchess requires me now."

She nodded and fairly flew off toward the duchess, who, she was sure, had forgotten her existence entirely for the moment.

She had convinced herself that the world's opinion did not matter. But yet it seemed, despite her best efforts, that one gentleman's opinion mattered very much. She discovered she could not bear the contempt in his eyes.

"Oh, there you are, Catherine," the duchess said, seeing her slip into the outskirts of the impromptu circle that had formed around her.

"This is Catherine Robins, my newest companion," the duchess said to the general interest of the group of elderly persons around her. "Rose and Violet you know of old. But Catherine here has only just joined me."

There were several murmurs of introduction and interested looks in Catherine's direction. A moment later, she found herself forgotten as the discussion turned to accommodations that were considered acceptable in Paris these days. Catherine had a good chance to covertly study the group that surrounded her employer.

They were all old, she thought with relief—indeed, some seemed ancient. A few of the gentlemen still sported periwigs, and the women were either thinned by age, as was the duchess, or blatantly plump. Some were dressed in high style and others sported garments that seemed to have come straight out of museums. One poor old gentleman, Catherine noticed, sat trembling in his bath chair, attended by an impassive valet. It was he who was going on, in a high, tremulous voice, about how the conditions of travel had deteriorated since his last journey to the City of Light.

"Of course," said the thin, pale old gentleman at Catherine's side, "that was before the flood, you know. Poor old Richard used to dance attendance on Pompadour herself, when they were both in nursery, I believe," he said, laughing. "And Cleopatra as well, I'll warrant."

Catherine turned to the speaker. He bowed and then looked at her with frankly approving eyes. She did not mind his obvious interest, because he was so very old and innocent looking. He had been tall, she guessed, in youth, but age had shrunken him, and now he appeared slender and almost translucently fragile. He had a thin coating of gray hair and his face was gentle and lined. His whole attitude, from the sober hues of his clothes to the quietness of his voice, gave her the impression of a gentle, kindly old fellow. So she smiled wholeheartedly at him.

"Ah, the duchess has picked herself a lovely this time," he said. "I hope you do not mind me being so personal, but at my age, alas, all I can do is admire loveliness in all its forms."

In truth, Catherine was growing weary of hearing nothing but references to her physical person, but it was impossible to mind anything this kind old gentleman said.

"Thank you," she said softly.

"Hah, look at the Vicar," cried the duchess. "Just got in a new flower and he's already buzzing around her."

"But never fear, little lovely," cackled one old female in a dizzying collection of shawls and scarves, "for he's lost his sting."

The assembled old people began laughing, and Catherine noticed that the man they called "the Vicar" laughed along with them.

"That is true," he said ruefully, "but Miss Robins seems to be a perceptive child, and so suffers my attentions nonetheless. We shall meet at Sir Sidney's, my dear, and show these doubters that I can still, at least, dance to a tune or two."

Catherine nodded her agreement, and further sounds of merriment were stilled as the vessel, now tied securely to the dock, began to let its passengers off.

The duchess debarked in state, leading her ensemble of four females—Gracie directly behind her, and then Rose, Violet, and Catherine—carefully picking their way down the gangplank.

"So exit the old hen and her delicious chicks," the marquis remarked to Jenkins from his observation point against the rails.

"I tell you, Jenkins," he said, in low tones, dispiritedly, "I cannot like this employment. Pitched into the midst of these posturing, empty, pleasure seekers. I'd rather be in the thick of some action or in any other company but this. Having to play at their games, play at being one with them is wearing. Fiend seize the old chap, I'll gather whatever I can and be quit of this charade as soon as possible. I cannot think I can learn enough of import for this trip to be worthwhile. I boarded this packet just to be in step with them. And what have I discerned so far? That Lady Scofield has left her lord for a dancing instructor. That he does not care so long as she takes care not to return too soon. That Lord Hunt is on the prowl for a French mistress, that old Bertie expects to make a killing at the gaming tables, and old Philip has to, else he cannot return home at all. That the Dirty Duchess has three females for hire in her train, one of them with the airs of a lady—oh, all of this, I am sure will thrill the old chap and save our dear country.''

"Aye," Jenkins said softly, "but you've not set foot on La Belle France yet. And you've not put your eyes or ears to work yet. It's in Paris where the meat of the matter lies.''

"And I have to stop off at Sir Sidney's and prattle with the lot there first,'' the Marquis sighed.

"That you do,'' Jenkins nodded. "For if you pass up an invitation such as that, they'll surely smell a rat. You're a pleasure-loving lad, and no pleasure lover would pass up such a treat."

"Then let's haul ourselves off there instanter," the marquis decided, uncoiling his long frame, "for the sooner it's over, the sooner we can go on. And,'' he said, eyeing the duchess's party as it disposed itself into a coach in the quay below, "I might just seek some pleasure there as well.''

"Well,'' said the duchess, with satisfaction, "now we're off. Sir Sidney has rented a house, and a great many good people are to be stopping off there before Paris. And so shall we. You've done well, Catherine," she said with pleasure. "The Vicar's an astute man, and he likes the cut of you. And I noticed that everyone is bowled over by my three companions, Rose, you were quite right. Now, I shall take a brief rest and hope that it is not too long till we reach Sir Sidney's. I grow weary of so much travel, but I think it is best not to chance some local hostelry this night. Far better to spend the first night at Sir Sidney's establishment. For while it may be a foreign house, it has an Englishman in residence.''

And, so saying, the duchess gave a satisfied grunt and closed her eyes. Rose, Violet, and Catherine sat rather closely together on the seat opposite the duchess and Gracie. Their luggage traveled in one vast heap in the coach behind them.

"I saw you in conversation with Sinjun, Catherine,'' Violet whispered, when she thought enough time had passed for the duchess to have found the slumber she sought.

"Sinjun?" Catherine asked, confused.

"The Marquis of Bessacarr, the handsome lord you were chatting up, on deck,'' Violet answered. "For his friends call him so.''

"Go on with you,'' Rose tittered. "Sinjun. Don't you just wish you called him so?''

Violet sniffed. "Well, I had quite a nice coze with him earlier. And he did ask after the new 'chick,' as he called her."

"But 'Sinjun' indeed." Rose snickered. "As if you two were bosom bows."

"He's too high in the instep for me," Violet said calmly.

"All he'd have to do is crook a finger, Vi, and you know it. But he never does. He chats with us, and he says such lovely things so charmingly, but there's an end to it," she told Catherine.

"Not," Violet put in, "that he's a hermit. But when he has the like of Gwyn Starr in London. And Belle Fleur, and almost any female like that, he doesn't tarry with us."

"And Lady Spencer last season, I hear. So don't be alarmed if he says things to you, Catherine, for he's only tarrying. And don't bother yourself about the Vicar's attentions either," Rose whispered, "for he's old as the hills. I hear he was a terror years ago, but now he just sits back and watches like the duchess. So rest easy about him as well."

Catherine nodded, both pleased and a little embarrassed about her two fellow companions' new solicitude on her behalf. But before they could offer her any further advice, the duchess opened one sharp eye.

"If you ladies want to prattle all the way, kindly let me know. I shall ride with the baggage."

And the three of them fell to guilty silence as their coach rolled on through the city and outward, into the unknown center of France.

Catherine was stiff in every limb by the time the coach rolled into the great courtyard. She did not know how a woman of the duchess's years could wake so quickly, and look about so brightly, as they reached their destination. It was true that the dowager had slept soundly for all the hours that Catherine had been looking out her window, trying to get glimpses of the life and people in this new land. But still, she seemed more alert and rested now than the girl who was decades her junior.

It was night, yet the great house seemed to blaze with light. Liveried footmen leaped forward to greet them and Catherine could see that other coaches were unloading other newly come passengers as well. In the gloom dispelled by the torches the footmen were bearing, Catherine could make out familiar persons from the boat, alighting from their carriages. The house itself, she saw with wonder, as she stepped stiffly out onto the circular drive, was massive. Gray and distinguished, it seemed a palace to her. She had never beheld so old and imposing a residence.

But neither her employer nor her companions seemed impressed. They had seen English country seats before, and this monumental old château was simply another stopping-off place for them. It had been the proud home of a French duke, who had fled during the revolution. Sadly, when the Bourbon had been placed back upon the throne and Napoleon left to lord it over only a small island, the duke was too impoverished and defeated by age to return. Instead, he hoped to better his heirs' conditions by letting the château out, for an exorbitant fee, to those who could afford it. And Sir Sidney and his shocking wife could afford it well enough. They had come over to France the moment hostilities had ceased, much to the relief of Sidney's more correct relations, and lorded it there in the ancient manner ever since. They never needed to journey to Paris at all for gaiety, Sir Sidney often said happily, since all those who mattered in Paris would be sure to come to him, either before or after they visited the great city. And so life in the great house had been a constant party since they had arrived.

Sir Sidney and his blatantly beautiful wife (an actress who had been lucky beyond her deserts, Violet whispered to Catherine as they went up the great steps to the front portals) were busily greeting their new guests.

"Ah, Duchess." Sir Sidney, a portly little man, beamed. "So you have come to grace our halls as well. And dear little Violet, and this must be Rose," he chortled, chucking Rose under her chin. "You see, we hear all here at Beauvoir. But who is this little darling? Never say, Duchess, that you have three exquisite companions now?"

The duchess permitted herself a little smile. "I do say it, Ollie. Good evening, Lady Sidney. So good of you to have us," the Duchess said, knowing quite well that Lady Sidney had nothing to say about who shared her house with her.

But her host and hostess had already turned to greet other arrivals, Sir Sidney chuckling that every time the packet came from France, he sent orders to his servants to make up the beds, for the British were coming. It was with relief that Catherine followed in the train of the duchess up the staircase, off the huge stone hall to which no amount of torches or candles could lend warmth.

A flustered housekeeper showed them to spacious, lavish rooms that Catherine was too weary to admire. Before settling in, Catherine scratched softly on the duchess's door. Being told by a perfunctory Gracie, already in her night shift, that the duchess was going to retire, Catherine was happy to wash and slip into bed. She had time only to murmur a silent thanks that she had gotten so far without difficulties before sleep took her far from the duchess, the château, and France.

Catherine knew that her employer never rose before noon, and in the hours that she wandered through Sir Sidney's house, she came to understand that no female of rank did otherwise. Only the lower servants and she herself were up and about in the morning. A few gentlemen, she heard, had gone out early to ride with Sir Sidney over his countless rented acres. But she was well used to being alone, and contented herself in prowling the halls and investigating the premises, storing up details to regale Jane and Arthur with on some later, quiet country evening.

Still, she thought crossly much later on, as she struggled to do up her buttons while changing for dinner, if she could only get into the habit of sleeping the day away, her state would be vastly improved.

Rose tapped and entered her room just as the early dusk of a winter's day descended. Catherine stared at her in awe. For the comfortable, companionable Rose of the day seemed vanished. In her stead stood a startlingly beautiful woman. Rose wore a low gown, the color of her namesake. Her blond hair was swept up in a flurry of ringlets, a sparkling necklace sat upon her ample breast, and she glittered when she walked. A heavy perfume hung over her, and her bright eyes seemed heavily lidded and glistened in the candle's glow.

"Oh, don't you look fine?" Rose said happily, turning to Violet, all in flaming red, with red plumes twined in her curls, as she stepped into the room behind her. "Don't Catherine look lovely? I told her to get rigged out fine, and so she did."

"And she didn't even ring for a maid. And so you should have, Catherine, to help you dress. Even though mine couldn't get out a 'how do you do' in English, and just chirped 'wee-wee' whenever I asked her anything."

Catherine could see nothing exceptional in her looks beside her two co-companions. She wore the simplest of light-green garments that she could find in her wardrobe, with a sash of darker green beneath her breasts. She had built up Madame

Bertrand's bold bodice so that only some of her white shoulders
and breasts showed above it—not at all like Violet and Rose's
deep expanses of exposed breast. At the last moment she had
bound up her dark hair with a green fillet, and the only ornament
she wore was a simple gold pendant that her mother had left her.
She felt she looked the servant to Violet and Rose's great ladies.

But they saw, tentative and graceful in the candlelight, a slip
and sprite of refreshing girl, so simple and refreshing as to
overwhelm their finery and make them seem tawdry.

Violet sighed. "You're either the boldest thing in creation or
the most innocent. I'm not sure I want to know. Come, we're dining
in state with the 'great lady.' After that, simply stay away from
darkened corners or stay at the old dame's side if you wish to
escape trouble."

"Don't rally with Sir Sidney, dear," Rose cautioned as they
went on slippered feet to the duchess's room, "for he's a right
old caution. And don't dance with Lord Lambert, nor Jimmy
Crawley neither. And don't flirt with Sir Harold, for he's up to
no good, and don't agree to see Viscount Hightower's collection
of snuffboxes, because he hasn't got any, and, no matter what he
says, don't offer to help Jamie Prendergast when he comes all
over faint, for he's fit as may be, whatever he says."

Rose's admonitions went on, with Catherine losing track of
her whispered warnings and only vowing fiercely to herself to
avoid all members of the opposite gender, footmen and waiters
included. At last the duchess appeared in her doorway, nodding
complacently at her entourage and quite taking their breath away.
For she was in her best looks, all in lavender, tall, erect, and
stately. She breezed down the stairs, as regal as a visiting
dignitary, with her three companions behind her and her devoted
Gracie watching from an unobtrusive darkened part of the upper
stair.

They dined in a great room with a blazing fireplace that was
big enough, Catherine thought, to accommodate a forest full of
logs. Their table was set up under two huge chandeliers whose
candles lit their plates and faces as daylight, but left the shadowy
retainers who filled their dishes and glasses as faceless as wraiths.
Catherine might not have been able to swallow a morsel if it
were not for the fortuitous fact that she had been seated next to
the gentleman she had met on the ship whom the duchess had
called "the Vicar." He was actually, he admitted, the Baron
Watchtower, but his intimates called him Vicar because of his

quiet, cautious ways. Catherine found him a dear, gentle old fellow and enjoyed his calm good humor and his easygoing ways.

She wondered what he was doing in this ribald company, for all about them the other guests, led by their host and hostess, were laughing loudly and drinking freely and calling to each other from all parts of the great table, in a manner, she thought, that was not at all seemly. But the Vicar spoke no more than the truth when he told her that though he was too old for such pleasures, still he enjoyed being part of such merry company. She could not know that in his time, the Vicar, so named because all his actions had so outrageously belied his manner, had been one of the most absolute dissolutes of his era. There had been no pleasure of the senses that he had not engaged in, no deeds too outrageous for him to attempt. He had never married, never having been so inclined toward women. And when he had noted an excellent nephew coming of age, he had decided the fellow would do a great deal better with his title than he ever had, and so had gone happily on with his own proclivities. Now he was truly burnt out and content, at last, to be just an observer of the scene. But since he had nothing in common with the tame socially correct world, he traveled in the duchess's set, preferring to spend the last of his years among those who understood his past rather than those who pretended to ignore it.

Catherine, he thought, watching her animated face, and seeing the candles reflected in the blue depths of her eyes, was in way over her head. This amused him, and he made a note to follow her adventures. For, for all his pleasant ways and gentle, amused acceptance of life, he was fully as selfish as the duchess and would never make a move to help a fellow creature if in some way it did not help him. Like the duchess, he had no interest in the passions between a man and a woman, but instead of spending his time gaining the attention of others, as she did, he derived pleasure from simply watching the follies of others. Catherine, he thought, would be an entertaining little creature to watch. There was every possibility she was what she appeared to be. And every possibility she was not. He was delighted to devote his attention to her throughout the long and riotous dinner.

After dinner, the ladies absented themselves from the gentlemen for only a brief time. The servants scurried to set up gaming tables in the great room to the left of the staircase, and musicians filed into the other room to the right. Catherine stood with Rose and Violet in the ladies' withdrawing room, but when the great doors opened, with a hasty farewell they both left her. She quickly sought out the duchess, who was seated at a card table with another elderly female and two middle-aged gentlemen.

Catherine, not wishing to call attention to herself to the point of summoning a chair, stood at Her Grace's shoulder in the shadows of the candlelight. After a few hands of a game Catherine did not know, the duchess glanced up at her.

"I thought so," the duchess grumbled. "My luck never runs right when someone's watching the cards. Run away, gel, I don't require you now. You're setting my luck to ruin. Run away, gel, and amuse yourself. I won't need you any longer tonight."

Catherine wandered out of the gaming room, for she did not wish to wager anything herself and could not just stand and watch others. She decided that as no one yet had gone back upstairs, it would be socially incorrect to do so. So she went into the large room where she could hear the music and watch the dancers swirl about, to look around for the Vicar to keep her company.

She stood in a dim corner, although not a truly darkened one, as Rose had cautioned. For in those dark recesses of the room she could make out dimly the figures of men and women, close together in intimate conversations. The waltz was played, and she saw Violet sweep by, her red gown swinging out with each step, in the arms of a tall, bulky gentleman with side whiskers. Rose, whom she could pick out by her dress, was in close converse with a short gentleman with a booming laugh. The Vicar, she thought, must be intent on remaining as unobtrusive as herself, for he was nowhere in sight.

So she stood and watched the scene before her. At one moment she saw the marquis dancing with a willowy woman in black; at another, she saw Rose again, this time with their host, laughing uproariously with him. She occupied herself with watching the changing couples for some time. But then her own hiding place was discovered. The aging gentleman she recognized as Old Bertie, his face gleaming with exertion, bowed and without a word hauled her, protesting weakly, off to the dance floor. She was not a bad dancer, she knew, but dancing with Old Bertie was one of the most harrowing experiences she had ever had. He gripped her too closely with his hot, wet hands. He trod upon her foot every other measure, and he clutched her closer to his protruding stomach every time she managed to get a little distance between them. When the music ended, he stood there and grinned at her.

"Right," he said, mopping his forehead. "Now how about it, eh lass?"

"Oh no," Catherine said quickly, to whatever he was proposing. And before he could reach for her again, she took advantage of the crowd and slipped away from him to the darkest corner she could find. But upon reaching it, she found that she had intruded upon a couple in intimate embrace, and, drawing in her breath sharply, she muttered an apology and made her way to another recess. Breathing more slowly, she found she had discovered an excellent outpost, very near to a window, and very near to some draperies, in only dim shadows, not absolute dark. She had barely caught her breath, when her heart sank as she saw the gentleman approaching her.

"Old Bertie's in a dither," he laughed. "He's searching for you everywhere. 'Where's that demned little green gal got to?,'" the marquis imitated perfectly in Bertie's accents. "However, don't worry, I won't let on a word. You're quite safe here. But I would suggest standing near to a green drape next time. This golden one sets your gown off too well. Come, dance with me this time. I have ten years on Old Bertie, and he won't trifle with you when you're in my arms. In point of fact, you'll be safer from him there than in the embraces of these curtains."

In some ways, Catherine thought, waltzing with the marquis was worse than dancing with Old Bertie. For although he was a graceful dancer, and although he did not hold her any closer than was seemly, she was far more aware of his lithe well-muscled body next to hers than she had been of the round mass of the older man's. He drew her near once, and the clean scent of him was sharper in her nostrils than the overheated miasma that had consumed her in Old Bertie's clutches. Far worse, though, was that he said not a word to her while they danced, and when she looked up, he gazed down at her with an unreadable expression. She was relieved when the music finally ended and he walked her back to a dim corner.

He stood next to her, looking down at her still while she searched for some light word to dispel the strange silence that surrounded them. At last, when she was about to begin to tell him some nonsense about what a lovely night it was, he spoke.

"Jenkins is right," he sighed, so close to her now, she could feel his warm breath on her cheek. "It is far better to find out for oneself. And the question has been troubling me more than it should. For though you do indeed, in this glittering company, look like Bertie's 'green girl,' the proof is in the tasting, isn't it?"

Before Catherine's mind could register what he said, she found herself in his arms, completely captured there, and being expertly kissed. The shock of his lips, so warm and unexpectedly gentle, quieted her for a moment. The experience was so oddly delicious that she stayed there, savoring it until a split second later the intensity of feeling that arose in her recalled her to her good senses. She was transformed into a fury the moment the realization of his action came to her from far beyond her amazed senses. She struggled free from him and, glaring up into his bemused, newly gentled face, she, her mind whirling with possible methods of retribution, kicked him forcefully on the shin.

It hurt her, she groaned, realizing suddenly the thinness of her dancing slippers, more than it hurt him. In fact, through her fury and the pain of her smarting toes, she saw him throw back his head and heard him roar with laughter.

"Oh, Lord," he laughed, his handsome face free of his usual cold expression, looking young as a boy's. "You don't kick a man who's just taken advantage of you, Miss Robins, not in the duchess's exalted set. It's just not done. In the first place, it doesn't hurt your attacker enough, and in the second, it's most unheard of. You take your hand, child," he said, taking her trembling hand in his, "and you put your fingers together and swing. You slap the fellow for all he's worth, if you want to make a point of purity.

"If you do not," he said, drawing her closer again, "you make some token gesture, such as a weak verbal protest, or perhaps a gentle little kick." He smiled. "And then, token protest being made and accepted, you submit gracefully to his and your own will."

And after this astonishing speech, Catherine found herself being held and kissed once again. This time she did not tarry to taste strange new sensations. She pulled free and, taking his excellent advice, swung her hand across his face. He seemed as startled as she was by her action. The sound her slap made, she thought as she turned to look for an exit through a cloud of outrage, should have stopped all the dancers in their tracks, although no one turned or seemed to notice. She raced quietly through the crowd of people and made her way up the great stairs to her room. Once inside, she locked the door and sank onto her bed. Unconsciously, she slipped off her slippers and massaged her aching toes. But it was only her lips, still tingling, that she thought of.

"She tasted sweet enough," the marquis smiled to Jenkins as they stood on the fringe of dance, "But I'm afraid she wasn't ripe for the picking, I forgot to discuss the going price for green girls this season. That seems to have been my major mistake."

"It could be," Jenkins said, "that she hasn't got a price, or leastways one that any in this room can pay."

"And it could be that I've taken too much wine, out of boredom. And attempted, clumsily, a highly bred doxy, for the same reason. It's just as well, friend, that I didn't find myself entangled with her. For we do have to be up and out early this morning, don't we? There's no more to be got out of this pack of merrymakers. We'll have to be off to Paris tomorrow, now we've made our token stop here."

"It seems," Jenkins said, carefully and conspicuously staring at the faint red palm print that still lingered on the marquis' cheek, "that some fruit hangs too high out of reach, even for you. You seem, lad, to have got lashed by some branches."

"But it happens," the marquis laughed, rubbing his cheek, "that she was only following my explicit instructions."

Chapter VIII

Catherine was furious with herself. She paced her room, for once gladdened that there was nothing to be done during the day in this great, rambling home the Sidneys entertained in. For she did not think she could bear to make polite converse and exchange idle pleasantries when she was so bedeviled by her own thoughts.

It had only been a kiss, she thought—there was no need for the incident to overset her so. But it had. And that was the fact with which she had to deal. She had, she told herself strictly, been kissed before, so there was little sense in making such a pother about it. In fact, she remembered, she had been kissed exactly three times before (she had kept careful track). Once, when she was just fifteen, and Fred McDermott had been seventeen. It had been a hasty little kiss, stolen while they were at a picnic. And had been memorable in that it had excited not her senses, but rather her pity, since Fred had been horrified by his impulsiveness and had spent the rest of that lovely summer Sunday apologizing to her and castigating himself.

When she was seventeen, Mrs. Fairchild's son-in-law, on a visit from Sussex, had taken too much port, surprised Catherine in the hallway of his mother-in-law's house, and delivered an overheated, messy salute upon her lips, along with a great deal of unpleasant fumbling, until she had broken away and run off. But then it had been a shameful incident, and Mrs. Fairchild herself, some months later, was overheard to confide to Jane that her daughter had not picked a "right 'un" and was suffering for it.

The third kiss had come when she was twenty and had gone walking out with Tom Hanley. Tom had been a pleasant-looking chap, an aspiring law clerk on vacation from London, visiting his aunt in Kendall. But that relationship had not gone beyond a few visits. For at their last meeting he had seemed preoccupied and solemn. And when he had left her, he had kissed her once—one brief chaste kiss—and then he had looked at her and sighed deeply. Within a month Catherine had heard of Tom's engagement to a young woman in London, daughter of one of the partners in his firm.

So, Catherine thought, it was not as though she was inexperienced. But nothing had prepared her for the embrace she had received last night. She could scarcely believe how overwhelmed she had been by the marquis' attentions. And she did not know how she could face him again, for surely he must have known how she felt. And if he did, she was sure that it would only reaffirm his belief in her immorality. And as for her kicking him! But in truth she had been outraged—she had never struck another being since her childhood. She had to do something, and, fool that she was, she had kicked a peer of the realm. And then slapped him. And that, she was sure, was worse.

When the pangs of hunger recalled Catherine to her immediate world, she decided that she must carry on as before. She must assume an icy dignity in the marquis' presence. She must not allow herself to look for him or to scan the company for his presence. For if she continued to be fascinated by him, she would, she chided herself, end up in the same case as Rose and Violet in some fashion.

As Catherine dressed for dinner, she took special care with her appearance. She rang for the little French maid and managed to communicate well enough, even though she realized with sinking heart that her long-ago French lessons were hardly adequate to equip her to ask for fresh water properly. She wore her finest new gown of a deep sapphire blue, just to show him that she had not been overset by him. And brushed her hair and drew it back in a severe and startlingly sophisticated style to show him that here was no little miss to trifle with.

When she went down to dinner, she looked neither to the left nor the right, but seated herself in the manner of a grande dame. She chatted lightly and superficially with the Vicar, who seemed vastly amused at something and who enjoyed her company in a very proper fashion. It was only when the dinner was over and the guests were at their regular pursuits of gaming or dancing, or meeting with one another in darkened parts of the house, that the

Vicar, who stood at her side watching the dancers told her that the marquis and his man had gone.

The house party, he told her in an aside, was already beginning to break up, and since the marquis had left, others were beginning to make noises about going on to Paris. "Which much displeases our host," the Vicar said, "since he needs to keep his house full. Otherwise he is left alone, with only thirty servants or so, a few constant hangers-on, and, of course, dear Lady Sidney."

Catherine felt deflated. And noticed that the music, dancing, and chatter all around her seemed suddenly less interesting, less enthralling. While the marquis was in evidence she had always felt on the verge of an adventure; now all this newfound splendor seemed oddly flat. And she murmured her sympathies for her host with compassion.

"Oh, don't pity dear Ollie overmuch," the Vicar said, grinning, "for he has found compensation, as you can see."

Looking up in the direction the Vicar nodded to, Catherine saw her host, smiling and whispering, deep in conversation with Rose. Rose towered above him by several inches and had to hang her head down to hear his whispered comments. But as they watched, the ill-matched couple seemed to come to some sort of understanding, and Sir Sidney, with a little bow and beaming smile, left the room. Catherine could see him going upstairs. It was rather unusual, she thought, for the host of such a great house party to absent himself from his guests, especially since if he needed anything above stairs, he had a clutch of servants he could summon.

But as the Vicar kept watching Rose silently, with a gentle smile upon his own face, Catherine did the same. And saw that within a few moments of her host's departure, Rose brushed some invisible lint from her skirt and then quietly left the room to go up the stairs quickly in Sir Sidney's wake. "Business as usual," yawned the Vicar. And Catherine felt her heart sink. It was one thing to know of Rose and Violet's interests; it was quite another to see them in action. Catherine felt deeply ashamed although she had done no more than watch.

Throughout the evening she clung to the Vicar's side like a devoted daughter. Her attendance upon him seemed to afford him great pleasure. And when he pointed out Violet's departure with an ancient viscount, she was so glad of the Vicar's presence, and so determined to stay with him, that he had to gently, and then less gently, hint to her that he wished to absent himself for only a few moments; he would return immediately, but he really had to be alone for a few moments. When she saw that he was gesturing vaguely in the direction of the gentlemen's withdrawing room, she grew dizzy with embarrassment and vowed to stop clinging to him like a limpet.

But when, in his absence, she found herself approached by no less than three other gentlemen with speculation in their bold, assessing eyes, she gave up her resolve and fairly flew to the Vicar's side again when he reappeared. And there she stayed till she saw the duchess making her stately way upstairs to her room.

For the next days Catherine stayed close in her rooms during the day, and took tea with her companions, but said little to them. For she had seen them disappear with such a variety of gentlemen each night that she felt she was not yet able to converse normally with them. She did not want them to see her revulsion, for in all, they were pleasant and helpful enough to her. And yet she could not reconcile their actions with her own standards, much as she lectured herself about tolerance and different values for different persons during the long days that she was alone in her room. At nightfall she would dress with care, for the duchess's eye was sharp, and on the one occasion when she tried to dress demurely and unspectacularly, the dowager had barked that she didn't employ sparrows—what was the matter with the gel anyway? And she would spend each evening in close converse or, at least, in close companionship with the Vicar.

She soon discovered that he thought her situation vastly entertaining, and, further that he really did not care about her predicament at all so long as it afforded him pleasure in observing it. Sadly, she began to discover that he was using her in much the same way that, she had to admit, she was using him. So it was with heartfelt relief that she heard the duchess declare, after a week at Sir Sidney's establishment, that they had tarried long enough. "The company's becoming flat," the duchess said, sending Gracie about her packing. "We'll take our leave tomorrow. I hear Paris is brimming with fashionables, and I'm eager to be off."

The Vicar had made one great sacrifice and was there to see them off the next morning. Their host and hostess were still abed, having made their good-byes in the night. As Catherine prepared to step into the coach with the others, the Vicar stayed her for a moment. There was a vaguely sorrowful look in his eyes as he took her hand.

"Good-bye, Catherine," he said. "I wonder if we shall meet again? I think not, for I do not go on to Paris. I am one of Ollie's constant hangers-on, you see. I am not one to lecture on morality, I fear, and I cannot offer you any assistance. For not only do I live upon the sufferance of my fellowman, but I am too old, too lazy, and, in the end, too unconcerned with my fellowman and woman now. But I do tell you, for what it is worth, that you do not belong here. Country chicks cannot keep company with parrots and cockatiels, you know. And it is mortally easy to become that with which you constantly associate, by slow degrees. You cannot hide forever, Catherine. And there are all sorts of lures in this wide world, especially for young things. I should know," he said, shaking his head. "I have set enough. Go when you can, Catherine," he whispered, bowing over her hand. "And go while you can. Home, where you belong."

"Thank you," she said, more chilled by his words than she dared show. "And I will. I promise, as soon as I am able."

He smiled sadly and then laughed quietly.

"Whatever you do decide, never fear, I shall know of it. For I hear of all things—that is what makes me so valuable a guest. Good-bye, my dear. It was pleasant being needed as a man again for a few days. Good luck."

He handed her into the coach, and, with a wave, they were off.

"Well you certainly made a conquest," the duchess grinned before she settled herself to sleep, in her usual traveling mode. "The Vicar don't give a demn for anyone in the world, but he seems to have been taken with you. But he don't spend a brass farthing on a female," she laughed, and allowed Gracie to tuck her up into a cocoon of wraps for the journey.

This time the duchess was in no hurry. For, she said to her companions as they dined that night in a small wayside inn, she was "shaken to pieces" by the journey and "wearied unto death" by the constant partying at Sir Sidney's.

They traveled on for two lackluster days, and it was only on the final approach to Paris that all of the company seemed to awaken at last. Rose and Violet were in full spate, commenting on the city, on the people they expected to see, and the fashions they glimpsed. Catherine was shocked to see that they did not even notice the poor, whose districts they had to ride through to get to the center of the city. The men and women in rags, far worse than any she had ever seen in England, the hovels in which they lived, and their hordes of huge-eyed starving children were not commented upon at all. But once the carriage drove through the wide white avenues where gentlemen and ladies of fashion promenaded, they noted every detail of every garment, and priced them down to their least penny.

The duchess beamed upon their excitement, but she told them she "had seen the town before." Yet even she was soon talking about hunting up some dressmakers and getting togged out in "Frenchie fashions again." By the time they rolled up in front of their hotel, the duchess was quite eager to alight and begin her inquiries as to where the gaiety was to be found.

The concierge was as obsequious as the duchess could have wished and groveled so much before her that she was in high good spirits when shown her rooms, even to the point of not beginning her usual tirade against the sanitation and grace of the establishment until he had bowed himself out of her presence. She had a large and airy chamber overlooking the street, and her companions' rooms were arranged around hers.

The duchess sat back with a grin of triumph.

"Well, gels, here we are in Paris. All dressed up with no place to go. Here, you Violet and you Rose, get yourself suited out fine and go down to the lobby; let the word go out that I have arrived. Then we'll see those invitations pour in. Catherine, you're free to do as you wish. Go tag along with the girls if you like. But be sure to tell everyone that you meet who you are and that the Duchess of Crewe has arrived. That should do it. Now, Gracie, my hair, if you please."

And sitting back and enjoying her hair being brushed, the duchess closed her eyes and planned a future full of balls and fetes and sensations.

In spite of the duchess's confidence, Catherine was amazed, when she answered the duchess's summons at an unusually early hour before noon the next day, to see her sitting at a little desk, sorting through what seemed to be a dozen invitations.

"Tonight," the duchess said to her companions, "dress up smartly, for we're off to no less than Count D'Arcy's ball. We've been asked to Lord and Lady Lynne's, and to Madame Martin's but we'd be fools to pass up the count's invitation, for that's the smartest of them all. Bound to be royalty there as well.

So do me justice, lassies," she said, in an unusually gay manner, "and who knows where we may be bound tomorrow night?"

"The old lady's in high alt," Violet said as they went back to their rooms to pick through their wardrobes for suitably dazzling gowns.

"She thinks," Violet explained to a puzzled Catherine, "that if she's daring enough, she'll yet get an invitation to an audience with the king. But she's out there, you know. For it may have been possible before all the nobs got their heads lobbed off for being royals. Now the throne's uneasy, I hear, and they don't want too much truck with a dizzy set like the duchess."

"And what makes you so worldly-wise?" Rose asked cheekily.

"I spent some time with old Ollie, you know, and he had a few words for me."

"A very few words, I'm sure," Rose said, laughing.

Catherine colored, but Violet shot back, "Jealousy won't get you anywhere, old Rose."

"It happens," Rose said, with suppressed laughter, "that I spent some hours with old Ollie too, and he don't waste much time on talk."

Catherine turned to her room quickly, so as not to hear much more of their chatter, which was turning more rancorous and more detailed than she wished to hear.

"Catherine," Rose called, giving Violet an admonitory poke, "do come to our rooms tonight before we leave. We'll have to see if you've togged yourself up in enough style. For when Her Grace gives orders for us to dazzle, you daren't do less or your head will roll."

Catherine gave herself one last glance in the mirror before sighing and turning to go to Rose's room. She could not, she thought, do better. She wore a high-waisted gown in creamy white satin, and bound her hair back with a pure white ribbon till only a crown of curls relieved the severity. The only touch of color was the azure of her eyes and the little gold pendant she always wore. She felt that if she were going to see royalty, she must dress in a distinguished, but unostentatious manner. The neckline of her gown, she realized, was lower than that of any of her others, but it had looked so perfect just as it had come from Madame Bertrand's that she had not dared tamper with it. Now, glancing in the mirror, even though the slope of her breasts showed daringly it no longer seemed so dashing—not, she amended, shocking at all compared to the dresses of the females she had seen at Sir Sidney's. The Vicar's words about becoming like the company one kept drifted into her mind, but she banished them quickly, and went out in search of Rose and Violet and their opinion of her dress.

When Rose called for her to enter, she stepped in, only to stand stock still and stare at Rose and Violet. For Rose was sitting at her mirror with the top of her gown down, chatting animatedly with Violet while at the same time carefully applying rouge from a little pot to the tips of her breasts. Catherine stood and goggled as Rose looked up. For a moment she looked only at Catherine's gown and cried out, "Oh don't you look a sight! Pure and cool and just lovely!"

And then, when she saw the expression on Catherine's face, she looked down at herself and sighed.

"It's to give my gown a better look, you see," she said hurriedly, rapidly completing the job of anointing her nipples with carmine, and then blowing upon them and lifting the top of her gown back on.

"It's to give the gentlemen a better idea of the wares," Violet said languidly.

Catherine looked at Rose in her thin salmon-colored gown and saw that the rouge did indeed emphasize the small part of Rose's bosom that was covered by cloth.

"And," Violet said, in a cool voice, "to give them an extra treat a little later. If a chap's going to spring for the pleasure of Rose's company, he expects to find something out of the ordinary. And a little color in unexpected places adds excitement."

Rose got up and looked daggers at Violet. She opened her mouth to make some rejoinder, but before she could, Violet moved.

"See here, Catherine," she said, walking over to her, letting her drink in the splendor of her spangled black and silver gown, "Rose here and I, we are what we are. And it's no good pretending that we're all jolly little cousins off on a spree. I've been fighting with old Rose here all day, and there has to be an end to it. We can't watch what we say and what we do every moment you're about. We're out of leading strings a long time. I told Rose there's no sense in our having a to-do every time I say something she thinks isn't fit for your ears, for we'll only come to cuffs all day if we go on so. If you're to travel along with us, you'll have to take us for what we are."

Catherine swallowed hard. And then she spoke.

"I know that, Violet. And yes, you are right, I cannot be an ostrich with my head in the sand. I knew that back when we met and I decided to accompany you. So Rose, there's no sense in fighting with Violet. She's quite right, you know."

Rose still seemed agitated, but then she had a sudden thought.

"You know, Catherine, it won't be all bad for you. For you will know what you are about. Far more than most young misses do. For there's heaps we can tell you about gentlemen."

"Oh Rose," Violet laughed, "now that far I would not go. We really cannot tell this little miss all that we know."

"Well, not all." Rose pondered. "But if more young misses knew what we know, fewer gentlemen would have to seek us out."

"And we'd be at a charity kitchen. Give over, Rose, do. We don't have to instruct Catherine. Not with her looks and style. It's only that we won't have to act so unnatural when she's about, and we'll all get on splendidly."

Rose seemed satisfied and went back to gazing at herself in the mirror. She adroitly rubbed rouge into her cheeks, applied salve to her lips, spit into a little dish of black and with one finger swept shape and sultriness about her eyes. Noting Catherine's silence, she asked anxiously, "Is what Violet says acceptable to you, dear?"

"Oh yes, of course," Catherine said, knowing full well that hypocrite that she was, she did not at all relish the thought of hearing all of their confidences. In fact, she wanted to hear none of them—she only wanted to run to her room and quake. But, she amended, she wanted more. She wanted to be home, safe at home again.

But as the silence in the room became ominous, with Violet smiling at her loftily and Rose looking at herself in the mirror uneasily, Catherine felt the burden of conversation fall upon her and searched for a safe, conciliatory topic.

"You can tell me how to go on," she said. "For if we are to be honest with each other, I do not know how to . . . ah, discourage a gentleman, without being rude."

Violet grinned wickedly. "That's hardly the sort of advice to be asking us."

"Oh Vi, give over, do; we can too tell Catherine how to go about things," Rose said, annoyed.

"What you want to know," Violet went on, "is how to stay

out of trouble. And I'm afraid we're poor persons to ask that of.''

"Well, Vi, you're a spiteful thing today," Rose said, angrily. "I think it's just because Catherine's looks knock ours all to pieces tonight. She hasn't got a spangle nor a feather," she said, eyeing the profusion of jet plumes set into Violet's elaborate coif, "and still she looks a treat. Well, then, I'll tell you, love. There's things you mustn't do with gentlemen and you'll find yourself safe as houses. You mustn't open your lips when you kiss, for one thing."

Catherine went pale. This was not at all the sort of advice she had requested, but before she could speak, Violet began laughing.

"Oh Rose, and what of Sir Alistar?"

"True," Rose said thoughtfully, "for he don't bother to kiss at all. Well, then, Catherine, I should say that so long as you stay upright at all times, you will avoid difficulties."

Violet held her hand against her bodice—she was laughing so richly.

"And what of young Perry and Lord Sulley, then?"

"Oh," Rose said, "and telling you to keep all your clothes on, which is what I was about to add, wouldn't do then neither, I suppose. Well then, Catherine, I'll tell you the best advice I can then."

Rose screwed up her face in thought and then smiled triumphantly. "You must never do a thing with a gentleman that you have not done before. And you'll go on splendidly, I'm sure."

At that, Violet's mirth got so out of control that she was gasping, and even Catherine had to join in.

Rose herself was chuckling good-naturedly. But when Catherine stopped, she decided to turn the subject as quickly as she was able to.

"Am I dressed properly then?" she asked.

"A treat," Rose agreed. "But perhaps a little too refined. You never know with Her Grace. She wants you to catch all eyes. Here," Rose said, plucking one white rose from the floral arrangement on her table. "Do put this in your hair, there on top, midst the curls, yes. That looks just as it ought. Now then," she said, squinting thoughtfully at Catherine.

"Yes, I'm sure I'm right. You do look lovely, Catherine. But who will see you across a room? Not that there's anything the matter with your coloring—it's all milk and cream. But there's the problem. In candlelight, you'll just fade away.''

"You're right, Rose," Violet said, taking a professional interest. "Footlights and party lights drab out a girl's coloring. A bit of lip salve, a bit of rouge, that's the ticket.''

And before Catherine could protest, they steered her to Rose's dressing table. Rose carefully applied salve to her lips, and though she was sure her furious blush would stay their hands, they carefully applied high color to her cheeks.

"Now don't blink or move," Rose warned, "or you'll blind yourself. S'truth.''

When Catherine gazed at herself in the mirror again, she dared not breathe. An exotic painted creature with darkly lashed huge blue eyes, pink cheeks, and violently red lips stared seductively back at her. Her hands went automatically to a cloth to wipe the vision away, but Rose stayed her.

"No, Catherine. That's just what Her Grace will expect. She'll dress you down if you come pale and ordinary. Now you look just as you ought. So leave it be.''

Rose and Violet accompanied Catherine to get her wrap, so Catherine could not even touch her face though she swore she could feel every gram of the cosmetics lying heavily upon her. They lingered in Catherine's room awaiting the duchess's summons. And when Gracie came to tell them to be ready, Rose took a small vial from her evening bag and went to Catherine's dressing table. She carefully put a drop from the vial in each eye and handed the vial to Violet, who did the same. Catherine saw, as if by magic, how huge and glittering their eyes now appeared to be, just as she had often noticed their eyes to be at night; she had assumed it was due to their excitement and candlelight.

"Belladonna," Rose explained as they prepared to go. "Gives your eyes a sparkle like nothing else. I didn't offer any to you, dear, for it's a thing you have to get accustomed to. It blurs things up, you know. So when you look your best, you can't see a blessed thing. The lights all dance, and sometimes you can't be sure of recognizing who you're talking to, for you can't make out their face properly.''

"Sometimes," said Violet cryptically, "that's a blessing, too.''

Rose and Violet proceeded to the duchess's chamber with the slow, stately tread that Catherine now saw was necessary for them when their eyes were so unreliable.

The dowager was swathed in silvery gray, with so many

diamonds shining at her throat and hair that Catherine felt sure her companions could only see a sparkling blur of her rich attire.

The duchess stared at Catherine. "Now, that's the way I like my companions to look," she crowed. "You'll have every eye upon you. You're finally getting the hang of it. And Rose and Violet, you two are bang up to the mark. Let's away. Don't wait up, Gracie, for this is to be a late evening."

Gracie nodded as they left, knowing full well she dared not slumber till her mistress was safely tucked in bed again.

Catherine tried to sink back into the shadows as she sat in the coach. And she tried to be less aware of the startled looks that James, the duchess's coachman, gave her when she stepped out into the blaze of light and torches outside Count D'Arcy's residence. She felt, as she trailed along behind Rose and Violet, deeply ashamed of her new appearance, and of the spectacular effect it was having upon those who turned to stare at her.

As their little party was announced, all heads turned to the top of the stairs to see the quartet make their way down the grand staircase to join the company. Her eyes almost as blurred and dazzled as Rose's and Violet's, Catherine saw that these were men and women in the most elegant clothes and jewels that she had ever seen. The company was composed of the titled and the infamous—poets, mistresses, wanderers and actresses, the rag and tag of émigré Europe, and the foremost pleasure seekers from her own land. All collected together and flashing their eyes and gems and costumes beneath the light of a thousand candles while musicians tried to drown their converse with light music.

Many stared at the haughty Violet and buxom Rose. Many gaped at the regal duchess and her train of demireps, whose reputations had preceded her here. And many gazed with delight upon the delicious child with the figure of a grown woman and the face, even beneath the paint, of a lovely gamine.

Catherine tried to ignore the sensation they had caused and that her employer was obviously reveling in. She stared about her in shame and despair . . . until her eyes caught and held one familiar face high above the crowd. A face that she had been unwittingly looking for. He had been watching her, she thought in deeper despair, and there was no doubt in her mind as to his thoughts. The marquis looked at her, at her face, at her neckline. His handsome face was immobile, but the contemptuous disdain in his gray eyes was readable even from across the room.

Chapter IX

"Sinjun," complained the petite dark-eyed woman, "you have been neglecting me. You've been here all night and you haven't danced with me once. You were not used to be so reluctant to enter my arms," she said coyly, tracing patterns with her fingertip upon his sleeve.

"Cecily," the marquis drawled, "you were not used to be Lady Smythe. Now that you are a respectable married woman, you cannot want to pick up our old ties. What would Alistar say?"

"Oh, pooh," she fretted, stamping one foot—an effect, he noted with amusement, quite lost in the throng of people. "I haven't seen him all night either. He's probably off somewhere with that Italian trollop of his. We have a very modern arrangement, Sinjun," she wheedled. "We each go about our own business, and no one's the worse for it."

"Cecily, my dear," the marquis said, beginning to edge away, "why should you try to reignite an old burned-out flame, when I have seen that devastating M. Dumont there has not taken his eyes off you for a moment?"

The woman wheeled and turned to look for her admirer and, not finding the rapt young face of M. Dumont anywhere nearby, she turned again to rate the marquis for his little jest and found herself standing quite alone.

With an exclamation of dismay, she flounced off to see her husband, to rail at him for his pursuit of foreign females.

"Oh, Lord, Jenkins," the marquis said in a low voice, when they met at one side of the card room, "for every true rumor, there are a hundred false ones. I have a list of many names now, it's true, but coming here this night has added nothing. For no sooner do I get on the trail of something, when there is an interruption."

"Your past catching up with you, lad?" Jenkins grinned.

"There's that, but I am quite expert at sidestepping. But more importantly, there's Beaumont. He's here, and he's everywhere tonight. He seems to be dogging my footsteps. And whenever I look into his eyes, I see tumbrels rolling. He suspects everything, but can prove nothing."

"He can do nothing," Jenkins said, lifting his glass of wine and holding it to the candle's light. "We're at peace now."

"Now. At this moment," the marquis sighed, "but if the scales tip, I would be first on his list."

"Whose field does he play in now?" Jenkins asked before draining the glass.

"Ah, now that," the marquis said, shrugging and then pausing as a waiter came close, "is a neat question." He took another glass of wine for Jenkins and one for himself, and they toasted each other until the waiter drifted off into the crowd and they were alone again.

The marquis began drinking his wine and then stopped suddenly to stare at his glass. "Now that," he said, "is criminal, such stuff to be even decanted in the land of the grape itself." He looked around casually, then continued, now sure of their privacy. "If we discover which pockets he has his hand in, we'll know for a certainty which way the wind is blowing. Our estimable commissioner . . . of what is it now? Taxes, water? No matter, our friend Beaumont is an excellent weather vane. He catches every nuance of the winds of fortune. That is how he has gotten and held his own fortune. Be sure that he will never put a foot wrong. In fact, I think that if we were but privy to the workings of his mind, there would be no need to compile all these names. For whatever the fate of France is to be, be sure that Beaumont will know it a half hour before the king himself."

"Aye," Jenkins rumbled, "but as he's not one to give an Englishman the time of day, best keep your ear to the ground."

"But not too obviously, of course," the marquis sighed. "Instead I shall ogle the ladies, drink more than is good for me, game for all I'm worth, and submerge myself in every bit of frivolous gossip. There are times, Jenkins, when I long for no more than a cozy fireside. I grow old, I think."

Jenkins gave a rude chuckle. "Oh yes. I can just see you

there, dandling your grandchildren on your knee, graybeard. But in the meanwhile, until you can delight in such homey pastimes, I notice you're spry enough at your job. You haven't taken your eyes off the duchess's newest doxy all night. Is it that you think she holds the secrets of the succession behind those lovely blue eyes?''

The marquis seemed taken aback for a moment and then drawled in the offhand languid manner Jenkins knew so well, ''No, that's an altogether different game. Miss Prunes and Prisms has arrived in Paris and finally shows her true colors. Or true paints, if you want to be more exact. She's obviously been after big game all the while. And I'm just curious to see to whom she attaches herself. For there's a lot to be learned from seeing to whom such a pricey little package delivers. Rose and Violet will ply their trade with whoever has the price of a night's entertainment. But these more expensive frigates will only sail off with someone who is prepared to come down handsomely for them. I think our little miss will show us the way the winds of fortune are blowing almost as well as our old friend Beaumont.''

Jenkins glanced around the room before saying dryly, ''But she hasn't sailed off with anyone as yet. The last I saw of her, she was trying to blend in with the furniture.''

''She's only waiting for her opportunity, Jenkins. She's after more than her weak sisters-in-trade.''

''You are too harsh on her.'' Jenkins sighed, shaking his head.

''Still thinking she is but a sweet little miss caught in the coils of misfortune? That's not like you, old friend. She comes to her first Paris fete, rigged out to the nines, painted and gowned like an actress. Did you see her entrance? She attracted more notice than a queen. The old girl's beside herself with happiness. 'The Duchess of Crewe is a *succès fou*,' they are all saying. That little rhyme will be the catchword of the season.''

''Look sharp, lad,'' Jenkins said, turning away. ''Beaumont's eyes are upon us. He's talking to that waiter. His men must be everywhere here.''

As the marquis drained his glass and prepared to leave, Jenkins smiled and whispered one farewell. ''You have to get your mind back on business. Why don't you just meet her price and then you will be able to forget about her and get on with it.''

The marquis walked over to the entrance to the great room where the dancers were whirling about together to the strains of a waltz. He watched them as he spoke with a young sprig just out of Cambridge on his first tour, who was chattering away excitedly. It was possible, he thought with a wry grin, to stand and chat with almost anyone at such an affair without even listening to half that was said. A sage nod, a small smile, or an occasional laugh when the speaker seemed to have delivered himself of a witticism was enough. He was the lofty, cynical Marquis of Bessacarr after all, wasn't he?

As the young man happily prated away, passing on all the secondhand tidbits he had amassed, Sinjun listened with half of his attention. The other half was focused on the amusing little playlets that passed before his eyes.

Lady Devon was playing her husband false with a handsome Austrian. Mademoiselle DuPres was batting her lashes at an old gentleman who had escaped the guillotine and come back to tend his lately restored estates. Mademoiselle DuPres knew, Sinjun thought, that the old chap would now need a wife to help him people his lands again. And Hervé Richard, who had been a man of substance and power when Bonaparte had led this land, was jealously watching his brother Pierre, who had been a beggar then and who was now a rich man deep in the Bourbons' confidences. The wheel of fortune had not yet done turning, the marquis thought, and that was why he was here tonight.

The marquis' eyes narrowed as he followed Hervé Richard's angry gaze. For his brother Pierre, as stout and overfed as his beloved friend Louis Bourbon, was dancing with Catherine Robins. Pierre smiled and bobbed, his red face beaming, while the girl seemed to be in an agony of discomfort. Was she never done with playacting? the marquis thought violently. She had captured the plum tonight. Pierre was a rich man now, and his presence at court gave him power and influence. And still she acted the shy virgin. But it seemed to be a useful ploy, for Pierre looked delighted with his little prize.

As the marquis watched, Beaumont, as neatly clad and unexceptional a little man as ever, came up to Hervé's side and began whispering to him. So Beaumont had some interest in watching the little playlet as well? Beaumont seemed to be consoling Hervé, who everyone knew burned with jealousy of his estranged brother. Now why should Beaumont be interested in Hervé? Sinjun's thoughts raced. Hervé was déclassé now, abandoned and impoverished. He had not followed his leader into exile, but he was financially and socially as much of an exile as Bonaparte. If Beaumont sought his company, then indeed something was in the wind.

"But, Sinjun, you say nothing. Don't you agree?" the little lord at his side asked.

The marquis recalled himself with difficulty. "Why, I'm sorry, Peter, I was distracted. What did you say?"

"I don't blame you. Not a bit. She's a smasher all right, isn't she? I wish I had the blunt to interest her," the young man said sadly, looking over to where Catherine danced.

"Now, now, Peter, she's too rich for your blood," the older man laughed. "And mine too, I think."

"Never say so," Peter replied, laughing. "Why, good English gold outweighs French any day."

The two men laughed, and then the younger, seeing the marquis' distraction, bowed and went off in search of more congenial company. It was good to have spoken with the marquis, for he was a man of the world and one whose name would excite much interest and envy among his friends when he returned home. But he was a strange fellow, after all, so bored that he seemed half asleep, those gray eyes half masted and quiet throughout their whole discourse. Peter essayed the same look as he made his way to the punch and found he almost stumbled against a footman as a result. Practice, he told himself sharply, that would be the answer.

But there was no boredom in the marquis' eyes as he watched the interminable dance go on in front of him. He watched Catherine dip and sway in Pierre Richard's arms. Her figure was exquisite and her face entrancing, even under all the paint. The swept-up dark curls revealed her white vulnerable neck. The marquis found that his hands were clenched. There was no use for it. He was interested in her. He had been from the moment he had seen her. Jenkins was right. Though she might be nothing more than a cyprian, certainly less discriminating than any of the wenches he usually consorted with, he did desire her. And his fascination with her was only getting in the way of his mission here. He must have her and be done with it.

In the morning, he knew, when he paid her, all the mystery would be vanished. He would have known all there was to know of her. Or all he wished to know of her. The attraction was strong, and it was dangerous for him to be so attracted. In the past, he had consorted with women whose conversation amused him or whose personalities somehow made the mercenary side of their relationship less sordid. He did not know if Catherine Robins could even read or write, much less make pleasant discourse. He did not care. For he had no wish to be ensnared by a woman ever again. It would be enough to have her, and thereby end the interest he had in her.

For he could neither gather information nor observe dispassionately when she was about. No sooner did he get on the track of some new development that might be of interest to his cause than she would appear and chase all such thoughts from his mind. For instance, he thought angrily, he should not be watching her dance with Pierre Richard and be as consumed with futile jealousy as Hervé Richard so evidently was. He should rather be at Hervé's side now, listening to his spiteful rage, as Beaumont was. For when a man was consumed by passion, he was often indiscreet, and when a man like Hervé Richard was being indiscreet, there was a chance that there would be a great deal to learn. No, his fascination with her handicapped him and he grew angry at himself. And so, indirectly, at her.

There was only one remedy he could think of. And he knew that before the night was out, he would have taken it. He was not such a coxcomb as to think he was irresistible. But he was experienced enough to know that she felt the same tug of interest that he did. And he did have money, money enough to assuage her conscience for giving up such a potential honey fall as Pierre Richard.

The dance finally ended, and while Pierre executed a courtly bow, Catherine took the opportunity to dip a sketchy curtsy and begin a hasty retreat to the wall where she had been standing before the weighty Frenchman had sought her out. But before she could return across the floor, she was intercepted by another gentleman. He looked much the same as the partner she had just abandoned, except that he was slightly taller, slightly less obese, and dressed in clothes that were far less grand.

He bowed, and the music struck up again. Before she could leave, he took her hand and led her into the dance. There were gasps and those on the sidelines broke into excited babble as the dancers swung into the first steps. The marquis was not the only one who stared at the dancers now.

And neither was he the only one who made his seemingly unhurried but nevertheless rapid way to her erstwhile partner's side. Monsieur Beaumont also began to make his way through the crowd to the flushed, angry gentleman. But Beaumont, whose legs were shorter, had to stop after getting halfway there when he saw the marquis lean to speak with his quarry.

"Good evening, Pierre," the Marquis said pleasantly in his perfect French. "I see that the new young English cocotte is becoming quite an attraction. Even your brother cannot resist her."

The stout gentleman muttered, as much to himself as to the marquis, "But he is a beggar now. What does he think he is doing? It was only through my intercession that he was allowed to stay on in Paris. For he is my brother, after all."

The marquis smiled sympathetically, knowing full well that Pierre would never allow his brother to go into exile totally, and thus miss seeing his more successful sibling's triumphs in society and at court. Just as Hervé had insisted on allowing his Royalist brother Pierre to stay on through his charity, when Bonaparte swept all before him.

"She could not refuse him, poor little sweet," Pierre said, never taking his eyes from the couple before them, "but I shall tell her, soon enough, that he has nothing to offer her. He forgets himself. It is through my sufferance that he is here at all tonight."

"Perhaps," the marquis said with a smile, "he thinks his fortunes are about to take a new turn."

"What?" Pierre said, distractedly, his attention so focused on his brother, who was whispering into the delightful young woman's ear, that he scarcely heard the question.

"No, no, never," he said vehemently, his attention reverting to the marquis. "I keep Hervé and his wife and children in food and necessities as it is my duty as a brother to do. But I assure you, he won't get an extra sou from me to carry on with a demimondaine. And so I shall tell her, never fear. Hervé shall not have her, never fear."

"Doubtless," drawled the marquis, watching Hervé clutch Catherine closer and shoot a triumphant look at his brother. "But I wonder what he is telling her now? Perhaps he feels he will soon be in clover again?"

"Never!" Pierre barked, his little eyes jealously watching the couple's progress. "For his star is no longer in ascendancy. It shines only on the little island of Elba. Paris is mine now."

"Perhaps," the marquis mused. For Hervé's bid at taking away Pierre's new plaything was not unusual. The two brothers were famous in Paris for their competitive relationship. The wags had named them Cain and Cain years before, because, as society said, neither one was innocent enough to be called Abel. Still, this was a daring gesture for Hervé to make. And one, the marquis thought, that might not have been made solely out of rage and jealousy. It might have been an ill-advised gesture; however, it might just as well have been only a premature gesture showing that Hervé thought the direction of his fortunes was indeed about to change. It was true, as he had told Jenkins, that one might learn a great deal from merely watching clever demireps. For they seemed to gravitate to money and power and point it out as surely as any compass could show the North Star.

When the dance ended at last, Hervé made as if to delay his partner, for he had seen how quickly she had fled his brother. But Pierre was quick off the mark this time, and as Hervé reached for Catherine's arm again, Pierre approached his brother and signaled forcefully that he wished to speak to him. While the two brothers broke into low and volatile argument, to the amusement of watchers, the girl made her escape. And when the marquis looked away from the snarling brothers, she was gone.

Beaumont looked about him rapidly and then turned on his heel and went into hurried conference with a footman. But the marquis only strolled away, seemingly aimlessly. He smiled to himself as he wandered off into the direction that he had seen the white flash of her gown disappear. An association with her, he thought, however brief, would be of some real value after all. For his own personal interest now seemed to dovetail with his professional interest in the girl. After they had parted, he might be able to work out some arrangement with her whereby she could report back to him on whichever of the two brothers with whom she finally chose to consort. A word from either camp would suit him well. He would have to be sure that he left her with pleasant memories so that she would be willing to cooperate with him. And he would have yet another partner in his inquiries.

He knew she would not fly to the duchess's side, for that was where the brothers would look for her first. Nor would she have gone to Violet or Rose. For both were deep in the process of securing business for themselves at this hour. Thus, the marquis reasoned, if she had disappeared into this section of the house, she must have sought a room where she could be alone to weigh the offers of the two brothers.

The marquis eased open two doors off the main hall before he found her, standing alone, holding her hands together tightly, staring into a fire in Count D'Arcy's unused library.

"What a problem," he sighed softly, entering the room and closing the door securely behind him. "Two such eligible suitors. And no one to give you advice as to which one to select. Hervé is, one admits, a trifle more comely, but after all he has four years on poor Pierre. But then, Pierre has the ear of Louis, and the purse and privilege as well. Yet again, as you surely must have heard, there are all sorts of rumors flying. And it is altogether possible that after one month of bliss with Pierre, you might find that Hervé was the one in power after all. His emperor is away just at the moment, but one never knows, does one?"

She turned and stared at him as he came up slowly behind her. Her eyes, he noted with amazement, were filled with tears and she wore an expression of grave despair. Had Hervé threatened her then? he wondered.

"I want nothing to do with either one of them," she whispered. "Nothing at all. I just want to be let alone and stay with the duchess just for a little while longer, just till I can get home."

As he watched, amazed, tears began to run down her cheeks. He took out a handkerchief and dabbed at them.

"Ah no," he said in his gentlest voice, "for how can you face the company again if you go on so? You shall ruin the work of art you have created upon your face. See? Although I can repair the damage, I will not be able to recreate the effect, for I've left all my cosmetics home again, alas."

At his words, she looked up in despair, and began to sob. He gathered her close in his arms and stroked her smooth bare shoulders. When she tried weakly to pull away, he only held her closer and whispered soft words of comfort to her.

"No, no," he said tenderly, pushing back some tendrils of hair from her face. "What can be dreadful enough to make you weep? It cannot be so terrible, can it? For here you are in the heart of society and you are so greatly sought after. Why, you are a stunning success tonight. So lovely that the world of Paris is at your feet. And you are so wretched? Come, come, tell me what is the matter. It may be that I can help you. For I have come to help you, you know."

He felt her warm and vital, close against him, and he held her close, whispering all the while, and then he laughed and planted a brief passionless kiss against her hair, which, he noted irrelevantly, had the scent of the rose she wore there.

"No, now you are turning my jacket to ruin. What will

Jenkins say? For it is not raining tonight. You will quite turn my reputation with him, you know, for I am not used to reducing females to tears. He will wonder what dreadful things I have been up to, to transmute lovely laughing girls into fountains.''

She drew away, looking ashamed. And after taking his hand-kerchief and dabbing at her eyes, she looked at him, he thought, with something very much like wonder.

"It's all such a mull," she said, controlling her voice with effort. "And I'm sorry to have wept all over you. But it has been so dreadful. I did not want to be a social success. No, I did not. I only wanted to fulfill my duties and stay in the background. But then that great fat Frenchman took my hand, above all my protests, and made me dance with him. I didn't want to create a scene, for I thought he could not understand English and my French is so poor. But once we were dancing, I found he spoke English as well as I. And he . . . he made me the most dreadful offer. That is to say, he supposed me to be something I am not. And no sooner had I gotten away from him when the other took me up. For a moment''—she smiled weakly—"I thought it was him again, but it turned out to be his brother, saying almost the selfsame things."

"What sort of things?" the marquis asked with a glow of interest in his eyes.

"Promising me all sorts of things," she said, closing her eyes and waving her hand in dismissal. "Carriages and gowns and jewels. And no matter what I said to both of them, they seemed deaf to my every word and only assured me that they were in earnest."

"They both promised great riches?" the marquis asked abruptly, an alert look upon his face.

"Yes, yes," she said. And seeing his abstraction, she said shamefacedly, "I am sorry to have gotten so familiar with you, Your Lordship, and I thank you for trying to set me right again. I shall be leaving now, for even though the duchess is at the tables, I shall ask her to give me leave to return to the hotel. I feel a headache coming on," she explained hurriedly.

"No, no," the marquis objected, capturing her hands and smiling down at her. "Let's have none of that. You owe me no thanks, for I have not done anything for you as yet. And let us have no 'Your Lordships' please; my friends call me Sinjun, and you are my friend. For we have known each other a long time, haven't we? Only we have let a lot of silly misunderstandings get in the way of our friendship. Tell me, Catherine, what is it you want of this journey that neither Pierre nor Hervé can give you? For I am here to help you. We are fellow Englishmen, in a matter of speaking, here in a strange land," he added, seeing her hesitate.

"I want to go home," she blurted, looking up at him, an incipient sob in her voice. "That is all. It was wrong of me to come. It is wrong of me to stay."

"Then why do you stay?" he asked in a low voice.

She hesitated again as he drew her a little closer and said, "Say it, Catherine. For have I not said I am your friend?"

"I must wait until mid March at least," she said gravely, not looking at him, "for the duchess pays me quarterly. And only then will I have the fare to go home."

The marquis stiffened imperceptibly, and then he laughed low in his throat. Ah, the little fox, he thought maliciously, it is true. A bird in the hand is worth all of a Frenchman's promises. So be it, he thought, we begin. Yet still he was aware of a strange surge of bitter disappointment. It is only, he thought rapidly, that it was, after all, so simple. Once they begin to speak of money, it always becomes so simple.

"Well then," he said, the lines of cynicism deep in his smiling face, "that is easy enough to remedy. No need to shed one more wasteful tear. For I have enough in my pocket at this moment to see you home. And more than that in my other coat at home. I shall see that you are able to travel home in style, little one, with even a companion of your own to see you safely arrived. I am only sorry that I cannot be that companion. For I must stay on here awhile longer and cannot now make any plans to leave."

"Oh no." She shook her head. They were standing so close to each other that he could feel the ends of her curls tickle his cheek. "I could not borrow from you, Your Lordship. . . ."

"Sinjun," he whispered, pulling her closer.

She resisted his embrace and went on in a small voice, "For I don't know when I could pay you back. Even though you are being so charitable, it would not be right of me to take your money. No, it would not be fitting. I can wait until March, truly I can. It is just that it is good to have someone I can talk to. Someone who understands."

"Why, there is no need for paying me back, little Catherine," he said gruffly, again wishing she would drop this game, and wondering if their whole relationship would be filled with this tedious denial of the truth. Would he have to ease her to bed above little halfhearted protests? Remove her garments, all the while quieting her sham of maidenly terrors? Would he have to put up with this mockery of innocence even as he bedded her? It would grow boring. He knew there were men who enjoyed simulated force in their amorous adventures, but he was not one of them. He wanted wholehearted cooperation. And so he sought to disabuse her of the notion and put an end to the charade.

"Little Catherine," he said, raising her chin with his hand and looking straight into her enormous eyes, "you would earn the lot." And seeing her eyes grow wider, he said quickly, "But I would, I promise, try not to make it a hardship. And I am generous. Although I usually prefer relationships that are open at both ends and can grow into long-standing ones, I am pressed for time. So I shall settle as much upon you for a few days of pleasure as I usually do for a few months. For it will not be your fault that we cannot continue. And though I do not pride myself upon being the answer to every maiden's prayers, I know I can be far more congenial than either of the Richards. You will find it more than pleasant, little one, I assure you. I have wanted you for a long time, and I know that you have not been unaware of me. So let's have an end to dickering. I will pay you—" He paused and then named a sum which he knew was more than generous, more in fact, than he had wanted to pay, but he was unsettled by the strange quietness in the room. "And I promise you will not have to exert yourself to earn it. Now, it grows late. Come, we'll go back to my rooms, and you will see for yourself how delicious it will be."

He drew her closer, bent his head, and kissed her lightly, and then, as he lost himself in the deepening kiss, he became aware of pain. For she was tugging sharply at his hair.

He released her abruptly. She was staring at him in horror.

"How could you?" she shrilled.

His thoughts reeled. Had she expected more? But that would be impossible—no man would pay more. Not even Louis himself.

"You are as bad as those others." She wept freely now, the cosmetics running across her cheeks, making her seem, not ridiculous, he thought, but somehow even more childlike.

"No, worse," she cried, pulling free of him and rushing to the door, "for you said you understood. And I trusted you."

"But what is it that you want?" he asked, standing alone and confused.

"I want to go home," she sobbed, and ran out the door.

The marquis did not go after her. He simply stood and stared after her, and then aimed a fierce kick at a chair, sending it flying.

What was her game, he wondered, savagely angry at her and at himself. Why should she come to this party painted like a doll and gowned like merchandise in a window if she were not looking for trade? Why should she be in the trail of the Dirty Duchess at all? Or thick as thieves with two other low tarts, if she were not what she appeared to be? And why should she maneuver so shamelessly to charm the coins out of his pockets? Somewhere, deep in his fury, the marquis felt the dim remembered pain of his past. He had been wrong before. Devastatingly wrong. And had sworn never to be so shortsighted with women again. But this time, how could he have been wrong? For it was not his perception alone.

How could he have been wrong when all the signs, all the world, and even she herself, in her request for money, had told him, unerringly, that he was right?

Chapter X

The duchess sulked for a day. She went on at tea about ungrateful little wretches, she complained at dinner about green little pieces, and went to bed grumbling about wicked, deceiving, brass-faced little hussies. But by the next day, when ever more invitations poured in, she had forgotten her anger at Catherine. For the chit was the talk of the town, and everyone had gotten a look at her, and wanted more, and then she had just disappeared.

The duchess was mollified when the spate of invitations flowed in. She had been a success, she knew it. What was it the Frenchies called her? Ah yes, "The Duchess of Crewe, le succès fou." A crazy success, that was it. That was one thing with these foreigners, she thought, pleased beyond her expectations at the evident splash she had made, there was no prudishness about them. No whispered condemnations. No sly little jibes. They took her to be a woman of the world. And a great many gentlemen had bent over her hand and looked at her with frank admiration. That was just as it ought to be, she sighed, holding the invitations as though they were a winning hand at cards. For though she had no interest in gentlemen any longer, nor indeed ever had for that matter, it was delightful to be so famous. When she at last returned home, there would be no more snickering. She would be such a success on the Continent that she would have to be admired not only in her own set, but in the highest circles in the land.

When Catherine crept in the next day, pale and shaken, the duchess only smiled at her benignly, all rancor forgotten. "Get some rest, gel," she said pleasantly, "for we're going to a levee

117

tomorrow night and I want my gels looking their best.'' And she
waved Catherine a royal dismissal.

Catherine walked slowly back to her room, where she had
hidden herself since the D'Arcy ball. She was in desperate case,
she knew, but she could not see her way clear yet.

How was she to get out of this coil? she mourned. She would
not beg Violet and Rose for funds, she swore; she must not. For
that would make her, in her own eyes at least, as culpable as
they were. She must find a way to tolerate this life at least for a
few more weeks, at least till mid March, when her quarterly
salary came due. For she knew the duchess would not advance
her a penny to go home, but surely, when the time came, her
employer would be honor bound to pay her justly earned wages.

She tried not to think of the marquis. For when he had
followed her to that empty room where she had sought refuge,
she had looked into his eyes and honestly thought she had found
honesty there. And so she had, but not in the way she wanted.
He had said he understood; he had neither said nor done anything
untoward. And had asked for her confidence. He was the only
safe refuge, she had thought. And so, like a fool, she had told
him her true situation. And discovered that he still thought her
no more than a conniving light-skirts. And, she thought, in
sorrow, how could she blame him? Her cheeks still reddened
when she imagined the construction he had put upon her telling
him of her need for money.

But he had seemed so genuinely friendly and caring. She had
looked into the depths of those softened gray eyes and had wanted
him to take all her problems on his own broad shoulders. Worse,
she remembered, when he had kissed her, for one tiny moment
of time, she had wondered what it would be like to stay in his
arms, to stay close to him, and go on further with him to taste
the ''delicious'' experiences he promised her. It was as the Vicar
had cautioned her—that if she stayed with her companions, she
would become as one with them. And so, she told herself
sharply, she had.

She had worn cosmetics and a gown that would have sent
Arthur and Jane to the top of the boughs. She had danced with
every lecherous gentleman who had leered at her, and capped the
whole thing by complaining to the marquis that she had no
funds, almost forcing his offer to her. She must, she knew, get
away before she actually became as Rose and Violet were. For if
she had doubted that such an impossible thing could ever come

to pass, she had only to remember the moment she had stayed, drowned in pleasure, in the marquis' embrace. How long before staying with him would seem like the only sane thing to do? She must go.

And if, she told herself strictly, staring at herself in the glass, she had to put up with insults, with sly appraisals, with comments about her condition, then she had merited it. She had brought it upon herself, and if, as a consequence, she suffered for it, that was all to the good. It would be a fit punishment for her. It would have been far better to have taken the ship on its turnabout journey home, once she had known about the duchess's companions and the life they led, than to have stayed and exposed herself to such an existence. Better, she thought, to have begged and scraped her way home alone than to go on in luxury under a false flag.

By the time that Rose and Violet came to her room for their usual afternoon tea, Catherine felt herself to be under control. And when Violet said, with a sneer, that Catherine had gotten herself quite a following, Catherine stood, and said firmly, "There has to be an understanding between us. I did not want this. I do not want this. If I could, I would leave now. But," she added, raising her hand in denial, "I want to make it clear that I want no charity, Rose. Nor any sympathy, for I've gotten myself into this coil. But, if you would be so kind, could you try to bear with me till a few more weeks go by? Then I shall take my quarterly earnings and go home, straightaway, as I should have weeks ago. Till then, please just try to accept me as I am, as I promised to accept you. And if you would, try, as you promised, to discourage any gentlemen that ask after me. Now let's forget about it. I have only to wait and let time pass, and it will all go right."

At first, it did. The next night, at the levee the duchess had promised them to, Catherine had to use all her resources to stay afloat. The gentlemen ogled her as before, and the ladies stole speculative glances at her. When the duchess went to the card room and Rose and Violet vanished with their own quarries, Catherine found herself pursued by the gentlemen again. She refused to dance, telling all who asked her that she had turned her ankle. But that only netted her a circle of admiring men, all vying to procure her a drink or tidbits or to keep her company. It was, she thought, better than having to dance, and the number of men who surrounded her ensured her safety from unwelcome suggestions as to her future.

She had worn a very conservative, almost demure gown and had refused Rose and Violet's offers of cosmetics, and so when she recognized the marquis as he strolled by her complement of admiring suitors, she raised her chin and met his eyes, unblinking and unmoved. He smiled at her and shrugged and then turned to his companion, a lovely Frenchwoman, and walked on. She felt a hollow glow of pride in herself and went on chatting with a very young, very charming Frenchman.

But toward the end of the evening, her dancing partner of the previous affair appeared. Pierre Richard seemed agitated when he saw her among her coterie of admirers, and stared hard at her and frowned. But then she noted that a smallish dark-haired man in conservative dress plucked at his arm and engaged him in conversation with many a smile and nod in her direction. This seemed to soothe him, and Catherine saw the rest of the evening out with relief, with nothing but a great deal of conversation filled with innuendos to parry.

At an émigré English couple's house party the following evening, Catherine saw both Richard brothers again. They seemed to exchange harsh words, and then each retreated to opposite corners of the room, from which they glowered at her separately throughout the evening. Really, she thought, it would be amusing—they were making such cakes of themselves in their admiration for her and their hatred for each other—if it were not for the fact that, separately, each had the power to frighten her very badly. They were like two overgrown evil children squabbling over a desired toy. But there was no dancing that night, so she could stay well away from both of them. The small dark man was there as well again, and he seemed to spend an equal amount of time with each brother, as did, Catherine noted through exaggeratedly careless glances, the marquis.

They met again at many parties and fetes as the days spun by. The same set of people seemed to revolve constantly about each other. When a fresh face appeared, everyone converged upon it with alacrity. Now she knew why the duchess and her followers had been greeted with such extreme admiration. For surely, Catherine thought, it was a very small world they allowed themselves, and since they insisted on partying constantly, and with the same persons, any newcomers must be met with joy.

By careful maneuvering, Catherine saw to it that she was

always surrounded by gentlemen. It was difficult to smile and pretend coy pleasure in the face of their incessant compliments, but it seemed to keep her safely away from any individual proposals. Her admirers ranged from callow young English boys residing in France for their education to dissipated roués who seemed to know her game very well. But all of them, by some miracle of fate, were content to beg only for her company at each affair. She could not know that they wagered nightly on the odds as to who the clever young doxy would eventually choose to be her protector.

The Richard brothers saw her many times after that night when they had each danced with her, but they no longer solicited her presence; rather, they watched her greedily from afar. The small dark man, she discovered, was a M. Beaumont. She learned that he was a person of some importance in the government, although his duties and title remained nebulous. Still, he was regarded by all with much awe and some fear. The marquis, she saw with an admixture of relief and dismay, no longer sought her out either, but only acknowledged her presence with a nod and a knowing smile. And each time she saw him, he was partnering a different but equally striking woman of the worldly sort. All the others whom she had met that first night in Paris she saw constantly as well.

Privately, Catherine now appreciated the quiet backwaters of life in Kendal. For she found that despite the fine apparel she wore and the fulsome compliments she always received, and the constant improper hints she had learned to refuse without shock, there really was no adventure or excitement in such a life. It was, she thought, fully as tedious in its own way as the many quiet evenings spent at home.

And while the duchess and her companions disported themselves freely in many homes and private ballrooms, they never received that coveted invitation to appear at court. Just as the dowager had been shunned in the highest circles in her own land, so she was ignored in a similar plane of society in France. The Marquis of Bessacarr might be welcomed to a fete in loftier circles, might even make his bow at the Tuileries, and have the ear of Louis himself. But the only time the duchess and her companions met the cream of Parisian society was when some of them came down to her level to gape at the goings-on of her notoriously wilder set.

Rose and Violet, she noted, were as busy as farmers during

the haying season, reaping their crops while the sun still shone. The only thing that shocked Catherine about their activities now was how steadily she grew less shocked by their activities. They were happy, and Catherine reckoned she was lucky to remain and pace out her days and nights unscathed, except in her sensibilities.

But Catherine grew uneasy and counted the days till mid March. And her uneasiness had little to do with Rose and Violet or even her own situation.

For there was a growing undercurrent here, in conversation and gossip, at the gay parties they visited, and even in the city itself, that she could not put a name to.

As it happened, she was not the only one aware of it. One afternoon, as she sat mending one of her frocks and gossiping with Rose and Violet in their rooms, Violet suddenly sat up and began to prowl about restlessly. These afternoons with Rose and Violet were some of Catherine's easiest moments as she counted the days till her release from the duchess's employ. She had grown used to their ways. She barely looked now when they sat about with their wrappers half opened, and barely blushed when they swapped stories about their gentlemen friends. For, Catherine noted with relief, with all Violet's speeches about their not minding their tongues any longer when she was about, they still greatly abbreviated their reminiscences in her presence.

Catherine had grown very fond of Rose, who, when not on her nightly errands, sat and sewed and smiled like the friendly farmer's daughter that she was. Violet was not so easily taken to, Catherine decided, for she had an acid tongue, and was not so scrupulously clean in her habits as Rose. In that, Catherine saw, she was not much different from many of the French ladies of fashion she had seen. For she had seen many a swanlike neck ringed both with diamonds and with grime. Still no one else seemed to mind, as both the gentlemen and the ladies appeared to be bathed in perfume and did not seem to consider water as useful as cosmetics.

Now Violet, pacing the room, cut off Rose's detailed description of a certain Austrian woman's tiara that she'd remarked upon the previous evening by saying sharply, "There's a lot going on here now, and, truth to tell, I wish to heaven we were in Austria too. There's too much afoot here, and too many whispers. I cannot like it."

"Whatever do you mean, Vi?" Rose asked, stretching

luxuriously. "It's ever so gay here now. So many dos, so many lovely people. Why should you want to hurry off now? The pickings are good enough."

Violet gave her a scornful look.

"You wouldn't know your hat was afire till you smelled the smoke, would you, Rose? It's like the top of a stove here now. I've been keeping company with an Italian, as it happens, and all of a sudden, last night he ups and informs me that he's off for home. And when I ask him why, he says, things are getting too hot in dear Paree."

"Why, Vi," Rose said ingenuously, "he must have been too old for sport, is all."

"Idiot!" Violet spat out. "Don't you see beyond your nose? There's talk Bonaparte is coming back. And where would that leave us?"

"We're English," Rose countered. "What difference does it make to us?"

"You talk to the fool," Violet said to Catherine in disgust.

Catherine looked up at Violet's worried face. "Have you told the duchess? Does she know? Perhaps she'll leave now if you tell her."

"The old cow is in the same case as dear Rose here. She wouldn't know the Little General was back till he was atop her."

"Not the duchess," Rose said, aghast. "She don't go in for that sort of thing."

Violet flounced back to her room in high dudgeon. But Catherine did not answer any of Rose's confused questions. All it needs is this, Catherine thought fearfully, Bonaparte returning. But perhaps, it occurred to her, her face brightening and reassuring Rose, if war broke out again, the duchess would return home. And all my troubles would be at an end. And then she felt guilty and shamed that she would be small spirited enough to actually welcome a war just to suit her own selfish purposes. Rose was quite worn out with trying to read the varying expressions that chased each other across the other girl's face.

"Really," she said at last, giving up the attempt, "Violet does take on when she's been dropped. Like the world was coming to an end."

"I think," the marquis said, as Jenkins helped him into his jacket, "that it's at an end. I think we can leave at any moment. Keep our gear in readiness. We have the names or, at least, all that we can humanly be expected to have. Enough of those at the Tuileries who are supposed to be supporting Louis, but who will stab him in the back if they have a chance. And enough of those who plot for Bonaparte's resurgence. We can do no more. If all the whispers have any credence, we shall be lucky to get out with our skins intact.''

"A few of Beaumont's lads have been watching this hotel,'' Jenkins said calmly.

"Yes, and a few are at every affair we attend. I should dearly love to know when Beaumont moves, to see what jump he makes. But he's too clever to move until the fat is already in the fire.''

"Aye, there's a lad who keeps his bread buttered on both sides. Last night, he kept the early evening with the younger Cain and lit the midnight oil with the elder. He's keeping all his exits clear.''

"He would not be alive today if he didn't,'' the marquis said, giving himself one glance in the glass. "For it's no small feat for him to have held power in both regimes. He bends enough to last out every storm. And as he has no true backbone, it's easy enough for him.''

The marquis strode to the door. "One last party, old friend,'' he said, "and then I think we'll be gone whilst we can. Beaumont shouldn't at all mind finding us in his net, if the tide turns his way. I only hope those other poor devils we'll be dining with have as much sense.''

"True,'' mused Jenkins, following him. "It's hard to think of the old duchess rotting away in the Bastille.''

For a moment the marquis paused, and Jenkins watched his face carefully to see if his arrow had landed.

Then the marquis smiled a cold hard smile that made Jenkins grimace.

"The old woman is so far gone, I doubt she'd know the difference. As to her camp followers—since that, I think, is what you were referring to—they are the sort that follow a trade that can be plied under any change of government. For men remain the same no matter what uniform they put on, or, as in their case, put off. Stop being a sentimentalist, old dear. I offered the girl a soft berth, and she turned me down. She's after a seat nearer the throne. Any throne. And good luck to her. And good riddance,'' he added grimly, motioning Jenkins to follow him.

*   *   *

Catherine gazed in wonder at the home she entered. She had been to a great many parties, so many that her head whirled thinking of them; they all seemed now to coalesce into one noisily splendid affair with richly gowned and garbed people saying the incessantly same things to her and to one another. But this home was so stately, so lavishly furnished, that she gaped anew. The staircase was decked with flowers; so early in March it was rare to see such perfect blooms. She saw many of the guests pause to stare at the masses of violets entwined everywhere.

Early on in the evening Catherine lost track of the duchess and her two other companions. She made her way to a chair in an unobtrusive corner, ready to plead distress with her ankle again, and was pleased and surprised to find that in the crush of people, her usual admirers seemed to forget about her.

She was sitting and watching the merrymakers when M. Beaumont came up beside her and bowed. Catherine nodded. In all the time that she had seen him, he had never approached or spoken to her. But now he smiled and asked her leave to seat himself. She smiled back and nodded again. She had learned much more composure in the weeks that had passed. Though her days were spent in her room, her nights had been filled with parties such as this one. She had gained so much aplomb that she turned to Monsieur Beaumont and was able to study him with candor before he turned to speak.

He was a neat man, she thought, of no special age. Small, well turned out, and unremarkable in every way.

"Mademoiselle Catherine," he said, with only a slight accent making "Catherine," sound droll, as if it were "Cat-arine." But so many of the French, she had often noticed, had trouble with the "th" in her name. "We so often have seen each other, I think. Yet we have never actually conversed. How delightful it is to find you alone, and on the very night that I wished to have private conversation with you."

Catherine kept her face impassive. She hoped this quiet little man had nothing improper to offer her, but he seemed to have nothing but calm appraisal in his small dark eyes.

"I see that you have been very circumspect, unlike the dear duchess's other two companions."

Catherine's eyes widened. She knew that she could not defend Rose and Violet, as it would make her appear a fool. But she did not like to hear them condemned, so she simply kept her face blank.

"No, no," he said sweetly, raising his hands. "I do not say a thing against them. They are two lovely English flowers, truly. And so many of my acquaintances have found their company so amusing. So I shall say nothing against them. But you, my dear, have been so much less . . . free with your person, shall we say? It has caused much talk among us. Why should the sweetest of them all withhold herself? they are saying. Why? I myself have wondered."

Catherine grew anxious—she did not care for the way this conversation was tending. For although she had become adept at countering flattery, and even immodest suggestions, this cool appraisal of her presence with the duchess disconcerted her.

"And then I thought. And then I knew. You are not a fool—no, not at all, Miss Catherine. You have refused my friends, even those of the highest rank. And you have refused even the much-admired nobleman from your own country. Yes, I know. And why?"

Catherine began to speak, but he cut her off with a shrug and a wave of his hand.

"No, no explanations please. The thing is clear to me. The others settle for small rewards, and small adventures. You are much wiser. You seek something more lucrative, more permanent, with more advantages. You see the long view, while your fellow companions see only the end of their delightful noses. We are two of a kind, mademoiselle. I understand you well."

"Indeed, you do not," Catherine flared, rising. "You do not understand at all."

M. Beaumont put his hand upon her arm and forced her to sit again. Catherine stared at him, for whatever insult she had been open to, no one yet had tried to forestall her physically. But this quiet man held her firmly in her seat, and, glancing upward, she saw many faces hastily avert themselves from her obvious distress.

"I am a man of some small influence, Miss Catherine," he said with a smile. "I would advise you to stay and listen to me. I have connections in many places, Miss Catherine, and if you do not listen to me here, I shall be forced to have you taken to some place where you will listen. I have that power, you see."

Catherine sat and looked at the small man. She quietened, and he took his hand from her arm.

"Much better," he smiled. "I do not like to insist upon my way unless I have to. Do not be alarmed, Miss Catherine. I appreciate your beauty—I am a man, after all—but I do not covet it. No, I am happy with my own dear, cher ami. I do not require your presence for myself, no matter how lovely you are. But you see, I do understand, no?

"Now if you go on as you are doing, you will end up with nothing. For you do not know how to go on, that is obvious. The dear duchess, she is quite old, and quite silly. And your two companions, they would advise you to squander yourself, as they do, on any fellow that comes along with a few francs jingling in his pocket. They do not understand grand designs. I do. As you do. But you do not know which way to turn yet, do you? Quite wise," he said, as she shook her head violently in demurral at his words.

"For my poor country is in such a state right now that even we do not know how to go on. He who rules now may be in the streets tomorrow. Change has only begotten more change. You are so right not to cast in your lot with one who may lose all in a moment. Take my dear friend Pierre Richard. Tonight he will go home and sleep on fine silks in a room next to a king. But tomorrow?" M. Beaumont shrugged. "So who could blame you for casting him down? Or, for that matter, for repulsing his poor brother Hervé? For at the moment Hervé has nothing. Nothing but his charming self."

Catherine sat trapped while the small man beside her smiled smoothly at her. She felt a danger emanating from him unlike any she had yet faced.

"But that is only for the moment. Great things are in the wind, my dear. And great things are called for. So"—he straightened and stared at her—"this is what I have come to say. Give up your ties with the duchess. She has served her purpose—you will get no more from her. In fact, she may soon have no more to give. Come with me; I shall steer a clear course for you to the rewards you have been seeking. I shall find you a comfortable arrangement before the week is out."

"You are wrong," Catherine whispered. "I shall not leave the duchess."

"Oh," M. Beaumont said deprecatingly, "you think I wish to share in your reward. Put that from your mind, please. I seek nothing from you. Rather, my reward shall come from seeing you well placed."

"No," Catherine said, staring at him, "such a thing is unthinkable. You misunderstand."

"It is quite thinkable. If you think the duchess will object, please speak with her. I have already, and she is quite willing to end her association with you, so you need not worry about any problems from her. And none in the future, I assure you. I have taken over your fate. You are in good hands, never fear. Just have your bags packed by tomorrow morning, and all will end more pleasantly than you ever hoped."

"Tomorrow morning?" Catherine gasped.

"Perhaps that is too sudden," he said with a smile that did not reach his eyes. "Tomorrow evening then. I know how you ladies have to make farewells and pack every little thing. Although, I assure you, you could come to him with nothing but what is on your back and he would be pleased. He will smother you in riches, I assure you."

"To whom?" Catherine asked, staring.

"To my dear friend Hervé, of course."

"Never," Catherine said, rising again.

"A very pretty show of reluctance. I quite see what has won everyone over. And I cannot blame you for thinking me misled. For until now poor Hervé has had nothing to offer. But things will be greatly changed, and quickly, I promise you. He will soon be able to afford you—more than that, to treat you as a queen."

"No," Catherine protested, "it makes no difference, I tell you."

"I have no time for playacting; the decision has been made without your consent. It is over, Miss Catherine," he said, rising with her and gripping her wrist till it ached.

"This is my country. It is my domain. It is my wish. You will please to make ready for your journey. My man there will see you to your hotel. And my man will take you to M. Richard tomorrow evening. We will meet again, and by then you will see how foolish your fears have been. But do not try to evade my orders, Miss Catherine," he said, pressing her wrist till she had to bite her lip. "For my name is known, and no good will come of it."

Catherine looked around her frantically and saw no one willing to come to her aid, even though she was in evident distress. Rather they turned and ignored her. Hopelessly, she craned her neck, looking for a glimpse of familiar gray eyes, familiar broad shoulders, but the marquis was nowhere in sight.

"You see?" M. Beaumont said. "I am known everywhere. Now go, Miss Catherine, and make ready for your new and more pleasant life. I do you a great favor, Miss Catherine, and someday you shall thank me."

He released her, and she drew back. An impassive man in footman's livery stood at her back.

"Take Miss Catherine to her rooms, Claude," M. Beaumont said, and he watched as the footman steered the dazed girl toward the door.

Done, he then thought with a sigh. That was a good piece of work. Hervé would babble with gratitude when he told him. Pierre would be beside himself with rage, but much good that would do him.

Henri Beaumont had weathered many political storms by catering to the right persons at the right moment.

He had never heard the old English folk song about his legendary English counterpart, the infamous Vicar of Bray. But he would have understood the chorus, in which the vicar supposedly boasted that "Whatsoever king may reign, still I'll be the Vicar of Bray, sir." For whoever took power, Henri Beaumont would serve him well. The trick was in knowing the precise moment to shift allegiances, the exact moment to bestow favors. It was all in the timing. And if foolish Hervé Richard wanted this little English miss, he would have her as a gift from his friend Henri Beaumont just before the tide rose, just before Hervé knew that soon he could have anything in France that he wished. Even his own brother's head, if he wished. Though—and here Henri Beaumont gave himself the luxury of a rare, real smile—Hervé getting the woman his brother wanted and flaunting her before him would be better than getting his brother's head on a plate.

He had separated the little English cyprian from that fool of an old woman. He would serve her up to Hervé, who would be undyingly grateful. For he did not know what M. Beaumont knew. He did not possess the small piece of paper with the few coded words scrawled on it that M. Beaumont had received this very night. The few words that let him know that Hervé's great good friend and former ruler would soon be his, and everyone's, Emperor again.

Chapter XI

"Her Grace ain't back yet," Gracie sneered. "As you should well know. Why, the clock ain't even struck twelve."

"Please," Catherine begged. "Please, Gracie, let me know when she arrives. At any hour, at any time. I shall be waiting, but it cannot wait till morning. I must speak with her this night, whenever she returns."

Gracie folded her arms over her narrow breasts, an expression of great satisfaction upon her usually grim face.

"It's Mrs. Grace to you, young woman, and don't you forget it," she said slowly, eyeing the trembling young woman. "And Her Grace needs her sleep when she comes in. Why, she usually is so done in, poor soul, that she just tumbles into bed and don't stir till morning."

"Mrs. Grace," Catherine pleaded, "it is of utmost importance. Truly. You must——" And seeing the expression on the older woman's face, she quickly amended, "Please, please, just tap upon my door when Her Grace returns. I am sure she will want to speak with me as well. I know she will," she pressed, seeing the indecision on the other's face.

"All right," the older woman grumbled. "But don't be surprised if she sends you off with a flea in your ear. For having a chat with her 'companions' ain't what she's used to when she comes dragging in after one of them big dos."

Gracie turned abruptly and closed the door in Catherine's face smartly. One of those cats got her tail caught in the door at last, she sniffed with contempt as she caught a last glimpse of Catherine's stricken face. It's the Lord's judgment upon all of them wicked females.

Back in her room, Catherine slowly removed her shawl with trembling fingers and sank down upon her bed. Her first thoughts were of self-condemnation. She had dithered, and her selfish, cowardly procrastination had led her to this. For if she had been truly virtuous and truly courageous, she would never have been caught in such a coil. If she had thought herself derelict in remaining in the duchess's employ, it now seemed that she never really understood the full extent of the danger she had placed herself in.

And yet, she thought, groaning to herself, she should have known. Step by step, her complacence had led her to this, as surely as in any morality tale she had ever suffered through at Sunday sermon. She had accepted all, by slow degree, just as the vicar had warned her. A few months ago, if anyone had told her that soon she would be able to accept as commonplace nightly invitations to strange gentlemen's beds, she would have been appalled. Or if they had said, straight-faced, that she would have permitted a nobleman's ardent embrace without deadly shame, or even, in the quick of her soul, welcome it, she would have thought them mad. And perhaps, worst of all, if they had hinted that she would have been able to suffer blithely the reputation of a light-skirts, she would have laughed in their faces. But all of this she had done. And see what it had come to.

One cannot wear the feathers of a bird of paradise without being hunted as one. Why should anyone believe her now? And, she thought, rising and pacing in her agitation, it had gone beyond explanations. For M. Beaumont would not care to hear weak excuses. He had seen her as a cyprian, so he had decided to use her as one. She must speak with the duchess, collect her wages, only a few weeks before time, and go now. For she wondered if even the duchess's influence could prevent M. Beaumont from going ahead with his plans. And yet a small persuasive voice in the deeps of her soul still whispered that she would not have to leave yet—that she would not have to brave the world alone as she went back to England, that the duchess was still her employer, was still a woman of title and influence, and would still protect her.

It might be, Catherine thought, as she paced her room and listened for every creak in the old hotel walls for the duchess's return, that now the dowager herself would have had enough and would wish to return home as well. And then Catherine would find the entire incident just a frightening, cautionary false alarm.

So she persuaded herself as she waited; so she consoled herself as the hours ticked by. For she could not face the thought that she was trapped, that her future had been taken out of her own hands.

When the tap came upon her door, Catherine started. It had been so long a wait that she was sure Gracie had not told the duchess after all, out of spite.

Catherine straightened, ran her hands over her hair, licked her lips nervously, and went into the dowager's rooms. She had practiced her speech, but it died upon her lips as she caught sight of her employer. For the duchess had changed, as if in a moment. As if she were some once-vigorous plant that had been touched by the icy finger of winter.

She stood, Gracie hovering by her side, waiting for Catherine. But she seemed not to stand so straight as before, and to be rather oddly shrunken and debilitated. No longer a regal and imperious peeress of the realm, but only an old woman. The icy eyes that had gazed sharply at life and its pleasures seemed watery and weak in the candle's glow, and when she spoke her voice was querulous and edged with self-pity. Catherine gaped at the transformation. She did not know that it was only that the duchess's brief late flowering was passed, that her moment of spectacular beauty was over. It had been inevitable, for no beauty remains forever, but its flight had been hastened by terror and anxiety.

"Well, good riddance," the duchess said, staring at Catherine, but instead of backing the words up with a haughty stare down her long nose, her eyes seemed to waver.

"Your Grace," Catherine began, recalling herself after the shock of seeing the dowager so transmuted, "there has been a terrible mistake."

"No mistake," the duchess said. "You've found greener pastures. Can't blame you. You're young, with the world ahead of you, and you've seen a better chance and grabbed it. Violet told me you would, and she was right. So go, and be demned to you."

"I don't want to go," Catherine cried. "I want to stay with you. M. Beaumont told me that you had agreed to my leaving, but I swear I don't want to go. I had no idea of what he had in mind. And I want to stay with you. Please tell him that he was mistaken."

The duchess sank into a chair.

"Why shouldn't you want to go, eh? He said there would be riches aplenty for you."

"But Your Grace, please," Catherine said, going to the duchess and sinking to her knees by her feet, "please listen. You know that I served you faithfully."

Gracie gave a short bark of laughter.

"No, listen," Catherine pleaded, "I came as your companion. I didn't know about Rose and Violet then. And when I discovered they were accompanying you as well, it was too late to turn back."

Catherine faltered, for how could she claim that the dowager's two companions were nothing but highly priced prostitutes and that she, knowing all, had not been the same?

"I have been only your companion," Catherine said fervently. "I have done nothing else, I promise you. I am not right for the life M. Beaumont projects for me. You must know that."

"I don't care what my girls do when I'm not about," the duchess said, turning from Catherine. "I don't know and I don't care. What they get up to is their business, so long as they don't involve me."

"But I have got up to nothing," Catherine cried.

"It was a mistake," the duchess mumbled, "all a great mistake. I should have hired on someone who was up to snuff, who wouldn't enact such tragedies."

"But it would be a tragedy for me," Catherine protested, rising to her feet and staring down at the duchess. "Can't you see that? Can't you just tell M. Beaumont that you refuse, that you wish me to stay on with you? I promise to be no further trouble."

The dowager avoided Catherine's eyes and instead began to talk rapidly to Gracie.

"I told him I wanted to keep the chit. I told him I was a woman of some influence. I told him that he had colossal nerve to try to dictate to me—the Duchess of Crewe. But he didn't back down. No, he didn't. Do you know what he told me? He told me I had no influence in France. That he had power over my life and death. That he could clap me in prison, duchess or no, and leave me there to rot away until my countrymen would extricate me. He told me that soon the English would all be in his power. And when I told him he was speaking fustian—and I did, Gracie, I did, I was so angry at the fellow—do you know what he told me?"

Gracie took the duchess's hand and soothed her with, Catherine saw in amazement, a look of great contentment upon her homely face.

"He told me," the duchess whispered, "that I was only a mad old woman. Only a senile old woman of no account. And that after a week or two in his cells I would be less than that. He told me I should be locked up for my own safety. That he had the power to do so. And that by the time my family found out, it would be too late for me. Too late for me! 'The Duchess of Crewe is a succès fou,' he said, and then he laughed and said it was no more than the truth, that I was a crazy old woman. And that everyone knew it and laughed at me, as they laugh at inmates in a madhouse. And then he said that that was just the thing! He would put me in a madhouse, and no one would question him at all. He had the power, he said. He does, Gracie, he does."

"Your Grace," Catherine said, but at the sound of her voice the duchess turned to her and cried with some of the old power in her voice, "Go, go from me. I never want to see you again. You have brought me nothing but misery. I should never have taken you on. Butter wouldn't have melted in her mouth, Gracie, I swear it. And now look at her. Begging me to let her stay. I cannot, don't you see? She will bring me to ruin. He wants her and he shall have her. Gracie," the duchess quavered, "I shall want to go home now. Yes, I want to go home."

"Let me come with you," Catherine begged.

"No, no," the duchess cried out in a strong voice, "for then he will not let me go. Get away. Get away."

Gracie marched to where Catherine stood. She placed herself so close to her that Catherine had to back away.

"You stop bothering my lady," Gracie commanded, suddenly forceful and demanding. "You let her alone. You and the others was nothing but a passing fancy for her, like I always said. She's come back to her own sweet self now and she wants to be shut of you and your kind. So the gravy boat has docked and you let her alone. I won't have you battening on her anymore. Take your things and go where you always belonged. To the gutter."

Catherine went white. The hatred in Gracie's eyes chilled her. There was no hope for her here, not anymore. She thought quickly and pleaded once more, "But if I am to go, please, Your Grace, my wages. For I haven't enough funds to get home alone.

And I have worked for you. Please do not strand me without funds.''

The duchess rose and went to her dressing table. She opened a drawer and with palsied hands withdrew a small box. She took a handful of coins and flung them onto the floor.

''Here, here. Take your money and go. I never want to see you again.''

Catherine went to retrieve the coins and almost stopped and let them lie when she heard Gracie sneer. ''It's the money all right. There's never enough for her kind.''

Catherine had to swallow back a biting reply and stifle the impulse to leave the money and flee with her self-respect intact. But she knew that self-respect alone would never extricate her from her problem. When she had hastily counted out the amount she knew she had earned, she stood again. There was some satisfaction in noting that she had left the better part of the coins still lying upon the floor.

''I have taken only what was due me,'' she said stiffly, ''and I am sorry, Your Grace.''

''Get out now,'' Gracie commanded, arms akimbo and advancing upon Catherine. ''Go and good riddance.'' Her voice softened as she looked back to the duchess. ''Leave Her Grace to me now. I'll see her right, just like I always have. I didn't desert her when she took to the wild fancies she did, and I shan't leave her now that she's come back to her senses. But you get out.''

Catherine heard the door slam behind her, and the sound was ominous. If M. Beaumont had such power as to terrify and override a duchess, what chance had she against him? She could not turn to the marquis, although her thoughts had turned to him a dozen times this evening. For if she went to him, he would only think she had at last decided to take up his offer. Somehow, she was sure that he could stand against M. Beaumont, or anyone in the world, for that matter. But to go to him would be to say she was his. Why should he believe otherwise? And in some small part of her mind Catherine knew that if she went to him, she somehow would become his. And even if he then took her to safety, she would then be lost to herself forever, and be in time no less than Rose and Violet. She would have become, no matter how she examined it, or how many excuses for her behavior she invented, a woman who sold herself to a man, and forever beyond the pale of decent people. And she was done with excuses for her outrageous behavior.

She knew she had enough money to reach the coast now. And enough to take a ship to England. But she knew that M. Beaumont would not let her get that far. So she waited for Rose and Violet to return. Now they were her last hope. They were clever and women of the world. Doubtless, they would have some idea of what she could now do.

Dawn was staining the sky with its gray light when Catherine at last heard some movement in Rose's room. She leaped to her feet and, after gazing anxiously about the empty hall, tapped on Rose's door.

"Who is it?" Rose whispered.

"Me, it's Catherine. Oh, Rose, let me in," she pleaded, suddenly afraid that Rose, too, would deny her.

But when she entered Rose's room, she saw only her familiar smiling face grow suddenly concerned when she glimpsed Catherine's ashen countenance in the growing light.

"Whatever is the matter, Catherine?" Rose asked, drawing her to the bed to sit. "You look as if you'd seen a ghost. Never tell me that Her Grace's heart's given out? That she's taken a bad turn and left us? For she looked like death itself when I last saw her. And when I went to her, she just shooed me away and told me to leave her be. I should have stayed," Rose mourned. "Poor old dear."

"No, no," Catherine said, "she's well. It is something else. Oh, Rose, you must help me. For I'm in desperate case."

Catherine took Rose's arm and, feeling the frozen hand which clutched her, Rose stopped chattering and sat quietly while Catherine poured out her story.

"Oh, that's a rum case," Rose sighed, when Catherine had done at last. "That's a fine predicament."

Rose stood and shook her head and looked consideringly at Catherine.

"You do have a problem, Catherine," she said, "and I have got to be right out with you, dear. The easiest thing for you to do would be to go with Beaumont. Hervé Richard ain't a bad sort. He's clean, and he's got something blowing in the wind for him. And," Rose added, absently rubbing her shoulder, where Catherine could now see in the brightening dawn light, there was a fresh set of bruises, "he ain't got any strange ways about him, so far as I have heard. No, he's a straightforward chap who wouldn't want nothing special from you."

Catherine recoiled and hastily averted her face. The look of horror, however, had not escaped Rose.

"No," Rose sighed, "I didn't truly think so. Ah, Catherine, forgive me. I didn't mean to hurt your feelings. It was just an idea, you know. Forget I said it, do. For I know you're a good girl, and I wasn't thinking straight. We have just to get you away from here without Beaumont twigging to it, and all will be well. How to do it is the question."

Rose and Catherine sat silently in the room as the light increased, each thinking alone. When Rose heard a movement from the next room, her face brightened.

"That'll be Vi. She's just the one. She's far more longheaded than I, and she's a wonder at getting herself out of tight corners. I'll just go get her."

Before Catherine could look up from her miserable contemplation of the carpet, Rose had fled the room, and before a few more moments had passed, she returned with a tired-looking Violet in tow. In the fresh light of morning, Violet's dramatic orange costume seemed tawdry, and her carefully made-up face seemed blurred and exhausted.

"Here she is," Rose sang. "Oh Vi, we need your help, for our Catherine's got herself into a terrible problem."

Violet turned her weary smudged eyes toward Catherine's woebegone form.

"If she's gotten herself in the basket," Violet yawned, "she's just got to turn round and go home. She can't be increasing in the duchess's employ. The old girl don't want a squalling brat on her hands."

"Oh Vi," Rose cried, genuinely staggered, "you know better. Catherine ain't in the family way. And she don't want to be in the game, neither, and that's the problem."

Violet flung herself upon the bed and lay so still while Rose explained Catherine's situation that, Catherine feared she had fallen asleep. But when the tale was done, she opened her eyes and looked at Catherine narrowly.

"You want to skip out, then?" she asked.

"I must," Catherine said. "But how? And I must do it now, for Beaumont will be here to collect me by nightfall. But how shall I go in broad daylight?"

"It's not impossible," yawned Violet. "I've done it myself. Remember in London, Rose, when that poxy viscount was after me?" She laughed. "I made a monkey out of him, didn't I?"

Rose nodded eagerly. "So you did, Vi, but this is Paris, and Catherine and I ain't so wise as you. What's she to do now?"

Violet studied Catherine's abjectly sorrowful face. Her thoughts raced behind her sleepy facade. So the Richard lout was about to come into riches and wanted a fine English female? Well, she'd do just as well to console him when he'd lost the one he had his heart set on, wouldn't she? She watched Catherine—she had nothing against the girl, but business was business, and it wouldn't suit her to stick her neck out and defy Beaumont. But if there was some profit to be made from the girl's disappearance, well, there were no flies on Violet. The problem was, she thought, how to get the chit safe away without Beaumont twigging to the fact that she'd helped. After a moment she smiled.

"Rose, you goose. The answer's plain as the nose on your face. Catherine, do you take those things you find necessary, and only a few things at that. Here, wait a tick," she said, suddenly galvanized, and the two other women stared at her in wonder as she leaped up and ran lightly to her room.

She returned in a few moments. "Here," she said, placing a worn portmanteau at Catherine's feet. "I always carry it in case I have to skip fast. It's old and battered, but it won't attract attention."

Catherine looked at the worn case and had to agree. Indeed, it looked as though it had been used in the days of Violet's grandmother.

"Now you take only a little with you, and when you've all secured, act sharp, because time isn't on your side. Then, you come back here. And then, Rose, you take Catherine down to the stables. James is there, and he's a right caution. What he don't know about Paris, the Frogs themselves don't know. He's a game 'un and up to anything. And if your pretty face don't tempt him to help, Catherine, your good gold coins will. For he's always on the lookout to make some extra. And he don't like foreigners above half. Now shoo, go to it, Catherine, time is wasting."

Catherine fairly flew to her room and collected those few items she felt necessary. She left all her fine dresses and bonnets and slippers without a backward glance, only taking those few dresses she had originally come to the duchess with. She flung toothbrush, hairbrush, and underthings into the portmanteau.

When she was done, she hurried back to Rose's room.

"Good," Violet smiled. "Now Rose, you take her down the servants' stairs and James'll do the necessary."

Rose paused and then asked, "Catherine, let me see your purse."

Dutifully, Catherine handed it over to her.

"Oh, this will never do," Rose cried, "for you're a pauper. Look, Vi, how far can she go on this?"

Rose hurriedly went to a box in her closet and came back with coins that she poured into Catherine's purse above her horrified protests. "No, no," Rose said adamantly, "I couldn't sleep nights thinking of you starving in a ditch. We're friends, aren't we?" she asked, suddenly stopping and looking hard at Catherine.

To refuse Rose's money, Catherine realized, would be to deny her friendship.

"So we are Rose," she whispered, "and I am grateful. Someday I hope to pay you back."

Satisfied, Rose nodded sharply. "Here, Vi, open the coffers. For you're fast with advice, but tight with your purse. What do you want Catherine to think?"

With ill grace, Violet left, to come back and add her mite to Catherine's growing treasure. "But understand," Violet said quickly, "if anything goes amiss, you're not to prattle about where you got the funds."

Catherine smiled bitterly and met Violet's worried eyes. "Do you think M. Beaumont will wonder at my riches?" she asked.

Violet seemed satisfied, but she added, "And I hope you'll not cry rope at us, if he does find you. Do you promise to leave us out of it?"

"Of course," Catherine said softly. "But I think if he does find me, he won't care how I failed or who helped me fail."

"But you won't fail, Catherine," Rose said quickly. "For James is as sharp as he can be. We'll have to think of something Catherine can wear to escape notice, Vi," she added, biting her lower lip.

"Leave it to James, Rose," Violet answered. "He's up to all the rigs. Now get her out of here. And then I'm to bed. For I'm worn out."

Rose bustled ahead to the door, to see if any servants or guests were in the corridor.

"Half a mo," she said cheerily, like a little girl up to some midnight pantry raid, "I'll go ahead and check out the stairs to see if all's clear."

"Violet, I thank you," Catherine said softly, when they were alone, "for I know it's a dangerous thing for you to do. And I know that you never really approved of me."

"I like things straightforward," Violet murmured, suddenly less bored. "And it may be, Catherine, that I don't like being constantly reminded what I am by some great-eyed innocent girl. It's well enough with Rose, and the gentlemen I accompany. And the old duchess is daft anyway, you know. But it just may be that I like to think of myself as only a clever businesswoman, and I don't care for the constant presence of someone who is so very much aware of what a bad business mine is. You don't hide your thoughts too well, you know. And while I've come to terms with myself a long while ago, you keep reminding me of what I am and where I'm undoubtedly going. I wished to be an actress once, and the trick of being a good actress is to believe in your part. You shake that belief, Catherine, and I don't mind telling you, I'll be relieved when you're gone."

"Thank you anyway, Violet," Catherine said, wondering whether she should give the older woman a farewell embrace, for wherever she herself was headed, she did not think they would, in any case, ever meet again. Violet settled the matter by taking Catherine's hand and shaking it.

"Good luck," she said simply, and then, with a smile, she added, "and stay away from wicked companions in the future."

"Come, come, don't just stand there, Catherine," Rose whispered in exaggeratedly conspiratorial tones. "Time is wasting. Come, come, let's go, for the stair is clear."

Violet lifted an eyebrow in Rose's direction and said with some asperity, "Stop looking so sneaky, Rose. You'd make anyone suspect you of anything. It's a good job you never tried for the stage. Good-bye, Catherine, keep a good thought." And then she gave a tremendous yawn. "Lord, I'm beat. I think I'll sleep the afternoon away, and if anyone knocks upon my door, they'll see that I haven't done a thing but sleep since I returned. I haven't seen a thing, I haven't done a thing. Just like you, Rose, just like you."

"To be sure." Rose tittered in her excitement. "And where dear Catherine's got to, how should we know? We've been just two sleeping beauties, haven't we? Come, Catherine, the time is right."

Chapter XII

Catherine followed Rose down the servants' back stairs, bumping her portmanteau against the wall at every turn. They went quickly, Catherine hiding, flattening herself against the wall at every landing as Rose scouted to see if the way was clear. But it was early dawn and they achieved the sanctuary of the stables without any mishap. Once there, in the dim light, with the strong scent of horses and hay in their nostrils and only the curious nickering of the horses to greet them, Catherine relaxed at last. Rose nodded with satisfaction, for none of the grooms or coachmen were afoot in the stalls area, and there was no sign of any human activity.

"Do you wait here now, Catherine," Rose whispered, and she bustled off down the line of stalls and disappeared up a stairwell at the back of the stables. Catherine absently stroked the neck of a mare and wondered how Rose knew her way so surely through the stables, for she herself had only seen horses and carriages emerging from them during the days and nights that they had rested at the hotel. After a few moments during which Catherine worried about the increasing daylight and started at every restless sound the horses made, Rose reappeared at the other end of the stable and motioned urgently for Catherine to follow her. Catherine followed Rose up the turning wood stairs and found herself on a level above the stable proper. There were several doors off a wide wood-planked hall, and Rose led her unerringly to the door at the end of the corridor.

"Are you decent now, Ferdie?" Rose whispered as she tapped softly at the door.

The door swung open and James stood there, stuffing his

141

shirttails into his trousers. He yawned, then grinned wickedly at Rose.

"Ah, Rosie, you never asked that of me before," he grinned.

"No nonsense now," Rose snapped, all business as she motioned Catherine to follow her into the room.

It was a garretlike room, with a wooden floor and a high sloped ceiling. A simple bed and dresser with a lamp occupied one wall, and the other wall had a large window overlooking the stable entrance. James gave Catherine and Rose a sweeping bow and then sat down on his bed and smiled sleepily at them.

"Your visits are always welcome, Rosie, my love," he said, "but you don't often bring me extra helpings. Whatever will our little Miss Catherine think?"

Rose flushed a bit and then said hurriedly, casting a worried eye at Catherine shrinking back against the far wall, "None of your games now, Ferdie. I told you. The poor thing is in trouble. And Vi said, and I agreed, that you're the very one to spirit her out of here. And quickly too, for that devil Beaumont is after her, and he's no easy boy to cozen."

"Ferdie?" Catherine whispered, wondering if her fear had turned her comprehension, for it was James, the duchess's coachman who was grinning happily at her.

"Oh, that," James laughed. "The old girl calls all her coachmen James, but it's Ferdie Robinson at your service. So you want to nip out and leave the old girl in the lurch?"

"No, that's not it," Catherine said quickly, "for she's washed her hands of me. M. Beaumont has frightened her badly." Catherine grimaced involuntarily. "He wants to give me to Hervé Richard. He thinks I'm . . . that is to say, he believes me to be . . ." Catherine found herself at a loss for words, since with Rose standing next to her, how could she describe what Rose and Violet were without giving offense?

But James/Ferdie just laughed and Rose looked on benevolently.

"Oh aye, I know. All of us here know, lass. You're not in the same game as dear Rosie here, and we've often wondered just what your game was. For I swear I've brought you back to the hotel a dozen times alone when you could have had company easily, and I knew back in dear old London town you was in above your head. I thought to drop you a word even back then, but I've learned the less said, the safer your head. So now you're in the soup, eh?"

"Oh James—that is, Ferdie—" Catherine faltered.

"Keep it James, lass, or you'll be stammering all morning."

"James then," Catherine said, gathering up her courage at the friendly expression on his plain, homely face. "I must go. I cannot do as M. Beaumont wishes. I cannot stay. Indeed, I should not have stayed so long. But see, I have all this money. I only need enough to take the packet back to England. You may have all the rest, but please, if you know of a way for me to leave safely, help me now."

"Keep your brass," James said, with a wave of his hand.

Catherine's heart sank and Rose bridled instantly.

"Why you are a beast, Ferdie Robinson. After all we've been to each other. And after I thought you were a right sort!" she shouted. "It's as well I never went along with you and your high promises. You'll leave my friend to go to strangers for help? Oh, you are a rum cove, you are."

"Hush, hush, Rosie," James said, quickly rising and going to Rose and capturing her in his arms. "Did I say no, love? I only said I wouldn't take her money. And so I won't. For she is your friend, love, and I wouldn't charge her for a favor. Anyhow, I don't like Beaumont, and I don't like the duchess, and I don't like this whole setup. I've only stayed on to earn some more shekels, puss, so I can set you up proper if you ever say yes."

Catherine noted the satisfied little grin on Rose's face with some shock. For she had never seen Rose so content as she seemed now as she coquettishly tapped James on the chin and sighed, "I knew I was right in you, Ferdie. You are a good lad. Ferdie is the wisest thing in creation, Catherine," Rose said comfortably. "So rest easy, he'll think of a way."

"They'll be expecting you to fly," James said thoughtfully. "We've got to confuse them a bit, that's all. We've got to get you safely away from here to Saint-Denis. That's only outside the city a way, and there's a diligence that stops there that goes to the coast. You've only to hop on it and you're in Dieppe again. Then skip on a packet and you're home."

"But how?" Catherine and Rose said in concert.

"Some sort of disguise," James muttered, pacing and thinking.

"A widow!" Rose exclaimed, clapping her hands together. "That's the very thing! With a long black veil. And you could pretend to cry a little, couldn't you, Catherine, dear?"

"And all they'd have to do is lift the veil," James put in, "and then she'd be crying in earnest. Rosie, love, when we do buy that inn, it's you who will greet the guests, and I that will run it. For it's your face that's your fortune, puss.''

Rose subsided sadly. She walked over to Catherine while James stood, lost in thought.

''It's true,'' she sighed, ''I'm not longheaded at all, you know. And I'm not getting younger neither. I most likely will buckle up with Ferdie. And follow his path. For he wants us to set up an inn on the road to London, and after this trip I think I'm done with this old life. I had such dreams of fortune. Now I think I will be very glad to be plain Mrs. Ferdie Robinson.''

''Never plain,'' James said, turning to them. ''It's a disguise we're after. Now how can we change this lovely English beauty into something Beaumont's lackeys will ignore?''

Catherine thought for a moment and then she clapped her hands together.

''James! Rose! I have the very thing. I've seen it done on the stage. And I've read about it often enough. I'm not very tall, you know. I can dress as a lad.''

James looked skeptical, but Rose was delighted.

''The very thing,'' she cried.

''I don't know,'' James said, but, at Rose's urging, he shrugged his shoulders. ''It's worth a go, I suppose. Wait here. There's a room downstairs with some old kit left over from lads that have stayed here and skipped. I'll be back in a flash. If Beaumont's coming to collect Catherine, we'll have to move smartly.''

Catherine wrung her hands in anticipation. ''I know I can do it, Rose. I've seen it often enough. And they'll be looking for a girl. I'll pull my hair back and I'll swagger a bit. . . . Oh Rose, it has to work. I cannot bear to think of what will happen if it doesn't.''

Rose's enthusiasm began to fade as she looked Catherine up and down. Some of her doubt communicated itself to Catherine, and by the time James arrived with an armful of old clothes over his arm, he encountered two white-faced grim-looking women.

''Try it,'' he said simply, handing Catherine the old faded clothes.

Cathering looked about nervously.

''Where can I change?'' she asked anxiously, looking about the room for an alcove or a closet.

''Yes,'' James grinned, ''there's no doubt, you are a lady. Here, Rose, let's go into the corridor and catch up on some gossip. The lads here have seen you often enough; it won't arouse comment. Might arouse something else though,'' he added, with a grin.

"Hush, Ferdie,'' Rose giggled, poking him in the chest. But they grinned at each other and turned to go.

"Open the door, when you're done,'' James whispered. "But Catherine, best close your eyes first,'' he added while Rose smacked at him coyly and simpered happily.

Catherine moved far from the window into a corner of the room. She quickly stripped off her gown and clambered into a faded, patched pair of pantaloons. They were tight about the hips, but, she reasoned, as she did up the closings, they felt so strange on her that she could not know if they fit or not. It's rather, she thought, as she quickly did up the buttons on a much-mended white shirt, as if a gentleman got into skirts. How would he know if they were the right length and fit? She felt a fool as she hurriedly pulled back her masses of raven curls and tied them severely with a simple black ribbon. But, she thought, as she stuffed her discarded gown into her portmanteau, she would gladly suffer feeling a fool for a space of time in exchange for freedom. She was so badly frightened that she felt she would go to any lengths—like a fox who would chew off its own leg to get out of a trap—to be free of her present situation.

Drawing in a deep breath, she glanced down at herself. She was barefoot, the pantaloons were fastened, the shirt seemed to fit. She slowly swung open the door, and, taking James's advice, she averted her eyes and whispered urgently, "James! Rose! I'm ready.''

And then she stepped back into the room, to await their approval.

Rose came in first with a little laugh and high color in her cheeks, and then stood, stock still, and gaped at Catherine. James followed languidly and then stopped at Rose's side and stared. He gave a low whistle and then said slowly, "I've never seen a lad like you, Catherine, my girl. But I surely hope there's more such about in this cold, cruel world.''

Catherine looked from Rose's shocked face to James's frankly admiring one, and then looked down at herself again.

"Don't I look right?'' she asked.

James started to laugh, and laughed till he had to hold on to the side of the dresser for support.

"Oh girl,'' he sputtered, "you do look right. But not in the way you could wish.''

Rose tittered as well. But then a considering look came into her eyes. "Oh, Catherine," she finally sighed, "you could have made a fortune. You could have had such a career."

"Here, Catherine," James finally said, steering her toward his dresser, where he had a small faded-looking glass in the corner. "See for yourself."

Catherine felt the color flooding her face as she stared at the image in the gray speckled glass. She might as well have been nude, she thought with shock, the blood roaring in her ears. The white shirt strained its buttons over her high breasts and emphasized them. And the pantaloons clung to her hips and legs like another skin. She was, she thought, in confusion, seeing her body's slim but rounded outline—the most indecent-looking female she had ever seen,

Desperate, she turned and blurted, "If I bound myself . . . here. And if there were another pair of pantaloons, but perhaps larger. . . ."

"No, Catherine," James said kindly, "for it wouldn't do. There's not a portion of you that don't look like just what you are, a full-blown woman."

"But," Catherine protested, "I've heard about it being done. I've read about it as well. Women can disguise as young men."

"Some women, maybe," James chuckled, never taking his eyes from her frame, "but you, Catherine, never."

"But you do look a treat," Rose said helpfully. "Ever so gay. Such a nice figure of a woman, Catherine. It's very flattering in its way, dear."

"Don't be a bufflehead, Rosie," James put in, wrapping one arm about Rose's shoulders as Catherine sat down wretchedly upon his bed. "She don't have to look good—she has to look different."

"All I look like," Catherine grieved, "is a fool. Which I undoubtedly am. I've landed myself in this wretched state because I have been a fool. So it's only right that I look like one. Like a fool, like a zany."

James's eyes narrowed as she sat there hanging her head and crossing her arms in front of her breasts.

"Now you've hit upon it, lass," he said unexpectedly, causing Rose to turn to round upon him for his unkindness. But before she could assault him for his cruelty, he was gone, out the door.

"Don't despair, Catherine," Rose said, sitting beside her and patting her shoulder. "I told you Ferdie is clever. He's not beaten yet. All he has to do is to get you out of this hotel and you'll be safe as may be. And I know he'll do it."

But Catherine only shook her head and did not try to restrain the tracks of tears that were slowly coursing down her face. She could not grasp the enormity of her failure. She could not imagine what she could do if M. Beaumont acutally came to claim her for his friend. She now knew that she had never really accepted that he would, or could. There had always been the possibility of escape in the back of her mind. Now, she felt, that was impossible. And now, for the first time, she had to face defeat. How, she thought frantically, ignoring Rose's murmured assurances, could she go on? It was one thing to bear the insult of being thought of as a prostitute. But she knew she could not actually be one. Her thoughts raced each other around in her mind, and she felt a despair such as she had never known.

"Here," James said triumphantly, suddenly appearing in the door and swinging it closed with his foot.

"Mop up, girl," he said, busily separating the garments in his arms. "Stand up, put out your arms. Come on, Catherine, buck up. Time's running. We have to be off now. We have a chance while it's yet early. Once morning comes up full and the light's better, we cut our chances in half. Now turn. No," he said, pulling off the jacket he had put on her and trying another. "Here, Rosie, you help. She's like a dummy. Get her arms into this. Aye, it's the very thing."

Catherine stood and let them push her about, buttoning up the jacket they had forced her arms into. She tried to wipe her eyes, but Rose was busily adjusting her sleeve. As she began to collect herself, James wheeled her round again and began to adjust a large battered hat upon her head.

"There," he said, standing back a pace and peering at her. "No, not quite. Half a tick," he said, and slipped out the door again. By the time he returned, Catherine had managed to slow her labored breaths and wipe her streaming face on the sleeve of the jacket they had put on her.

"Hold still," James ordered, and while Catherine stood dumbly, he, to her dazed horror, took some of the dirt from the handful he had acquired in the stable yard, streaked it across her cheeks, and added a dab to her nose. Then he pulled the brim of her hat further over her forehead.

"Perfect," he exclaimed, and then he steered her to the glass again. "Now look, Catherine, that's the ticket."

Catherine saw a bizarre vision facing her in the looking glass. It was small and woebegone. It wore a battered sloping hat down over its eyes. Its face, the part that was visible, was streaked with tears and mud. The patched and misshapen jacket that it wore hung to its knees. Its sleeves ended inches below its hands. Just the bottoms of the pantaloons showed, and bare feet completed the vision.

"A zany," James breathed. "A want-wit lad. Just a scruffy little lack-brain French boy."

Rose gave out a long satisfied sigh.

"There was a lad like that in the town where I grew up," she said with amazement. "He had a good heart, but he was a simpleton. You look just like him, Catherine. Oh Ferdie, you are a one!"

"They'll be looking for a desperate lovely young beauty. They won't cast an eye at a little simpleton wheeling along with a coachman. We'll walk right out of here, under their noses. And we'll go by foot to my friend Jacques, the other side of town. He's a Frenchie, but he's all right. We can't take any of the horses from here—they'll know them. But Jacques owes me a few favors," he smiled reminiscently, "and he'll lend us the nags. He works for some jumped-up tradesman. I'll get you to Saint-Denis right and tight. Then you board the diligence and you're off!"

"Shall I use this voice?" Cathering said in gruff tones, her spirits rising by the moment, infected by James's enthusiastic confidence.

"Oh, Lord," James said, "you still sound a female. And your French ain't too good, is it?"

Catherine nodded sadly.

"Never mind," James said briskly, "we'll get us a note. In French. From your folks saying as how you're just a poor simple lad going to visit your grandparents in Dieppe, and would any stranger kindly direct you right. Then you don't have to speak at all. Just be mute. You can show the note, and your fare, to the coachman on the diligence. Then when you get to Dieppe, you board the packet. Get out of your disguise. Then get the captain aside and tell him the story. Tell him all. He's bound to be an Englishman and he'll see you safely through."

"I can't write French too well, but if someone dictates it . . .''
Catherine said doubtfully.

"Never mind," James said dismissively. "Your hand's probably too good. Our simpleton's not from an educated lot. We'll get Jacques to pen it. It will look better if it ain't spelled or written too fine. All set?"

"But she has no shoes!" Rose cried, aghast.

"Now I'm thinking like a noddy," James groaned. He went out the door again swiftly, mumbling that time was wasting.

"I told you," Rose sighed happily, "didn't I? He's a caution. And he's right. For you do look a fright. Nothing like the pretty lady they're on the catch for."

Catherine peered at herself from under the worn brim of the hat and laughed merrily.

"Thank you, Rose. That's the finest compliment and the most welcome one that I've heard since I came to France."

She amused Rose by striking foolish poses in front of the glass and flapping the long arms of her jacket. She looked, she giggled to Rose, like a ninny, there was no doubt of that. The worn jacket must have belonged to a giant, she opined, and its threadbare shape could have accommodated both herself and Rose. With the hat pulled over her eyes, she cavorted for Rose's delighted applause, looking, they both agreed, a veritable model of a fool. James returned carrying a pair of scruffy well-worn boots in his hand.

"Boots is the one thing they never leave behind unless they're dead," he grumbled, " 'cause they cost the earth. But here's a pair someone must have outgrown and then couldn't flog to anyone before they left. They're in sad shape, but that's all to the good. Put them on quick, girl, for folks is beginning to stir already."

Catherine struggled to fit the boots to her feet.

"I can't get them on," she cried in anguish. "My feet are not so large, but these must have been a child's, for I can't fit into them."

"Here," James said, bending and helping her to tug them on, "it just needs some force."

With concerted effort, Catherine and James managed to pull the left boot on. When she stood, Catherine stifled a cry of pain.

"Oh, Ferdie," Rose complained, "you never are going to send her off squeezed into those. Why, she doesn't even have stockings. She'll be in agony."

"There's no stockings about," he said sternly, "and the agony will be worse if Beaumont finds her."

Catherine bit her lip. If these were the only boots available, she would not quibble. She would wear them if they had hot coals in them. It would be poor spirited to lose all for the sake of momentary comforts. She reached down for the right boot, but James stayed her hand.

"Where's the blunt you've got?" he asked.

"In my portmanteau," she answered, puzzled.

"Get it out, Rosie," he said.

Rose looked at him with consternation, but obeyed. She handed Catherine's purse to him with a questioning look.

He spilled the coins and scrip into his hand.

"Here," he said, wrapping the coins in a square handkerchief he pulled from his pocket.

"Frenchie scrip won't be worth beans in England. Take the gold, wrap it like this, and keep it for home. There's pickpockets," he said, wrapping the little parcel tighter and tighter, "and thieves, and portmanteaus can be lifted too. You use the poor man's safe, Catherine, and you'll be right and tight. Here," he said, "stow it in your boot."

"But there's hardly room for her foot," Rose protested.

"Then she can swim to England," James thundered, "for if someone lifts her good British gold, she's a beggar."

"But," Catherine said, "if someone robs me, they'll discover what I am."

"Even if they do," James said grimly, "with your money safe in your boot, you can still go home."

Seeing her sudden stillness, he went on more slowly, "So you don't speak to a soul, and you just nod and show them the note. And even if worse comes to worse, you'll always be able to get home. For whatever else they may take off, it won't be your feet they're interested in. But if you're clever, they won't go near you, for you look poor as any beggar boy in Paris. So calm yourself. And hurry."

Catherine took the little cloth-wrapped parcel from James and firmly laid it in the bottom of the right boot.

"Lay on, Macduff," she said bravely, as James helped her tug up the boot.

"Talking warm don't suit you, Catherine," Rose sniffed.

Catherine laughed shakily and stood. When she began to walk

to the door in response to James's hurried admonitions, she had to limp.

"All to the good," James commented, seeing her altered gait. "It completes the picture."

Catherine and Rose waited in the darkened entry of the stable while James sauntered out casually to get the "lay of the land."

"Rose," Catherine said, clasping the other woman's hand, "I shall never forget you. You have been more than good to me. I do not know if we will meet again. I hope not in France, at any event. But I shall never forget you."

Rose clasped Catherine to her and hugged her tightly. As Catherine returned her embrace, Rose gasped a little, and, drawing back, Catherine again saw the fresh red bruises on Rose's shoulder.

The older woman looked down ruefully at the angry marks on her shoulder.

"You see, Catherine," she shrugged, "it's not a good life. And not one that I wanted for you. I choose it, so it's not the same for me. But not for you, love, for you are a lady. Anyway"—she smiled seeing Catherine's eyes glitter suspiciously beneath the downturned hat brim—"I'll be leaving it. We're to start that inn, Ferdie and I. So do you look for it one day. On the road to London. With a stable, and fine food, and flowers in the back. And Ferdie says he'll call it The Rose and the Bear, after us two. Now you go on, dear, and never look back."

James came back to the door of the stable.

"Say your good-byes, girls, for we're off, my simple lad and I. It's a lovely clear cold morning. Get back to your rooms, Rosie, and sleep the day away. You don't know a thing, Rosie, you don't know a thing."

But Rose hovered in the doorway and watched the lanky coachman and the small, ragged, limping little urchin flapping by his side swagger out into the street together. Clapping his hand around the young innocent's shoulders, the man began to sing a simple French rhyme, and the mismatched pair thus ambled on down the street. M. Beaumont's man only looked up and noted their passing. Then he turned his eyes up to the window where the English miss was, waiting and watching for any movement there. He doubted his employer's warnings that she might try to leave by stealth. Why should she, he mused, as the ragged pair of layabouts passed him, when she was set to go straight into the lap of luxury? Some females, he thought idly, blowing on his chilled hands after his long night's vigil, had all the luck.

Chapter XIII

Even though her feet ached, even though her right foot felt like it trod upon a fiery cobble every time she took a step, Catherine kept pace with James, and even swung her battered carpetbag in rhythm with the little song he chanted. For she felt freer and lighter than she had in days. They had walked blocks from the hotel. And no one seemed to give them a second glance. James marched her through the poorest district in the city, through crowds, yet no one bothered to take note of their passage. In her disguise, in dirty borrowed clothes, she suddenly felt more herself than she had all the nights she had been gotten up in her new finery. For that disguise, she reasoned, had been more alien to her than this one.

At least, she thought, as she gratefully rested on a barrel outside of the stable where Jacques, James's friend, worked, she would have a tale to tell her grandnieces and nephews when she grew old. For even now she was beginning to turn her thoughts homeward. Home, toward Arthur and Jane and the haven she looked forward to enjoying again. She might not, she thought, swinging her feet aimlessly as she waited, ever be able to tell Arthur the entire story. But she would tell Jane. And Jane would understand. Her adventuring days were over. She would be glad to go home and be a good auntie.

But the worm of ambition still gnawed at her. She might, she mused, someday be able to write of her adventure, perhaps under an assumed name, and earn a few guineas so that she would have some money of her own, and not be a burden upon Arthur forever. Then she hastily put her thoughts away. For it was ambition that had landed her in her difficulties, and she vowed to

be done with it. Still, a sudden thought made her laugh aloud.
And a nearby groom looked at her and shook his head over the
way even a stray current of air could amuse a simpleton. For she
very much doubted if Arthur would ever believe that his correct
sister-in-law could be dressed as a scruffy idiot, chewing a straw
and giggling to herself in the heart of the city of Paris. Oh Lord,
she thought, drawing in a breath in sad realization, what a
desperate pass I have come to.

James came out of the stable looking very pleased with himself.

"Here," he whispered, bending over her, "Jacques believes
you to be the son of a friend of mine. The less said, the safer your
head. I decided to name you Henri, in honor of your friend
Beaumont." He laughed. "And I thought 'Gris' would be a nice
short last name for you. Now," he continued, puttting a bit of
paper in her pocket, "there is your note. It says, as best as
Jacques could pen it: 'Here is my son Henri. He visits his
grandparents, M. and Mme. Gris, in Dieppe. Please see him
safely there, he has not much wit.'

"And now," James said, rising, "here are our horses. They're
too good for peasants such as us. But we have to stir stump. I
have to be back at work by evening. That's when the old woman
stirs. So mount up and we'll be off. You can ride, can't you?"
he said suddenly, in her ear.

Catherine eyed the huge black mare she was to ride and
swallowed hard.

She nodded. She had ridden back in Kendal, when Mama had
been alive. But always sidesaddle. Still, she thought, as James
threw her up atop the horse, she would do what she had to.

Seeing her there, clutching the reins with whitened knuckles
and struggling to stay right, James nodded.

"You look just as you ought," he grinned wickedly. And as
they rode off, he laughed to himself, watching his companion
struggle to stay upright. "Just as one would expect."

It seemed to Catherine that they rode for hours. But she knew
that it was only her body protesting her means of transport. The
horses steadily made their way through the crowded city streets,
and when the crowds began to thin, she thought she could see
James relax. "Now, we must travel," he called to her, and they
picked up their pace.

By the time the sun was high in the bright afternoon sky,
Catherine didn't know which part of her anatomy ached more,
her feet or her seat. But she was curiously happy, even in all her

discomfort. Once they reached open country, she even found herself humming in time with the beat of the horses' hooves. She wanted to whisk off her absurd hat and sing. For she was free. The air was cold and sharp and clean against her face. The decision had been made. And it did not matter what sort of a fool she looked, for no one knew her. And in her anonymity lay her safety and her passport to freedom.

She was almost sorry when James drew the horses in at a farmhouse and signaled her to dismount.

"I will go and make arrangements for the horses to be watered here. Then we'll walk to the inn where the diligence stops. For it never hurt to be extra careful," James said consideringly. "These nags are too good for the likes of us and you never know who notices such things at an inn. So we'll hoof it there ourselves. I'll collect the horses on the way back."

While James went to the back door of the farmhouse, Catherine leaned upon a wooden fence. When the farm wife came out to look at the horses and glanced curiously at Catherine, she quickly drew her hat brim down further and gazed at the ground.

James dickered with the woman in his rough French, and then he came back to Catherine and slapped her on the shoulder, almost knocking her from her feet.

"*Allez idiot!*" he roared, "*Il est tard. Allez, allez.*"

She strode after him and breathlessly kept pace with him till the road turned and they were out of sight of the farmhouse.

"Did you have to be that convincing?" she complained, limping quickly after him.

"It does grow late," he said worriedly, glancing at the sky, "and she wanted to offer us some cider and a bite to eat. But I couldn't risk it. It wouldn't do for me to be gone when Beaumont comes. He'll twig to me in an instant when he finds you're gone too."

Catherine felt extremely guilty. For she hadn't realized the penalty that would fall to James if it were discovered that it was he who had helped her. So she merely nodded and tried to keep pace with his long strides. Her feet burned in the tight boots, and her right foot felt as though it were afire with each step she took upon her secret cache of coins. But she knew it would be selfish and dangerous for James if she slowed her pace, so she held her lips together tightly and forced herself to match his steps.

As they walked, James offered advice.

"It might be crowded on the road. And if it is crowded, there are always folk who'll take advantage of a half-wit. So push yourself. Wave your note around if they tell you there's no room in the coach. Someone's bound to take pity on you. You look sad enough. But remember, don't speak. Don't trust anyone. Keep to yourself till you get aboard an English ship. Keep that portmanteau by your side. Sleep on it, if you have to. And don't take off that boot. That's your bank account.''

Catherine puffed along with James, nodding at his every suggestion. The cold afternoon eased her pain. The ground was so cold, and the sole of her boot so thin, that her right foot was numbed and the pain seemed bearable. She would board the diligence and suffer quietly. But, she vowed, the first thing she would do aboard ship, even before she took off her hat, would be to rid herself of her accursed boots.

The inn was a sorry-looking place, Catherine thought, as they came to it. It was weathered, in need of a coat of paint, and grimy. James sniffed disparagingly as they passed the pungent odor of the stables. There seemed to be a great many people, mostly peasants and tradesmen, milling about in front of the place and talking loudly to each other.

"Stay by my side," James whispered urgently as he mounted the steps to the entrance.

Once inside, James pushed his way through a group of angry-looking farmers and went up to a high desk. A harassed, very fat woman was arguing loudly with a red-faced farmer. James waited until the farmer had finished his argument and stomped off before catching the woman's attention by rapping a coin on the desk. He flipped the coin repeatedly in the air as he held a whispered conversation with her. Catherine could not catch his words, but he, too, seemed to be growing angry. Finally, he sighed and flipped the coin at the woman, who caught it adroitly and then moved on to speak to another patron.

James drew Catherine aside at the entrance to the inn, near a large crowded taproom.

"Ahh, bad luck," he sighed. "The diligence broke down further down the line. And it won't come till tomorrow. So you'll have to spend the night here. These others, most of them live nearby and will go home and come back tomorrow. But still others are staying overnight. So there's no room for a rat, she says. You can't sleep in the stable neither, for there's a whole crew of rowdies putting up there, or share a room, for they're all parceled out. So I offered her a pourboire and she says a little chap like you can sleep safe enough right there.''

James pointed to the massive fireplace that took up one whole end of the taproom. Catherine looked at him in puzzlement, a little smile on her lips, for surely he was joking.

''No, not in the fire, nit,'' he laughed. ''But on the fender there—it's wide and brick, and there's room enough to curl up warm there.''

The fireplace, Catherine saw, did have a wide brick lip that ran in a semicircle along its circumference.

''Not the best accommodations,'' James shrugged, ''but keep your hat on, curl up tight, use your carpetbag as a pillow and you'll be safe enough. This side's for the common lot. There's private rooms on the other side. I gave her a tip so you could stay and she would see you on the diligence tomorrow. So,'' he said, looking around him, ''this is as far as I take you, sweet. I have to go now. But is there anything else I can do for you before I go?''

Catherine shifted from foot to foot in embarrassment. There was one other problem, but she did not know how to ask him about it. He saw her consternation and after a moment began to laugh. He cuffed her on the shoulder again.

''I'm a looby too,'' he grinned. ''Come with me.''

Keeping her head down, Catherine followed him out a back door near the steaming kitchen. There was a small vegetable garden and then nothing but a field of weeds. James picked carefully through the garden and led her around to the side of the house. Two ramshackle outbuildings stood there.

''Go into the one on the right,'' he whispered. ''I'll keep watch.''

When she came out of the little building, the smile disappeared from James's face.

''See you don't go in again unless there's absolutely no one about,'' he warned.

''I'd like to wash up,'' Catherine whispered.

''Forget that,'' James cautioned, leading her back into the inn and the taproom, ''for it's dirt that makes the man in this case. Now,'' he said quietly, as he sat her down by the fireplace, ''there'll be a spot of dinner later. Then curl up and sleep. And then, after breakfast, board the coach and go. I don't care if you have to ride atop it, go.''

"I'd like to pay you," Catherine said in a very little voice. "You've been so very good to me."

James grinned hugely, swept her into his arms, and kissed her soundly on both cheeks.

"Payment," he said. "The French," he whispered, "kiss all the time. Take care, Catherine, and luck be with you."

She watched him go and sank down at her seat by the fireplace. Suddenly the light seemed gone from the day, and she almost, imperceptibly, shrank into a smaller shape. She was on her own, at last.

The afternoon passed slowly. True to James's predictions, the crowd of people slowly filtered away, grumbling as they went. Still, the inn remained filled, but few people entered the taproom and those who did, ignored the simpleton sitting and staring at his boots by the fireside. As night came, it grew colder, and soon the landlady huffed into the taproom and brushed at Catherine.

"*Allez, allez,*" she roared, as people do at those they think are lacking in wit, as though volume alone will get their meaning through. "*J'ai besoin d'allumer le feu,*" she screamed, indicating the logs stacked in the fireplace.

Catherine stepped back from the bricks and let the landlady, puffing from exertion, bend to touch a match to the tinder. Soon a comfortable fire was roaring, and the landlady grunted in satisfaction. She waved at Catherine again.

"*Asseyez-vous. Asseyez-vous,*" she commanded, and, after what she deemed to be enough of a confused consideration, Catherine sat back down again as requested.

The taproom slowly filled, and a few tired slatternly-looking kitchen maids brought bowls of stew, tankards of beer, and bottles of wine out to the guests. One stopped and placed a bowl of stew and a glass of cider on the bricks at Catherine's side. She smiled at the poor waif, and Catherine ducked her head and began to eat, badly frightened because she had almost said "thank you" without thinking.

Most of the diners finished, puffed at their pipes, and then grudgingly left the warmth of the taproom and made their way upstairs to their rooms. The heat and a full stomach should have made Catherine drowsy enough to curl up to sleep. But the heat had thawed the anesthetic of cold from her leg, and the pain was sufficient to keep her sitting upright in distress. The hour grew later, and she sat almost alone by the fire, rocking unconsciously to the beat of the throbbing in her foot. The warmth had made her feet swell and the boot was now like some medieval torture device. Catherine was in agony, both in spirit and body. Her every impulse told her to strip off the boot and be done with the pain. And her every thought told her that James had been right and on no account should she part with it. But the walking and the heat were taking their toll, and she felt her leg would burst.

The interior misery she was suffering had become so acute that she did not take note of the altercation at the desk in the little front room for some time. But finally the sound of raised voices reached her pain-deadened ears and she looked up. She could see the front entrance clearly from her seat. The landlady was shrieking at a troop of men who had straggled in. They were a bad-looking lot, Catherine thought. Some wore uniforms that were tattered and grimy. Some wore work clothes. But they were tough desperate-looking fellows, and Catherine shrunk into herself, looking at them.

Even with her poor grasp of the local patois, the sense of what they were shouting at the woman was clear to her. These men were traveling to Paris, they protested loudly. For they had heard that their emperor was returning. And they were volunteering to be of service to their country again. One great fat fellow was roaring that the emperor would be very displeased with a female who denied free room to his soldiers. The woman shouted back, equally loudly, that as far as she knew Louis still sat upon the throne and no one was going to take over her inn as housing for an army that didn't exist. She was not turning over her establishment to the rag and tag of an army without orders or compensation.

Catherine listened to the battle rage. The gross fellow who was the evident leader of this disorderly troop finally banged some money down disgustedly on the counter. And then, to Catherine's horror, the landlady pointed to the fireplace and to Catherine.

"*Allez. Avec l'idiot,*" she said.

The troop of men, grumbling, coughing, and cursing, made their way into the taproom. Catherine was afraid to budge, so she simply took her portmanteau, put it on her lap, and tried to look as insignificant as possible. The men eyed her, and then disregarded her and began to call for food and wine.

After they had eaten, they sat and continued to drink and talk. Catherine was desperate for sleep, for an end to the pain in her foot, but she was afraid to close even one eye. The fire was dying and the night advanced. But terror kept her wide awake.

As she sat there, hoping that they would soon settle down to sleep, the fat man who was their leader looked over to her. He shouted at her in a rough patois. She was not sure what he was saying, so she simply sat still, hoping he would lose interest. But he rose and came over to her. He was huge and unkempt, with a burgeoning belly and a sly look in his eye. He shouted down at her. She drew back, both from the violence in his voice and the dark heavy smell that emanated from him.

Then, to her horror, he reached down and lifted her by the shoulders and threw her aside. She stumbled against the edge of the fireplace.

"*Je dors là,*" he grunted, and, sitting where she had been, he took her portmanteau and began to open the straps on it.

It was sheer despair that caused her to launch herself soundlessly at him, cluching for her portmanteau in a frenzy. He waved her off with one large paw and kicked out at her. When his booted foot connected with her aching leg, she heard some-one howl in a high keening scream of pain, and only when she fell, cradling her leg, did she realize that it had been she herself who had made that terrible cry. The tears were streaming down her face as she watched him begin to undo the other strap, and she was sobbing in earnest, when she heard an incredibly famil-iar voice say in French, "So this is how brave Frenchmen disport themselves."

The landlady bustled into the room, clucking.

"*Non, non. Ce n'est pas bien.*"

Catherine, looking up from under the brim of her hat, saw in the wavering light of the drying fire, as best she could through misted eyes, the tall straight figure of the Marquis of Bessacarr striding into the room. Jenkins, she saw, was behind him.

"Now why does a grown man torment a child, do you think, Jenkins?" the marquis drawled in English.

"Let it be," Jenkins said, with a worried look at the men in the room. "And for God's sake, let it be in French."

"We are not yet at war, Jenkins," the marquis said. "There'll be time enough for that."

The man who held Catherine's portmanteau put it down and slowly stood up. But she saw, from where she crouched on the floor, even when he stood up fully, the marquis still towered over him. In a caped driving coat, immaculate, disdainful, and straight, the marquis presented a picture of authority and command. Though hate glittered in the other man's eyes, he was the first to drop his gaze, and he walked back to the fireside and threw Catherine's portmanteau at her.

He muttered something about the boy being only an idiot. And the landlady began to explain rapidly to the marquis, Catherine surmised, who and what Catherine was.

"*Pauvre petit,*" the landlady cried, helping Catherine to her feet. Then she went on to assure her in many ways, by shouting loudly and by hand signals, that she was to go back to her seat by the fire, that the kind gentleman had interceded for her, that she was safe now. Then she turned and scolded the other men, who looked at her sullenly.

The marquis looked around him.

"And how long do you think it will be, once we are in our rooms, Jenkins, before they take extra good care of the poor lad?"

"Let it be," Jenkins repeated. "You surely don't intend to stay the night down here to watch over some wretched simpleton?"

"Hardly," yawned the marquis, "but, as I recall, there's a spacious hearth in my room as well. I'll let the lad spend the night there. For these oafs will tear him apart by morning, just to revenge themselves on me, if I do not protect him now."

"Surely not," Jenkins said, genuinely appalled, "for he's flea-ridden, or worse."

"I didn't say my bed," the marquis said coolly. "I said my hearth."

Jenkins shook his head in demurral, and Catherine stood still and watched as the marquis explained his plan to the landlady. She beamed at him and hastened to Catherine.

"*Allez,*" she shouted in Catherine's ear. "*avec le gentilhomme. Allez. Allez,*" she screeched as Catherine stood frozen to the spot.

Still, Catherine noted that the marquis did not look at her again. He merely turned and went to the stairs and began to go up. Jenkins turned once and shook his head in disapproval. But the men in the room grumbled to themselves, and Catherine knew she would be safer away from them.

As she mounted the stairs behind the marquis and Jenkins, she realized that neither of them had seen through her masquerade, and that the light was dim, and she would be expected only to curl up and sleep by a hearth. And, she thought wildly, she could be gone by early light. Safe from the marquis and from the brutes below stairs, for they were traveling in the opposite

direction. Gratefully, she limped up the stairs in the marquis'
trail. For a moment when she had recognized him and heard the
firm assurance in the deep voice, she had longed to throw herself
upon his mercy and reveal herself. But then she remembered
where he had last seen her, and what James said. But tonight's
safety would do well. She hugged her bag to her chest and
entered the marquis' room as quietly as she could.

His room was spacious and well appointed. It was obviously
the best the inn had to offer. The marquis flung off his cloak and
sighed.

"This will be my sheet for the night, Jenkins. I expect these
bed linens are inhabited. Perhaps they contain more livestock
than the garments of that poor soul over there."

"English?" Jenkins asked with a lifted eyebrow.

"The poor creature hardly understands his own language. Do
you think him fluent in English?" The marquis laughed.

"Right," Jenkins said, and then, seeing Catherine sidling
toward the fire, he said softly in French, shooing her, "Sit, sit.
Go to sleep. Go to sleep, boy."

Catherine obediently put down her portmanteau and, gathering
herself up in a small heap, lay down upon the stone hearth with
her bag as her pillow.

"Take off your hat, child," Jenkins said again in French,
reaching down.

Catherine sat bolt upright and clutched her hat tightly to her
head.

"He's terrified of us. Let him be," the marquis said.

"Gladly," Jenkins said stiffly, "but I'll sleep with my door
open, for I think he's not above theft."

"I wouldn't worry," the marquis yawned. "At least not about
him. But I think we ought to speed up our pace a bit. That's the
second group of volunteers I've seen headed for Paris. The
moment hostilities arise, we are fair game. I disliked to stop over
here, but I refuse to ride through the French countryside in the
dark of night. Tomorrow, if all remains the same, we'll leave the
horses and get on the coach. With luck, we'll reach England
before the week is out. And then let them march on Paris all they
wish."

"Aye, lad. I think they'll accommodate you. But pray it's
after we're safely asea."

The marquis and Jenkins continued to talk softly about lists
and plans and plots while Catherine lay quietly at the hearthside.

She would very much have liked to have done with the whole scheme and was itching to leap up and tell them who they shared the room with. She yearned to have the burden of escape taken from her shoulders. But, she reminded herself as sternly as she could, it was in seeking the easy way, the comfortable way of life, that she got into difficulty. It was time that she took responsibility for herself at last. She sighed heavily.

"The boy's aching for sleep," the marquis said, hearing her gusty sigh. "And, for that matter, so am I. I give you good night, Jenkins. We have a long day tomorrow."

Jenkins shot Catherine a suspicious look as he went quietly into the connecting room. Once there, he did not close his door all the way.

Sinjun blew out all but one candle by his bed and lay himself down upon the cloak that he had draped over the unreliable sheets. In the semidark, he could only make out the outlines of the poor boy's form by the dying fire. Satisfied that all was quiet, Sinjun lay back and rested his head against his laced hands.

All was done, he thought. The lists lay sewn firmly in the seams of his coat. Now there would be a reliable guide as to whom they could trust, whom they would have to name enemy, and who would sell to the highest bidder. A smile touched his lips as he thought of the list. There was really no need for it, he knew them all by rote. And as for highest bidders, his thoughts wandered to the man he knew ached to arrest him on any premise. If he could leave this benighted land before the emperor returned, there would be no need of the list, and if not, he thought resignedly, he could find a way at least to get the list out safely. It was not as if there was anyone in England who would mourn long for him—it was not as if his oblivion would matter at all. He felt a twinge of despair and pushed the thought firmly away as he had trained himself to do. He was wide awake. Company in his bed would eventually bring sleep, he thought. But the serving wenches below stairs looked in as sad a state as the linens his cloak protected him from. And as for that female in Paris—his lips wrenched into an unpleasant smile—she had probably been long gone to a higher bidder. Sinjun lay back silently and waited resignedly for sleep to at last steal over him. It would be, he thought, a long wait.

Catherine sat up slowly. It had been a long time since she had heard any movement from the marquis. She had lain still for a long time—she could endure no more. Her leg ached with a steady throb that began to encompass her whole body. Whatever James had said, she knew she must get her boot off. She would take her money and conceal it somewhere else upon her person, for no one, she told herself, should really be expected to endure such travail.

The sound came to Sinjun's ears immediately and his face twisted into a disgusted grimace. He raised himself slightly and looked over toward the boy. The fool was sitting up, slightly hunched over, and the sound of his rhythmic panting was clearly audible. Sinjun lay back and gave himself points for his own idiocy. Jenkins, of course, was right again, as usual. See how he was repaid for a moment of compassion. Sinjun had spent his boyhood in boarding schools, and he had traveled in the thick of many various armies. Lovely, he thought grimly, I give the waif a safe harbor and he repays me by using my room to abuse himself in. Ah well, he thought angrily, at least it won't go on for long. And I think I won't tell Jenkins in the morning, for it will delight him no end.

But after several long laboring minutes had gone by, the fool of an idiot was still at it. Sinjun wondered at his perseverance, for the harsh breathing went on, not only unabated, but considerably louder. Slowly, with the stealth that had surprised many enemies, Sinjun raised his long body from the bed and padded slowly on light feet to see what the devil was going on. He felt a moment's self-recrimination when he saw that the poor fool, far from attempting to enjoy himself, was merely struggling to get his shabby boot off.

With an exclamation of impatience at himself and the world which sent poor half-wits out into it with no protection, he approached the boy.

"Here," he said gruffly in the local argot, "let me do it."

He had expected the boy to be surprised, but not to the extent that he was. For he jerked up to a sitting position and cowered away.

"Come," Sinjun demanded in the same dialect, "I will help you. Do not be afraid."

And without waiting any longer, he made a gesture of impatience and reached down to grasp the boy's boot. He held it firmly and began to wrench it off. As he gave it a twist and the final tug to free it, three things happened almost simultaneously.

The boot, freed from its grip on the boy's foot, came off in his hand. A small packet flew from it and landed on the floor with a damp thud beside him. And the boy cried out in English in a high, clear woman's voice, "No. Do not touch me. Please, don't."

And then as he stood dumbfounded, the boy flung his hands to his head and fainted away.

Sinjun bent over the boy and stared at him. Then, still shaking his head, as if to clear his sight, he gathered the boy in his arms and carried the insubstantial weight to his bed. Once he had lain the lad there, he gently removed the ridiculous hat and stared long at the still white face. He pushed back one dark curl from where it had fallen onto the forehead and continued to stare, genuinely staggered at the sight of the unconscious form.

"Well," said Jenkins slowly from behind him, as he sheathed his knife carefully, "it looks as though you've finally gotten her where you wanted her, lad. In your bed."

For once the marquis did not return Jenkins' sally with another. He only stood and watched the closed face beneath his.

"Here's a pretty sight," Jenkins grunted.

Sinjun wheeled around to see Jenkins holding up the bootless leg. The small white high-arched foot was blood-smeared and torn.

"This," Jenkins snorted, holding up the small bloody linen-wrapped packet, "is what did the trick. A boot's a good place for treasure, as you well know, but not when there's scarcely room for a foot there as well."

"At least," said a small frightened voice from the bed, "it was safe till I disturbed it."

Sinjun turned and looked down into a pair of wide terrified eyes.

"That," he said, with a slow smile, "is more than I can say for you, child."

He let his eyes linger on her as he lowered himself to sit beside her, and trailed one finger slowly across her jawline,

"A great deal more than I can say for you," he smiled.

Chapter XIV

Catherine's voice faltered as she brought her story to a close. The marquis had sat beside her silently as she had told it. She had no idea what expression he wore, as she had been afraid to chance a look at him. Instead, she had watched the far less threatening, more sympathetic play of expressions on Jenkins' concerned countenance. And it had been Jenkins who had insisted that she tell all in such a gentle fatherly manner that she had complied. If she had been alone with the marquis, there was every possibility that she could not have uttered a word, for when she had woken from her pain-induced swoon, his face had held menace, and his voice had implied further distress for her at his hands. But she had taken heart from Jenkins' presence. For no matter what the marquis' intentions, she doubted he would initiate any ploy against her with Jenkins in the room. Now, risking a glance at the marquis from under her lashes and seeing the unblinking gray gaze fixed upon her, she did not know which she feared more—his anger, his disdain, or his easy seductive acceptance of her.

But there was nothing seductive in the look which he now bent upon her. There was only outraged incredulity. He rose and paced a step and then wheeled back to her.

"Do you mean to tell us that you actually believed you were to be no more than a companion for the duchess? That your duties were only to be to hold her knitting or sit and have pleasant little cozes with her about her grandchildren or her rheumatics?" he asked.

She shrank back from the force of his voice, but then found herself growing angry at the tenor of his words.

"How should I have thought otherwise?" she argued, "for she was a duchess and she seemed to live at the height of respectability. Even Arthur—he's my brother-in-law, you know, and he is a stickler for propriety—could not claim otherwise. Indeed, he would have been glad to have thrown an obstacle in my path, for he did not want me to earn my own way at all. If he had had even an inkling of anything amiss, he would have thrown it up to me."

Seeing the patent disbelief upon the marquis' face, she went on with more spirit and a genuine sense of outrage, "Women such as the duchess may be common coin in your set, Your Lordship, but I assure you we have none such in Kendal. Why, if any woman behaved so, her relatives would have her clapped up somewhere to protect her from herself. Mrs. Blake is the only true eccentric we have," she mused, "and that is because she is so overfond of cats. And even so," she added triumphantly, "her children have told her if she adopts one more, they'll have the whole lot out on the streets, for people will begin to talk."

Sinjun ran a hand through his hair while Catherine could hear Jenkins' low chortling. But then the marquis turned again and said with a certain slyness, Catherine thought, "And yet, even you must have realized what her game was by the time we met upon the packet to France. For both Rose and Violet were in the duchess's trail then. Never say you thought those two particular prime bits were there to complete a cozy sewing circle? Or that they were too reticent to tell you the whole of it?"

"No," Catherine admitted in a little voice, hanging her head, "by then I did know."

"Then, in the fiend's name, why didn't you just throw up the whole bad business and hie yourself home to Kendal and rejoin your eccentric cat-loving old ladies?"

"I hadn't the funds," Catherine answered softly.

"Why didn't you appeal to someone you knew? Or tell the duchess the whole game was off?"

"She wouldn't have paid me," Catherine said sadly, "for she had already advanced me my wages for the first months and told me the rest would only come quarterly. And I did not think she would take kindly to my denouncing her and demanding un-earned money for my return home before her journey had truly begun. And I knew no one else."

Sinjun stood still and then said with a softer voice and an expression she found hard to read in the dim light, "But you did know me. And I'm not known to be pinch-pursed, and, certainly, I had not been distant with you.''

"Oh yes," Catherine flared suddenly, "you have not been. But you took no pains to conceal your opinion of me. And I was going to tell you twice, in fact. But that first time aboard ship you only began to give me advice about which gentlemen I should attach myself to for profit. Wouldn't I have presented a pretty picture if I had asked you for money after that recitation?''

The marquis, Catherine noted, looked abashed for the first time since she had met him. A brief uneasy silence fell over the room which was at length broken by Jenkins' query. "And the second time?''

Catherine, remembering the moment in the marquis' close embrace, only flushed. And the marquis, instantly remembering the same scene, for once was speechless. He only gave a low muttered curse and walked to the fire to stare at its dying embers.

Well then,'' Jenkins said with suppressed laughter in his voice, "we should see about binding up that limb of yours, Miss Catherine. For one-legged companions are not in too much demand this season. Just sit back. I'll go to fetch some clean water. No need to worry, for His Lordship can tell you I've some experience in that line, and I'll have you up and ready to travel by first light.''

Jenkins went quietly out into the passage. Finding herself alone in the room with the marquis, Catherine sat very still, not daring to break into his seeming reverie. But before long he was back, standing beside the bed and looking down at her. She did not dare to even look up at him this time, being too aware of his proximity and of her embarrassing position, occupying his bed.

"And how," he asked finally, "did you think to come through the whole of your adventures with your reputation intact?''

"Oh," she said slowly, "as to that, it hardly mattered, for I intended to go home to Jane and Arthur immediately upon my return. One's reputation in Paris and London wouldn't count for much there. For no one I know travels further than to market most of the time.''

"And how," he persisted, "did you think to return with your person intact?''

She looked up at him in anger when the meaning behind his words became clear to her.

"As to that," she said with some heat, "I felt that I could rub on well enough if I remained alert and circumspect in my dealings with the gentlemen in the duchess's set. And so I did. Except, of course, in your case. For you were the only one who attempted liberties. The others were content to accept "No" and look around for easier game."

"Liberties!" he exploded, shouting loudly enough to make her wince. "Do you consider a few brief embraces liberties? When you were prancing about Paris, painted and half clothed in the company of acknowledged tarts? I think," he said, sitting down abruptly beside her again and taking her chin in one hand and forcing her head up to meet his blazing eyes, "that you should know more of 'liberties' by now. Didn't those two expensive bits of muslin you were cloistered with all these weeks tell you more about liberties?"

"No," Catherine protested, drawing back from him and his touch. "No, they didn't. They were actually very prim with me. They said that they did not think they should tell me anything I didn't already know."

The marquis dropped his hand and shook his head, as if to clear it. He gazed at her steadily till she shrank with embarrassment. She could see belief and disbelief battling in his expression. Then he smiled a slow easy smile that curiously both melted and chilled her, and went on in a low sweet voice, "But there was nothing you did not know about embraces, was there, little Catherine?" He took a curl of her hair in his hand and toyed with it as he spoke. "I do not remember that there was need of too much further instruction in your kisses. You are not totally inexperienced then, are you? Mine was certainly not your first kiss, was it?"

"Of course not," Catherine blazed, striking his hand away, "yours was the fourth. I did not grow up in a clam shell. And if you count Roger Scott's, it is five. But," she admitted carefully, "I do not usually count Roger Scott's for that was only upon my cheek, and I have never been sure if that was his intention or if he missed. But it makes no matter, for I was very angry with him anyway and did not speak to him again."

The marquis looked at her speechlessly, but any reply of his was cut off by Jenkins, who had appeared by the foot of the bed and who shooed him away by saying briskly, "I have to do up the lady's foot now. And if you two persist in quarreling at midnight, you'll call the whole inn's attention to the presence of a female in your rooms. Here now, My Lord, do you hold her hand. For I have to put some medication upon the wounds and I think she'll be glad of something to hold on to, for it will smart a bit.''

"No thank you," Catherine said loftily, snatching her hand from the marquis' grip.

But when Jenkins poured some of the fine French cognac he had produced from his bags over her aching foot, she involuntarily grasped the marquis' hand again and bit her lip to keep from crying out.

"That's the worst of it," Jenkins said cheerily as he began to spread some unguent and then carefully wrapped her foot in strips of linen. "It will hurt like the devil for a few more moments, but then it will ease off enough for you to sleep."

True to his words, by the time Jenkins had straightened and begun to pack away his medicants and remove the ewer of water, Catherine's pain had subsided to only a low cranky aching.

Jenkins retreated to his room after bidding her a pleasant good night, and Catherine had a moment of alarm as the marquis straightened but still stood looking at her. She was about to rise and hobble back to the hearthside when he said curtly, "I'll retire to Jenkins' room. I hope you're an early riser. For we have to be off by first light."

"You may be off wherever you choose," Catherine said sleepily. "I shall wake early and go from here and bother you no more."

"Don't be absurd," he snapped. "As a woman traveling alone you'll never get past the door by yourself."

"But I shan't be a woman traveling alone," she said, smiling. "I shall be a poor zany French lad."

"In the night, you might have gotten away with it for a few hours," he said sternly, "but never in the day." He cut off her next words by saying swiftly, "And if you think you can, I beg you to remember what might have befallen you if we had not interceded with that pack of mercenary curs below stairs this evening. So you shall travel with us, unless you really do desire Pierre Richard's fevered embrace and are only trying to up your price by being a little inaccessible when M. Beaumont comes to call."

"I shall not travel with you," Catherine whispered fiercely. "And, at any rate, it is not Pierre Richard, it is Hervé, that M. Beaumont intended me for. And I would rather face a horde such as I met this evening than—"

But she could say nothing further, for the marquis had taken her shoulders and gripped them hard. "Hervé?" he said fiercely. "Are you sure he said it was to be Hervé?"

"Yes," she answered fearfully, for there was a terrible expression upon his face, and she could hear Jenkins give a low whistle from the doorway, where he stood watching them.

"Then we shall awake before first light," the marquis said grimly, releasing her and turning to go. But before he left her to the sleep which exhaustion was drawing her to, swiftly and against her will, like water flowing down an open drain, he said harshly, "And if I discover you have taken one step from this room without my knowledge, you will wish we had left you to those misbegotten wretches downstairs. You will pray for Beaumont to come and save you, I swear it."

While Catherine abandoned her struggle against the weariness that was closing her eyes to his retreating form and her mind to the thousand questions that assailed it, the marquis was ordering Jenkins back to the bed from which he had risen.

"I'll take the floor," he said savagely. "It won't be the first time and I feel the need of some penance. Hervé! There's a turn. Bonaparte must be closer than we had thought. For if Beaumont is beginning to shower Hervé with gifts, it's certain that his little corporal has quit his island empire and is on his way. Henri's not a fellow to squander his riches or to take chances with fate. He takes no risks."

"Aye," Jenkins agreed, as he took the bedcovers and rolled them into a makeshift bedroll for the marquis over the latter's angry protestations. "And he'll be like a hound on the lass's traces if he's already promised her to Hervé. For nothing makes a fellow more of a no-account than promising something he fails to deliver. And Beaumont can't afford being thought a no-account, not with big things in the wind. And won't it be sweet for him to deliver up to his new master a fine English gentleman that he can prove is a spy once hostilities are opened again? He'll have your head neatly from your neck, lad, the moment Bonie's got one toe back on the throne. It will be a double risk, traveling with the lady."

"Lady?" snorted the marquis, settling himself for sleep. "But no matter. Whatever she is, I can't leave her here. For whatever she is, she seems to have no more talent for self-preservation than she had for companioning."

"Oh, I think she's a lady," Jenkins said softly in the darkened room, "for there's no cause for a trollop to put herself to such rigs when she's been offered such a plum. And, at any rate," he yawned, "you have only to look at her and listen to her to know she's telling the truth."

"A courtesan has to be a good actress," Sinjun whispered, almost to himself.

"Ahh, you're just narked because you're merely the fourth fellow to kiss her," Jenkins laughed lightly. "Fifth, if you count the lad with the bad aim."

The reply was a pillow flung across the room and a curt, "You're a cat-footed sneak. Go to sleep. We have to be up early."

But as he drifted off to sleep, there was no look of anger on the marquis' face. Instead, one would have thought, looking at the small easy smile that he fell to sleep with while thinking of the female in the next room, that his was the best of worlds.

It was an early hour and the few birds that had braved the chill rain to greet the first light of a March morning were unheard in the finest room the inn at Saint-Denis had to offer. For a low-voiced but fierce battle was raging there.

Catherine stood, backed up against the fireplace mantel, dressed again in her outsize gentleman's jacket, with her low-brimmed hat pulled over her forehead. The marquis towered over her, advancing upon her with his hands on his narrow hips, dressed as a gentleman of fashion, but raging like a low brawler.

"You shall not go on by yourself," he said adamantly. "You shall travel with us and there's an end to it."

Catherine shook her head stubbornly.

"I know what you think of me," she insisted, "and your saying that it's your position as a gentleman to defend me makes no difference. I am capable of looking after myself."

The marquis groaned in annoyance and she went on bravely, "So unless you intend to carry me out kicking and screeching, you shall have to let me go on alone. For I do know that you have no wish to draw undue attention to yourself. I'm not entirely stupid, you know, just unlucky. And I do not desire your company," she said defiantly, tilting up her chin to get a better look at him from under the brim of the hat.

His face softened unexpectedly. Really, he thought, she looked such a complete waif in her bedraggled getup that the absurdity of her appearance and the spirited defense she was offering irrationally combined to make her irresistible.

A new train of thought occurred to him and he shrugged and turned from her.

"All right," he said quietly. "I can, as you say, do no more. I can but let you go your own way. Of course, it is true that you do know a great deal more of Jenkins and my doings than any other man in France. In fact, if you were indeed a man, we should not be expected to let you go, if only for our own safety. For there is little doubt that Beaumont has unpleasant but extremely persuasive ways about him" he added grimly. "And there is also little doubt that as much as he needs you to build up his own personal empire, he needs poor Jenkins and me. Our heads in a basket would only add to his prestige. And once he has caught you, it will be the work of a moment to get our direction from you and then, of course, capture us."

He heard a little gasp from behind him.

"I should never tell him," she said stoutly.

"Oh, you should not care to, I'm sure," he sighed. "But, of course, he has ways of making strong men tell all."

In the small space of silence that fell as Catherine remembered M. Beaumont's implacable smile and strong hands, the marquis continued, "If you were a man, I make no doubt that Jenkins would either have dispatched you already or, failing that, enlisted you in our cause. But as you are a woman . . ." He shrugged again.

"There is no need to make an exception," the little voice said sadly. "And as I do not care to be, however inadvertently, an accomplice of M. Beaumont, I shall come with you. But," she added, as she turned, "I shall expect you to treat me as you would any man."

"As a lady, never fear," he corrected her.

"No," she insisted, her voice rising again, "just as you would a man. I ask no special courtesies of you. Treat me as an equal."

When Jenkins returned to the room, there was another acrimonious dispute being waged. He smiled to himself and then called their attention to his recently acquired burdens.

"The kitchen maid was glad to part with her second best dress, as a present for my own little French friend, you understand, and for a substantial price. And, My Lord, you and I are pleased to be the owners of these splendid garments, courtesy of the landlord and his stock of repossessed clothing from guests who stayed the night and went forfeit on their baggage when they could not ante up the price of their accommodations. We shall be a trio of right Frenchies till we reach Dieppe. And," he went on triumphantly, "there's a sadly used old mare, for a gift to my little French mistress's father, that I managed to persuade the innkeeper to part with. For a staggering fee," he said sadly, "but it is done."

"A good morning's work," the marquis said.

"I can't wear a dress," Catherine said nervously, "for the landlady saw a little boy come up here last night."

"And so she shall see a little lad leave this morning," the marquis said over his shoulder as he inspected the garments.

"And as soon as we take the turn in the road, the little simpleton will disappear forever. In his place will be a comely peasant lass. In this," he said, holding up a simple faded-blue long-skirted frock.

"I'll bind up your foot well," Jenkins added, beginning to fold up the clothes for storage in his traveling bag, "And slit the boot so you can get into it. We'll bind it on with rope. It will only be a little way to walk," he assured her, seeing her distress.

"It's not that," she said. "It's only that I dislike being a burden to you."

"Think of it," the marquis commanded, snapping his bag together, "as being a necessary evil, if you will. For your own safety, and ours. And," he added jauntily, as Jenkins bent to help her with her boot, "I think I'll carry your treasure with me for a while, seeing as how now your strong box has been breached."

So it was that at an early hour the landlady of the inn at Saint-Denis saw the two fine gentlemen off. They had decided, they said, not to wait upon the coach, as it would no doubt be sadly crowded. The simpleton, she noted, limping badly and dragging his battered carpetbag, came down the stair a few moments after them. As her other guests were beginning to descend for their breakfast, she did not see the lad hobble off out her door. And by the time other patrons began to throng her front room, waiting for the delayed diligence to arrive, she had forgotten that she had not seen the quiet little ragged simpleton come to breakfast.

The marquis and Jenkins stood waiting for Catherine, atop their horses, as she finally hobbled to the crossroads they had indicated was far enough from the inn. But before they let her mount the speckled gray they had procured for her, they insisted she divest herself of her costume and put on the peasant's dress.

In the chill rain, Catherine stood behind some bushes at a distance from the road and changed quickly. Then she gathered up her things and emerged again by the side of the road.

The sight that met her eyes made her heart stop beating for a moment. For there were two evil-looking rogues atop the marquis and Jenkins' horses. One was a swaggering younger fellow with patched trousers and a once-white shirt open at his throat. He wore a scarlet bandanna carelessly tied about his neck. The other was a gruff, grizzled fellow with a slouched hat and a none-too-clean jacket tied about his waist with a frayed belt. She was about to dart back into hiding when she heard the marquis' deep voice call out to her. He slipped from his horse's back and bowed to her, a wicked smile upon his lips.

"You haven't seen the devil, child, just two vagabonds set on keeping you company. *Vite, vite.* We have some traveling to do."

He helped her up into the saddle, and let his hands rest upon her waist for one extra insulting moment, and then laughed at her uncomfortable expression.

"Now, now. You did say you wished to be treated as an equal. Now I'd never keep hold of a lady for so long, but any fellow would only thank me for making sure he was well seated before we took off."

Catherine tossed back her head and pretended not to hear Jenkins' snort of amusement. She was fully prepared to brood upon the marquis' impertinence, and to worry whether he had noted the shock of pleasure she had felt at his touch. But once he had remounted his horse, he slapped her old mount sharply on the rump to get her started, and they were off. Riding in the cold wind-blown mists soon took her thoughts from his warm touch and turned them irrevocably to thoughts of the fine chill rain that found its way unerringly down her collar to trace icy fingers along her back.

By the time they drew their horses to rest beside a farmhouse, Catherine was thoroughly chilled. Not much conversation had been possible as they rode the muddy lanes in the gusting wind. And now it was with a distinct shock that she felt the marquis help her down and heard his low voice whisper in her ear, "The good wife here is curious. So say nothing. Your grasp of the language, I recall, is inadequate. You're my woman, for the remainder of the trip at least''—he laughed at her upturned face—''and very shy. But your brother and I will take care of you. We've bargained for a rough luncheon and then we're off again. So sit as close to the fire as you're able.''

Catherine was grateful for the bread and cheese and rough wine that the farm wife provided, and loath to leave her perch by the fire when the marquis arose and bade their hostess farewell. But she was determined not to be a hindrance to them, and duly remounted and rode off without protest when they indicated it was time.

The remainder of the afternoon became one wet, miserable blur to her. Even in later years she could not remember the route they had taken that day. She kept her gaze firmly on the horse's ears and prayed for some benevolent god to stop the wind and rain.

By the time dusk fell, the rain had mercifully stopped, and the increasing winds were drying the lanes they traveled, turning some of the ruts to ice.

''This must be the house Madame indicated,'' Catherine heard the marquis say. And while she was still gazing numbly at the tilted roof on the weatherworn house at which they had stopped, she felt the marquis swing her down from her saddle.

''It's in bad shape,'' Jenkins said, as they entered the simple one-room house through a door that was banging in the wind.

''War takes curious turns,'' the marquis agreed, ''for when the master of this hovel died in glorious battle and his wife had to go beg to relatives, I doubt they could have guessed their home would ever provide succor to their dearest enemies.''

Seeing no chairs or furniture, Catherine simply lowered herself onto a wooden box by the side of the fireplace.

''You do have a propensity for gravitating to hearthsides,'' the marquis noted. ''I wonder at such a sit-by-the-fire being able to pick herself up to travel the Continent in such high-flying fashion.''

But seeing how weariness had stilled her tongue, he left her and set about building up the fire and held low converse with Jenkins about securing the horses in the half-timbered barn that remained.

After a welcome dinner of cheese and bread that Jenkins had foraged earlier, and after warming herself thoroughly by the fire, Catherine stretched and began to take lively note of their surroundings again.

The marquis sat at ease across from her on a box he had found in the barn, and Jenkins sat cross-legged on the floor, gazing into the fire.

"I suppose," Catherine said conversationally, "that it won't be too long before we reach Dieppe, will it, Your Lordship?"

"Oh, Catherine," the marquis answered. "Have done with 'Your Lordship.' We are not precisely in a drawing room here. I doubt the mice will be offended if all the proprieties are not observed. At any rate," he went on, pleased to see blush upon her cheek, "It would be nothing wonderful if you did not blurt "Your Lordship" the next time we were in a crowd of Frenchmen, if you persist in calling me that. I should hate to lose my head due to an overnice attention to the correct social forms of address.

"But no, I am sorry for it, but it will be long before we reach Dieppe. It will be never. No, don't startle. I haven't formed the intention of becoming a lifetime resident here. It is only that too many people knew you were bound for Dieppe. Indeed, I think soon half the English in Paris will be bound for Dieppe, and it will be the logical place for Beaumont to pick up your trail. No, we will journey to Le Havre. And we shall not find ourselves berths upon a tourist packet for we will be snugly accommodated on some fishing vessel. Brandy, lace, and smuggled souls are high trade on the coast. And I think that, sly as he is, still M. le Commissaire Beaumont will not look to find one of the duchess's doxies sharing her seat with a haddock."

Sinjun looked up to see Catherine's face blanch. She looked as though he had slapped her, and he turned in sudden uncomfortable contrition to Jenkins.

"It grows late, old friend. Let's gather in some hay to make this wretched floor pass for a feather bed."

As they rose to go to the door, Sinjun looked back at Catherine, who was ostensibly studying her fingernails with concentration.

"Forgive me," he whispered back to her. "I have a rash tongue, and I'm sorry for it."

Resting upon her pelisse, which lay over the mound of straw Sinjun and Jenkins had provided, Catherine stared into the darkness. Sinjun lay not far from her on the other side of the fireplace, and Jenkins, nearer to the door, breathing heavily.

She was warm and full and the two men in the room gave her a feeling of comfort and security such as she had not known in many weeks, but still she could not sleep. Her conscience twinged. Perhaps it was because she was just where she wished to be, she thought with sudden alarm. The sense of contentment and pleasure in the marquis' company was so overwhelming that, try as she might, she could not imagine a place where she would rather be. And yet she felt that if he but knew her deep contentment, he would be somehow displeased. He would be, she thought further, convinced that she was no better than a light woman. For what decently reared girl would be so pleased in such bizarre, irregular circumstances? She ought to be, she thought sternly, fearful and trembling in distress, not as contented as a sleepy puppy.

"Catherine," came a low whisper in the dark, "do go to sleep. For we must travel hard in the morning. We go a roundabout route."

"How did you know I was not sleeping?" she whispered back.

"I could hear you thinking," Sinjun chuckled. "And I could not hear you snore."

"I don't snore." Catherine giggled, thinking again, as she had all evening, that the marquis seemed to have put off his cold, cynical manner as he had put off his immaculate garments. Now he seemed so much younger and more carefree that she had a difficult time remembering the aloof aristocrat she had met a hundred years ago in another life, in London.

"Nonsense," he replied softly. "Hear old Jenkins sawing away over there? I'll wager between the two of you, I won't have a moment's rest this night.

"Catherine," he said again, after a pause, "do not worry. We shall see you safely home again. But I wonder—how shall you explain your travels away to your family when you get home? Should I expect your brother-in-law at my doorstep at dawn with a pistol clutched in his hand? For while I consider Jenkins an excellent chaperone, I do not know if William will."

"Not William," Catherine smiled; "Arthur. And I assure you, you need not fear. Indeed, he will be grateful to you for seeing me safely from my own muddled affairs."

"I don't have to make reparation for sullying your good name?" he asked lightly.

There was a moment's silence, and then he heard her reply in a suspiciously low, broken tone. "Indeed, I do not see how anyone could have sullied it more than I."

Sinjun silently cursed himself for an insensitive clod, and then went on as if he had not heard her, "I must admit that if I knew my sister was traveling with me, that is to say, if I were not myself, and heard that my sister was traveling with me, I should be outraged and fly to her defense.''

Catherine gave a little laugh. ''I did not know you had a sister.''

''Well, I was not hatched from an egg,'' he protested, in mock affront. ''Of course I have a sister, and I had a mother and a father as well, you know.''

''Tell me about them,'' Catherine said sleepily.

And so the lofty Marquis of Bessacarr lay back upon his straw pallet in an abandoned French farmhouse on a cold March night and spoke into the darkness of his sister's wild extravagances and her complacent husband, and their brood of unruly children. Encouraged by Catherine's delighted response, and prodded by her questions, he told her in less merry tones about his wastrel father and his invalid mother. By the time the natural progression of his story had led him into deep water and he fell silent, wondering how to tell her of the mistakes he had made in his career, he noticed she did not urge him to continue. Instead, he only heard her muted, even breathing.

He rose and went to her. She lay like a child with one hand under her cheek and the other flung out in sleep. He knelt to cover her more securely with her coat. If she were an actress, he thought almost angrily, seeing the easy peace sleep had brought her, she was the best he had ever met.

''I make no doubt''—Jenkins' amused voice came from the shadows—''that you have put many females to sleep of nights. But I do doubt that you've ever just talked one to sleep before.''

''Go to sleep, you old pretender,'' the marquis grumbled as he sank down upon his bed of straw again, ''or you'll wake her.''

Chapter XV

Their journey was not half so simple as Catherine had anticipated. The weather was against them. First rain, then cold to freeze it where it lay, then wind and more rain slowed their forward movement. They dared not go by coach, and yet increasing numbers of coaches, private and hired, passed them on the roads. It was as the marquis had predicted: The English—at least some small portion of the more than fifteen thousand who had arrived on French shores since Louis had been put back on the throne—were beginning to go home again.

At every stop either the marquis or Jenkins would engage the inhabitants of the small villages or farming communities in easy conversation. Rumor was everywhere, and while the farrier in one town would insist that they were at war with the pigs of England again, the one in another town would steadfastly maintain that Louis still held sway and the adventurer Bonaparte was still at Elba, safely out of harm's way.

Other incidents impeded them. Catherine's horse, never in the best condition, began to founder as they traveled further toward the coast, and they had to stop and search and bargain till they could trade it for another, younger bit of horseflesh that an avaricious farmer near Vironvey agreed to part with. When Catherine insisted on paying Sinjun for the expense, he grew angry, and their bickering caused Jenkins to comment that he felt as though he were seeing two children home from an outing that had overtired them.

Jenkins, for his part, had insisted on calling Sinjun "lord" and "sir" till Sinjun had cursed him and snarled that Catherine would understand if he dropped the pose and continued to call him "lad" or "friend" or "enemy," for fiend's sake, so long as he was done with posturing as a correct gentleman. Jenkins had looked wounded and explained that those names were only for Sinjun's ears alone, and not for use in company. And when Sinjun rejoined that Catherine was by no means polite company, she looked so stricken that both the marquis and Jenkins together had to jest and make up foolish verses to old songs till they had jollied her out of her depression.

One day they had to sit and wait out the weather in the shelter of a disused barn. For the rain and wind were so fierce that they knew neither the horses nor they themselves could have traveled far. They had passed the time telling stories, speculating on the fate of those they had known in Paris. When, at noon, Jenkins produced an old, limp deck of cards, they had cheered as though they had been given the rarest treat.

They had traveled together for five cold, unpleasant days. They had slept in abandoned houses and begged night's permission to camp in barns. Their food had been rough, their beds usually straw or their own folded garments, yet Catherine could never remember being happier.

And the cause of her happiness, she had thought on the fifth day, rode alongside her. Though they had been constantly together throughout the journey, and only for a few moments of the day was she ever alone, she grew uneasy when he was not with her. She had stolen glances at his straight back and noted the way the wind tossed his demon-black hair back from his forehead. Each night, like the small children Jenkins had commented on, they had chatted happily in the dark till sleep overtook them. He had been a courteous and charming companion, and every last vestige of the cool autocrat she had envisioned him was gone. And, above all, never once since they had begun their trek had he looked at her with the salacious, burning looks he had used when they met in society. He did indeed, she thought with a mixture of relief and disquiet, treat her as an equal.

He had often made her laugh, there in the night, when they spoke to each other as disembodied voices. And she counted among her life's greatest triumphs those moments when she in turn reduced him to helpless mirth. Sometimes they spoke of their past lives, and though she found nothing in hers that she thought might interest him, still he pressed her to tell him more. So she had recounted her mother's sad story, and told him of

Jane's beauty and Arthur's primness, and even, as the hour grew late and Jenkins seemed to snore in earnest, of her own desire to be a free and independent person rather than an obligation for her sister's new family to bear.

Sometimes after that first night she told him of Rose and Violet, and tried to make him see that they were nothing like one would have thought, simply common harlots. She told him of their hopes and fears and attempted to let him see that their lives, apart from their trade, were much as anyone else's. And she felt he did try to understand.

She thought he was far too hard on himself. He did not seem to be able to speak of his past without disparaging it and demeaning himself in jest. He did not appear to be able to speak of the woman he had offered for without congratulating her on her perspicacity in rejecting him. He held himself in low esteem, and she found herself tightening her hands to fists whenever he joked, there in the night, about what an empty, idle fellow he was. For she dared not let him see how very much she wished to disprove what he said. One night, as he was speaking, she almost blurted out, "No, how can you say that? You are a man any woman would give her life to please." For where would she proceed from there? If he rose and came to her and asked her to prove that, how could she then say, "No, I didn't mean that."

The only discomfort Catherine had felt beyond the physical on their journey toward home was the discomfort of knowing that if he knew her feelings—worse, if she displayed them—he would think her to be the easy female he had originally thought her.

So she kept herself under restraint. They spoke of books they both had read and liked. They joked about the people they both had met. They giggled in the night like small children afraid to wake their nanny, Jenkins. But they did not touch. And they did not speak about their new friendship. Catherine kept herself on a tight rein. She was so busy keeping her feelings tightly to herself that she never saw the looks he bent upon her, obliquely and often during their journey.

The next day the sky cleared and it was a cool morning—one of those strange mornings in the earliest spring when the air holds only a tantalizing promise of the splendors of the months to come.

"We're allowing ourselves a treat today," Sinjun said as he rode beside her. "We've come more than halfway and the coast will soon be in sight. I think we deserve a day of rest. We are on

the outskirts of Rouen, and since we have heard no bells tolling
or cannon fire, I think we can safely assume the throne lies
secure still. So we will stop at an inn. Then it will be an easier
day's journey to the coast.''

"And," growled Jenkins, "he neglected to mention that my
horse's shoe is coming off."

"Ungenerous Jenkins," Sinjun said. "Here I was convincing
Catherine it was all due to my magnanimous nature and you have
to tell her the blunt truth."

"Bless your horse," Catherine cried, "for I think I would
trade my soul for a chance to wash my hair and sleep upon a bed
that a horse hasn't used first."

"And," Jenkins stressed, "we must go out, His Lordship and
I, to nose out the land. We'll be convivial in the taproom,
Catherine, whilst you launder your hair, and find out what's to
know. We need to know if we have to skulk about in Le Havre
or if we can ride in like free men and charter a vessel openly.
Things depend upon what state the land's in. And whether there
are any looking for us or not."

Catherine sobered at the reminder that there might yet be
danger. For she had felt so secure thus far that she had almost
persuaded herself that the night in Paris when M. Beaumont
approached her had been nothing but a mad fancy of hers.

The inn they chose heartened her. It was clean and in far
better repair than the last one in Saint-Denis.

They had spoken for two rooms. One, Sinjun had explained,
was for himself and his good wife, and the other for his brother-
in-law. Catherine's room, she saw with joy, when the proprietor's
daughter had left her at last, after filling the large basin of water
Catherine had bespoken, was as lovely as the faded beauty of an
old genteel lady. The carpet upon the floor yet bore the outlines
of soft spring flowers. And, best of all, Catherine thought as she
immersed her hands in the warm scented water, there were soft
towels and a cake of soap at the washstand.

She stripped off her peasant dress and washed herself from top
to toe.Then, as she knew she would have more time alone, since
Sinjun and Jenkins had the horses to see to, and then would
undoubtedly luxuriate in their own room for a space, she
allowed herself the bliss of washing straw and dust from her hair
in the large enameled rose basin. Glowing with good feeling, she
shook out a plain blue frock from her bag and got into it. Clean

and dressed, she sat in a chair by the fire to comb out and dry her tresses.

But afternoon came and began to fade, and her hair was completely dry and silky soft, and still there was no knock upon the door. She began to worry and went to the window to look out. There was little activity in the stable yard below. It was only a tranquil late-afternoon scene that met her eyes. There was a small millpond, deserted save for a few geese that patrolled its tiny shores, and the only soul she could spy was a stable boy, drawing water from the well's pump.

As the hours went by, all sense of ease and delight faded from Catherine. They had been gone too long, and she worried over the dozen misfortunes that might have befallen them. She had almost gotten up the courage to go downstairs by herself, against all of Sinjun's express orders, when she heard a light tap upon her door.

She fairly flew to the door and flung it open. Sinjun stood there, looking down at her with surprise.

"I hope," he said, entering the room and closing the door behind him, "that you have no intention of stepping outside in that garb."

The joy in her face faded.

"This is just an old garment I had when I came to the duchess," she said in confusion, looking down at her simple high-waisted blue muslin gown.

Her hair, newly washed, fell riotously around her face, and she had to sweep it back to see him when she looked up at him again.

A curious spasm, almost of pain, crossed his face for a fleeting moment.

"It might not be," he drawled, in a voice she had not heard for many days, "High fashion on the Champs Elysees, "but here it is decidely not what a simple little peasant wench wears to dinner. It's as well, I suppose. For it would be better if you did not go down again till we leave."

She searched his face for the reason for the solemnity in his voice.

"We've been out, we two hearty French lads, chatting up the local gentry. And, it seems, they don't understand why we're not marching in the other direction, toward Paris. For all the able-bodied young chaps hereabouts are off to war again. They've heard that their little corporal is on the high road to glory once more. But it's not confirmed, of course. So we'll have to dine without you tonight, Catherine. We'll get you a tray in your room and we'll sit and drink with every local know-something we can find.''

Catherine tried to essay a smile. ''But Sinjun, you said it's only a day's ride to Le Havre. Surely, we can get that far before a war breaks out.''

''Catherine,'' he said, his gray eyes serious and steady, ''we may well be at war at this moment. I do not know. And if we are, then Jenkins and I are very wanted men. We are not an English peer and his valet—we are also labeled 'spies' in some quarters. I do not care to spend years skulking about the French countryside in disguise. And neither do I wish to be clapped in irons in Le Havre. For the ports are the first places the soldiers go to comb through the refugees for profit. So stay in this room and say only a shy little *non* if a maid or anyone comes to this door tonight.''

Catherine nodded and then, as he turned to leave, tugged at his sleeve. ''Must you go out?'' she whispered. ''Could you not stay and just wait till morning?''

''I must go out. There's little danger here, I think, and we have to discover how much is fact and how much is rumor. And, oh Catherine, if you get the notion of creeping below to aid us by eavesdropping or some other strategy your fertile mind conjures, there is one other bit of news. It seems that there is talk of a reward offered for the apprehension of some vile Englishwoman who stole a fortune from her employer, a certain English lady. And the word is that the miscreant is most probably headed for the coast.''

Catherine shrank back.

''You know I stole nothing,'' she gasped.

''Of course. Your purse is in my keeping, remember? It's a meager treasure you hoarded. And I don't even know if you are the female they are seeking. But M. Beaumont is a desperate character and dislikes having his will crossed. So stay safe inside, my little French 'wife,' and no harm will befall you.''

''Sinjun?'' Catherine asked softly.

''Yes?'' he answered, his hand already on the knob of the door.

''Will you come back tonight and let me know what you have discovered?''

''Of course,'' he agreed. ''Otherwise I think you'll stand and shake all the night through. Don't trouble yourself so. I said it is all rumor. And you know you are safe with us.''

Jenkins brought her a tray a short while later.

''Best if the maids stay far from this room altogether,'' he said, putting it down for her. ''When you're done, wait till there's no one about, peek out the door if you must, and when the coast is clear, put the empty plates outside. They'll understand below stairs.''

''They'll think me a poor shy retiring lady,'' Catherine said with a smile.

''There's that,'' Jenkins agreed, ''and also the fact that His Lordship explained how his little wife was enceinte, and feeling very poorly after her ride.''

Catherine gasped in indignation, but Jenkins only continued blithely, ''He's a lad who has a fine tale for any occasion. It's what has made him so valuable in his work. You should see him below stairs, drinking and gossiping, like he was a born Frenchie. All out of sorts, of course, because he's itching to go off and join up with his emperor's forces, and he's stuck with a pretty new wife, expecting her first babe, and he's got to deliver her to relatives before he's off to war. He's even made me feel sorry for him.''

Jenkins displayed her dinner by whipping a serviette off the tray with a flourish.

''There's good fresh meat—best not to inquire too closely as to its origin, though. And bread and lovely green beans. And a bottle of the landlord's best, with His Lordship's compliments. He's got a nose for good wine, you know, and he's very impressed with this local vintage. Even to the point of regretting not being able to take a case or two home with him. So he's trying his best to take as much home with him as he can hold.''

Catherine, remembering her stepfather's bouts with spirits, grew uneasy.

''But if he gets light-headed, he might let something slip.''

Jenkins only laughed.

''I've been with him years now, and I've never seen him let slip one word in his cups. He's got a hard head, Catherine, so don't you worry. But you drink up, for it'll ease your mind and let you get a good night's sleep. 'A little wine's a lovesome thing,' I once heard, and a little of anything can do no harm.''

When Jenkins had left, Catherine sat to dinner, thinking she would be lucky to be able to peck at something, her fears had so encompassed her again. But the wine was good, and the dinner miles above anything she had eaten for days. By the time she was ready to place her tray stealthily outside in the hall, she noted with amazement that she had finished every scrap upon her plate and reduced the bottle of wine by half.

Catherine did not like the sudden inactivity she was forced to here in her faded, but elegant little room. She was restless and impatient, itching to be off and doing rather than to be just a passive creature awaiting whatever fate had in store. That, she thought, was gentlemen's main advantage in life. For they could go out and meet fate head on, while a gentlewoman was expected to sit back and watch what the tides of fortune brought to her feet.

Women like Rose and Violet were able to go out and face life and try to turn it to their advantage, but a properly brought-up female could not. Perhaps, it was that, Catherine thought moodily, sipping her wine, that turned them to such occupation in the first place, rather than inherent lechery. A part of her was appalled by the new train her thoughts were taking, and yet another applauded her new expanded vision. Whatever else this trip provided, she concluded at last, it was certain that the Catherine Robins who returned to Kendal would never be the same who had left it.

The hour was late, the muted sounds of activity and voices in the inn had all but faded away, and Catherine was sitting sleepily in her chair, when she heard the faint tapping at her door.

"Catherine," Sinjun's voice called in low, conspiratorial tones, "it's Sinjun, reporting back to you at last."

She was glad to ease the door open to admit him.

He strode in and grinned at her. She sensed a high excitement emanating from him, and saw that his tanned face held a faint flush along its high cheekbones.

"All the lads are planning how high to hang old Louis. Some are even talking of how to spend their prize money when they take over London. Oh, spirits are running high downstairs," he said, walking carefully to the table and lifting the bottle of wine to peer at its label.

"Fine vintage," he commented, almost to himself. "It's a great pity I can't reason out a fashion of getting it home with us."

There was a recklessness to his speech and a glitter in his eyes, and Catherine wondered if he had indeed partaken too much of the wine he so admired. But she well remembered the condition of her stepfather when he was in his cups, and the marquis did not stagger—he walked erect, perhaps with even more of a careful tread than usual. And he did not wear a foolish grin or slur his words or sing or say inconsequential words as her stepfather had done when he came reeling home after an evening with his friends.

"And what is said of the Englishwoman who was branded a thief?" she asked.

"Oh, as to that," Sinjun said airily, "there's no description of her hereabouts save one. And that is that she is traveling in the company of two English gentlemen."

Catherine gasped.

Sinjun grinned again.

"It seems that you disappeared from Paris the same day Jenkins and I did. So Beaumont has reasoned, and one can't blame him for it, that I ran off with you just to tweak his nose. Which is a bit conceited of him, but a lovely thought nonetheless. Still, they're looking for three English citizens, and here we are, three sturdy citizens of the Republic. So there's nothing to fear. But here," he said, seeming to see her for the first time since he had entered the room, "it is far past midnight. Why aren't you in bed?"

"I waited for you," Catherine explained. "I was worried."

"And," he went on, frowning, "not even in your nightclothes. You don't have to share your room tonight. I thought you would make yourself comfortable and sleep like a proper lady, not in your clothes again. Catherine," he said, marching toward her and glowering "get into bed and go to sleep. At once."

Catherine sat back upon her bed and and told him that she would go to bed as soon as he had left her room.

"Now that," Sinjun said, sinking down to sit beside her, "truly wounds me, Catherine, it does. For we have shared our rooms for so long and you never were so punctilious before. I only came to tuck you in tightly, as a good brother should. And I have been a good brother to you, haven't I?"

He sat close to her and ran his hand gently across her hair, seeming to become engrossed in the texture of it.

"I have tried very hard to be brotherly, Catherine, though Lord knows, you are nothing like my sister. And I have been extremely circumspect. Yes," he agreed with himself, as if, it seemed to Catherine, he were speaking only to himself, "extremely circumspect. A perfect gentleman, in fact. And the wonder of it is that all these months I had thought you so available, and when at last I had you to myself, I treated you with perfect courtesy. And it has been hard, Catherine, very hard to do so. Now don't you think I deserve a reward for being such a paragon? Especially,'' he said, looking down into her eyes and bringing his other hand up so that he held her face between his two hands, ''especially since . . .''

But he did not finish his train of thought, for he bent and kissed her, gently and sweetly, and she was surprised at the eagerness with which she involuntarily returned his kiss.

Although it was only Sinjun who held Catherine, she was so lost in the warmth and delicious pleasure of his embrace that she had no thought of holding him closer to herself as well.

He moved his lips to her cheek, to her throat, and then gathered her still closer with a groan.

''Catherine,'' he whispered against her hair, ''you are lovely.''

And then he kissed her again, a deeper, darker embrace that began at last, to waken Catherine from her stuporous pleasure.

But it seemed that as she became aware of exactly what was beginning to transpire between them, he became less aware of her reaction and more lost in their embrace. His hands drifted from her back and moved to begin to trace the outlines of her breasts and waist. He began to call her still further into his provenance as she retreated from him. His kisses became more profound, his mouth as warm and rich and fragrant as the wine she tasted upon it. But these were not the sweet light movements that had so enticed her. He now seemed to be setting something urgent into motion, something that she could not control or know how to respond to. So she began to try to pull away from him, to force his searching mouth from hers.

''Catherine,'' he breathed as his hands became more insistent, ''no more pretense. Come, I know what will please you.''

But now all thoughts of pleasure, for herself or for Sinjun, were gone from Catherine's mind. In their place was panic and the realization of what he thought her willing to do with him. She struggled to be free from him and finally repelled him, crying out, ''Please, Sinjun. No. No more.''

He released her immediately when she spoke and sat confused.

''No, Sinjun,'' she cowered, fearful of the changed expression in his smoky eyes, fearful of her own reaction to him.

''What is it you want, then, Catherine?'' he asked, genuinely puzzled. ''Have I gone too fast for you? I promise to go slower then. Lord knows we have the entire night before us. I can be patient. Come, Catherine," he said, pleased with himself for being reasonable, and reached for her again.

But she pulled away and stood and when he rose to take her back, she cried out again, "No. Sinjun, Your Lordship. Please, it is late. Please leave."

He let his hands drop to his sides and stood shaking his head, but no longer reaching out for her.

"I don't understand," he said slowly. "Why are you so afraid, Catherine? You've never been so afraid of me before."

"It's only that I startled her," Jenkins said, coming up from behind Sinjun, and indeed startling Catherine with the sudden soft-footed grace of his movements. He seemed to have appeared from nowhere.

"I've something important to tell Your Lordship. Indeed I do. Come with me. Make a good night to Catherine," Jenkins said, propelling Sinjun from the room with him, "and come with me, for I've something to tell you. That's a good chap," he said, talking steadily to the marquis and leading him away. "Lock your door, Catherine," Jenkins called back to her, "and go to sleep. His Lordship and I have something to discuss."

Catherine collected herself and rushed to her door, not to lock it, but to see what Jenkins and Sinjun were about to do. But instead of leading the marquis back to his room, Jenkins, still talking softly and rapidly, led him down the stairs. From the top of the stairs Catherine could see them going to the front of the inn.

She ran back to her room and went quickly to her window and flung the casement up. Cold night air rushed in, making her realize how warm and flushed she had been. She leaned out to see where her two companions were going.

But she could see nothing in the darkness. All was quiet, no one seemed about. Then she heard a splashing coming from the pond. And a sound of thrashing water, as though some large animal had stumbled into it. She stood listening, straining her ears and eyes, but after a few moments all was quiet again.

The room grew cold as the night outside, so Catherine lowered the window again and went back to her door. She was trembling with the cold and with the force of her emotions. She had welcomed his embrace—she could not deceive herself as to that. And she had pulled away from him not only because of her fear of the unknown, but because of her horror at having let him see what her innermost emotions toward him had been. Now, she told herself dumbly, he will think me no better than what he always thought me.

After a long while she heard Sinjun and Jenkins return, heard them coming slowly up the stairs in silence. When they neared her door, Catherine's eyes widened. Sinjun was drenched. His hair was plastered to his head, and his clothes were dripping water. She thought she could perceive a slow shudder race across his wide shoulders. He turned to her and bowed before he passed her door.

"My apologies," he said stiffly. "I bid you good night, Catherine."

Catherine could only gape after him, but Jenkins paused as they returned to their room.

"Lock your door now, Miss Catherine," he said sternly. "There'll be no further disturbances tonight."

"But," Catherine whispered, "what befell Sinjun? Was there trouble with footpads?"

"No, no," Jenkins said soothingly, "no trouble at all. His Lordship only decided to go for a midnight dip. Just a moonlight swim."

"But it is freezing outside," Catherine said in horror. "He'll be ill. He'll take a chill."

"No, no," Jenkins demurred. "He *needed* a chill was what it was. The poor lad was overheated from all that fine French wine. He's a hot-blooded fellow, never fear for him. And I'm sure he'll be all apologies for his behavior in the morning. He'll be fine now, I assure you. And glad, I'll be bound, to forget this night."

Jenkins bowed correctly and then waited till Catherine had closed her door and locked it.

Sinjun toweled himself dry in silence as Jenkins climbed into his bed.

"I made a cake out of myself, didn't I?" he asked.

"Yes," Jenkins answered.

"I frightened her, didn't I?" he asked.

"Of course," was the only answer he heard.

"Well, blast it," Sinjun shouted, throwing the towel across the room, "it was the wine."

There was no answer.

"It was the wine," Sinjun said softly, "and the last vague

hope that I was right and she was just another cozening fancy piece.''

"And the fact that she said no changed Your Lordship's powerful mind?'' Jenkins growled.

"And the fact that she wouldn't have known what to do if she said yes,'' Sinjun admitted.

His companion made no reply save a disgusted snort.

"But,'' Sinjun said, lying down upon his bed, "I will make amends. Never fear, Sir Galahad, I shall put things to rights. For I've attempted to seduce a decent young female of good birth, and I know the penalty for that. I am,'' he said righteously, "a gentleman, after all. Not completely lost to propriety.''

"Go to sleep,'' was the only reply Jenkins made as he turned his back with an irritated ruffling of his bedclothes.

Sinjun lay back and gave a deep sigh. The cold water Jenkins had toppled him into had cleared the edges of his mind, but he still felt the vaporous waves from the wine cluttering up his thoughts. He had, he thought wryly, not gotten himself so inebriated since his youth, and all, he now knew, because of that damned female.

For he been a pattern card of behavior. He had watched her—noting the curve of her neck, the tilt of her nose, the inviting sway in her walk—for all these days and had pretended he saw nothing. He had been entranced by her in London, and then again in Paris, and then when he had grown to know her, she had captivated him completely. And he had shown nothing of his feelings all these days by word or action.

She had completely enticed him, he thought angrily. For by the time he had offered for her favors in Paris, she had ruined him for other women. There had been an Italian countess when he first arrived in Paris, but her embraces had palled by the time he met Catherine again. And when Catherine refused him, the little unfaithful wife of a diplomat had offered him solace. But he had lightly rejected her, thinking then that it was that he did not care for the tone of her laugh, or for the way she had of constantly clutching onto his sleeve. But, he admitted now, it had been that he had looked up and seen Catherine across the room and the sight of her had turned the diplomat's fluffy wife into something like a toad. No, there was no escaping it—he was, he admitted, well and truly caught.

Well then, he thought, so be it. He would offer her marriage. And then a small repressed uncomfortable thought wriggled into his mind from its dark hiding place. He could not bear to think of the answer she would give him. The answer that would be like another's so long ago. The remembered sad pitying look, the soft glance of sympathy, the mournful little syllable that would accompany all the unspoken sorrowful gestures: "No." And then the torrent of words about understanding, and friendships and respect, followed by the reasonable explanation that there could be no acceptance where there was no love.

Very well then, he thought quickly, I shall put it so that there has to be no word of love. Where love has not been offered, it cannot be refused. I shall put it on a basis a girl like Catherine can understand. And wait until we get back to that infamous town of Kendal, for surely her prig of a brother-in-law will understand and encourage it. For I have traveled unchaperoned with a young woman of good birth and spent many nights with her. No man of even sterling reputation can do that without destroying a decent female's hope of ever being received into polite society again. And my reputation, especially with women, is far from clear. Moreover, Sinjun thought with some satisfaction, as he lay in the dark and built his reasonable case for a reasonable marriage, I have overstepped the bounds of a decent gentleman. I have attempted her virtue. All the tenets of society demand that I offer her my name.

I do not, he thought, have to offer her my love as well. At least, he amended, I do not have to let her know that is what is being offered. For surely it is not deception, he told himself, to withhold an emotion that can only distress her. She was horrified at my embrace, but perhaps, he thought with sudden hope, she will come to love me in time. It is not unheard of for a wife to come to love her husband, even in a forced marriage. But I can protect her. I shall have her for my wife. And that will be enough. More, he thought with a last sleepy grimace, than I deserve.

Chapter XVI

Three very solemn travelers mounted their horses in the stable yard of the inn early the next morning.

Sinjun had come into Catherine's room at first light, with a breakfast for her. He had been stiffly correct and unsmiling, and had apologized sincerely for his actions of the previous night, explaining that they had been caused by the amount of wine he had partaken. His words were gracious, his manner contrite, his gaze half-lidded and impersonal. His very correctness toward her froze Catherine. For she read disdain and revulsion in his every word and gesture. And so she had meekly accepted his apology and thanked him for it. He had turned and left her room, convinced that she held him in the deepest abhorrence.

Jenkins, seeing his companions' uncomfortable attitude toward each other, only sighed heavily and kept his own counsel. And so, though it was an easy ride to Le Havre for the last lap of their journey, it being a clear and sunny, bracing day, it was the uneasiest trek in spirit that any of the three could remember making.

Their conversation was minimal, merely an asking after each other's physical comfort and brief consultations as to their direction. By afternoon, as Catherine saw the houses growing more clustered together as they rode past and when she scented the distinct salt tang of sea air, she was heartsick and disconsolate.

They rode through the main streets of the seacoast town. Many other travelers thronged there, but not so many, Catherine noted, as there had been in Dieppe. In Dieppe she had seen all sorts of crested carriages and equipages taking on finely dressed, happily chattering noble visitors. Here in Le Havre there was more of an assortment of humanity.

There were fishermen and ragged urchins and small family groups. The English people she saw were not the sort she had seen either in Dieppe or in Paris. There were knots of schoolboys with their masters and soberly dressed couples. There seemed to be a hush over the town and an atmosphere of uneasiness that could not have sprung just from Catherine's own uneasy perception of the world this day. It was as though the village were holding its breath either in fear or anticipation. All those she passed conversed in low voices and even the local people seemed to be in clusters of whispered conference. She repressed a start when a screaming gull soared overhead. She would be glad to be gone from this place.

They stopped at yet another inn. It seemed the most ordinary of places and when they dismounted, not one of the stable boys looked at them with any particular interest. Sinjun led Catherine to a table in the inn's front room. She was amazed to see his countenance change to that of a hale, jocular, rough sort of common fellow when the serving girl came up to them.

In loud happy tones he ordered some refreshment for his little wife and himself. And he added, with a huge wink, he would be pleased if she would bring some sour wine for his brother-in-law, who was joining them, for the fellow was a sour enough sort as it was. Soon Sinjun had the French girl laughing and simpering. Soon, Catherine thought sourly, he would have the girl agreeing to bring him anything, including her own person on a plate.

He looked handsome enough, she thought. His shirt was unbuttoned to the chest. The red bandanna emphasized the tanned muscular neck, and his hair had been artfully arranged by the March wind. Catherine saw the girl give her a speculative sideways look. She probably wonders, Catherine imagined, what such a fine fellow is doing with such a drab quiet little mouse of a wife. She could not know that her own eyes sparkled bluer than the tone of her simple peasant frock or that the wind had flung her dark hair into exquisitely curling tendrils. The serving girl smiled lovingly and helplessly at Sinjun again and went off to find refreshments for the beautiful young couple.

When Jenkins joined them, they fell to their food in continued silence. Only when Catherine had done and looked up did she find Sinjun watching her with a troubled expression in his eyes. It was gone in the moment she saw it. He looked at her coolly and then said in a low voice, "Catherine. Jenkins and I now have to go and find lodgings. We'll try for this inn, but I fear it's too crowded here. Then we will have to saunter over to the waterfront and look up a few local fellows well known for turning a blind eye to the cargo they carry. More importantly, Jenkins knows of a few English fellows who might be ready to start home again. For if we had our way, we'd rather go home with an English crew than find ourselves at sea with a crew of suddenly patriotic Frenchmen. So it will take time. Stay here and sip your chocolate. Speak to no one. If you spy your own sister walking by, do not speak. Do you understand?''

Catherine nodded.

"Buck up, Miss Catherine." Seeing her quiet compliance, Jenkins put in softly, "With any luck, we'll be out of here by the rising of the tide.''

Catherine watched as Sinjun and Jenkins strode out the door, telling her in French that they'd return shortly.

But the afternoon lengthened and Catherine sat mutely stirring the third cup of chocolate the serving girl had brought her, and still they had not returned. She had sat impatient and feeling as cramped and bottled up as an ill-tempered genie as the time had gone by. She watched all sorts of people pass the window of the inn, and had difficulty swallowing when she noted that there were soldiers in the town, strolling by and looking at all the passersby. A few had looked in the window at her. But aside from one cheeky young fellow who had winked at her, they seemed to pay her no special attention.

She was wondering whether it might be possible that she could be on English soil again before another day passed, when she noted a group of people who had entered the inn and had come into the room where she sat. So she turned and stared out the window, pretending to be oblivious to her surroundings when she realized that one of them had come up to her table.

"Good evening, Miss Robins," Henri Beaumont said silkily. "It is a great pleasure to find you here. I do not care for your new style of dress, but I must say you do nonetheless look as enchanting as ever.''

Henri Beaumont pulled out a chair and sat smiling benignly at Catherine. He noted the shock in the girl's eyes and the distress which had sent the color flying from her cheeks. It pleased him to see her in such distress for it had been a long and uncomfortable chase, and at least her consternation in some small way repaid him for his discomfort.

He did not blame her, he thought, watching her sit and blink at him as though he were a specter, for opting to go off with her countryman. Even he could see that the English marquis was a better example of manhood than his poor friend Hervé. After all, she was a woman as well as a businesswoman. When he discovered she had flown, and that the marquis had flown as well on the same day, his chagrin had been genuine. Still, he would have been content to shrug the whole matter off if it had not been for two unexpected factors.

One was that Hervé had been horrified to find that he was not to be presented with the English miss his brother had been so sure he would have for his own. For, as Hervé had explained, sputtering and banging upon the table, Beaumont had promised the woman to him. And he had told his brother he was to have her. And now, he had gone on, flapping his arms in fury, he would look like a fool. For while it would be delicious to be in power again, to live in splendor and deign to give charity to his brother, it would be as nothing if he had not the whole of it. What use, he had screeched, to be generous and dole out coins to Pierre? What use to see Pierre give up his splendid apartments to live in a hovel? It would not be complete if he could not see Pierre dying of envy as he nuzzled the neck of the very woman Pierre had thought to have. And implicit in every furious gesture Beaumont read the message: If Henri Beaumont could not procure him all that he desired, what sort of a friend was he? And what did he need him for when soon his beloved general would reward him so well for his loyalty?

The other factor that had precipitated Henri Beaumont's chase across the country was the man that the English female had fled with. For there was no question that the Marquis of Bessacarr was on clandestine business in Paris. Beaumont had known it, but had been helpless to stop it while peace and Louis reigned.

But now that the regime was changing, matters were different. The moment Napoleon once again set foot upon the throne, all the marquis' immunity would vanish. Even now at this delightful moment as he recovered the girl, he could not take the Marquis of Bessacarr. For, with all his far-ranging network of informants, still he had not gotten certain word of Napoleon's arrival in Paris. That he had left Elba, Beaumont knew. That he was coming to Paris was also certain. But as yet there had been no word of his triumphant arrival. And he had to wait upon that word.

Still, he thought, it had not been a wasted trip. Here was the girl. She was not a titled Englishwoman; she had no immunity. He could deliver her to Hervé and be in the excellent position of having Hervé Richard deeply indebted to him. He looked at the girl as she sat, pale and transfixed with terror, gazing at him. She was lovely, he noted dispassionately. Fleshly passion was not one of Henri Beaumont's sins. Women were in all, he thought, rather boring creatures. Power was Henri Beaumont's only passion, and he felt a distinct twinge of pleasure as he contemplated the girl he had gone to such lengths to discover.

"So," he said, placing his hands upon the table, "now you will come with me, Miss Robins."

"No," Catherine said, "I shall not. I told you so in Paris. And I say so again. For I am an English citizen and I am free to go home if I wish."

"This is so very tiresome," he said. "I know you are loath to leave your good friend the marquis, but I assure you Hervé is a generous man. While, admittedly, he is not so fine a specimen as the marquis, he is a good enough chap in his own way and you will be recompensed more than adequately for your services."

He stood and motioned to two of the soldiers who had entered the inn with him.

"Please stand and go with them quietly, Miss Catherine," he said, "for it will be no use for you to make a to-do."

Catherine rose and began to walk with the two soldiers. She knew she could leave a message for the marquis, but she feared even letting his name slip in M. Beaumont's presence. In her confusion Catherine could only hope that Sinjun had seen what was happening and was wise enough to stay away in safety.

But as they approached the door she saw Sinjun and Jenkins enter. Jenkins was breathing heavily, as if they had run a long way.

Sinjun stood and stayed the soldiers with one imperious up-lifted hand. He turned and stared at M. Beaumont. Even though Sinjun was dust covered and dressed as a peasant, still he had an air of command that communicated itself to the soldiers.

"M. Beaumont," he bowed, "how unexpected to meet you again."

Henri Beaumont stood quietly, a solemn gray-coated insignificant man beside the marquis. The two men measured each other with their eyes.

"Not entirely unexpected, Your Lordship," M. Beaumont

smiled, returning the bow. "For surely a gentleman such as yourself would have patronized finer establishments than stables and barns on his journey if he had not been at least halfway expecting to see me again?"

Sinjun acknowledged the words with a tight smile.

"And," M. Beaumont went on glibly, "I admire your caution. But you could not know that the landlady in Saint-Denis wondered why the little simple lad never got on the diligence. Nor could you have known that Mme. Boisvert in Louviers noticed that your charming French wife spoke English when she thought no one was listening. And I pride myself on reasoning that Dieppe would be too obvious a place for you to return to and Calais too far in these so troubled times."

"Very reasonable pride," Sinjun said, "but why are you taking my lovely companion away? Is it sheer revenge?"

"You know better than that," M. Beaumont said. "I must deprive her of your company. Alas, she is lovely, but she is also a thief. See what I have discovered she had upon her person when I apprehended her."

He dug into his pocket and held up a chamois purse. Lovingly, he withdrew a strand of pearls. As Catherine gaped, he took an emerald and diamond brooch from its folds and, lastly, held up the duchess's finest sapphire and ruby pendant.

"And not only that," he said sadly, "but I have also the dear lady who owns these trinkets to testify as to their theft."

He nodded to one of his minions, who quickly went out into the street to a waiting coach.

"Now what magistrate could deny the word of a titled English lady against her former companion?" he asked.

As Catherine watched in horror, M. Beaumont's man returned with the Duchess of Crewe following him. She appeared supported by Rose on one side and a wretched-looking James on the other. She was blinking in the light as though she had just been awakened from sleep. No trace of her former dignity showed, and when she spoke, it was not with command, but with a cranky querulousness.

"Yes. Those are my jewels," she said immediately upon entering, never once looking at what M. Beaumont held up in his hand. Her eyes wavered over to Catherine for a moment and then hastily darted away from her.

"And that's the gel. Now I must go. You said I could go home now. Give me my jewels back and let me go."

"I must keep the stolen goods, for evidence," M. Beaumont said calmly. "Surely you do not object to that? For if you do, you can always wait until the matter is settled and then claim them from me."

"No," the old woman gasped, "no. Keep them, but you said that I could go home now. I've told you all I know. I want to go home. Rose, tell him he must let me leave now," she whined.

"Certainly," M. Beaumont said, as he dropped the jewels back in his pocket. "Now that you have spoken in front of witnesses, you may go."

"But, Your Grace," Catherine called, unable to restrain herself, "and Rose. And James. You know I did no such thing. Oh, why don't you tell them it is untrue?"

But the dowager only hastily and ungracefully made for the door. Rose's face was red, but she and James only helped the old woman on her unsteady way and did not look back.

"So you see," M. Beaumont said helplessly, spreading out his hands, "I have no choice. I shall keep Miss Robins here securely for a day or two. Then we shall return to Paris and justice. But," he said slyly, "you may visit her in her incarceration if you wish, My Lord. I am not a heartless man, after all."

"And you hope I visit often, often enough to let time pass and tides turn?" Sinjun snapped.

"Oh, well," M. Beaumont shrugged, "time has a way of doing that, hasn't it?"

"Time enough," Sinjun said bitterly, "for news to come from Paris, no doubt?"

"We both await such news, Marquis," M. Beaumont said smoothly, "for even as we stand here talking, such news may be old in Paris. But, alas, there is no glass to see so far nor any voice to carry."

"And," Sinjun said carefully, "there is even a chance that such great events might miscarry, is there not? For otherwise, I think, you would not be so content to let me go."

"All things are possible," M. Beaumont said, "and I am a careful man. You are free, of course, M. Marquis. But the moment you become Citizen Marquis I shall know of it. Mlle. Robins will be safely kept in the jail here. But the tide runs high tonight, so you may visit or you may go. It is all the same to me."

He signaled to the soldiers to proceed and they motioned

Catherine to go with them. She stared at Sinjun and shook her head fiercely.

"Good-bye, Your Lordship," she said tersely. "Please do not fear for me. Please leave while you can, for I see this is a coil you cannot extricate me from. Good-bye, Jenkins. Good luck."

And, head held high, Catherine looked away from Sinjun's despairing face and followed the soldiers from the inn.

Catherine sat on the wooden bench in her cell and actually smiled to herself. For, she thought, M. Beaumont was a great one for effect. She knew that there were large clean cells above stairs, for she had seen them when she had been brought in. But here in the dank basement the cells looked like something out of a picture book of medieval tortures. They were made of cold gray stone with an ancient vaulted ceiling. The bars were thick enough to keep in a ravening murderer, and the one high window only showed a patch of light while it was still day.

She was the only prisoner, and her jailer, a close-mouthed dirty old fellow, spoke no English and seemed to be more interested in catching up on his sleep than in observing her. But M. Beaumont had been set upon proving his power to her. She shivered in the musty chill of the cell. He had succeeded. She had spent the last hours feverishly rationalizing her situation, and knew that she had her emotions under only the most gossamer-thin control. The only way she could stay rational was to tell herself over and over that at least Sinjun was free, and that perhaps he would find a way out of this for her.

Now she felt even that meager lifeline of hope slipping away. For now that she had sat here and night was upon her, a new cold voice rang in her head. Why should he risk all to save her? And even if he did, how could he possibly win her freedom? M. Beaumont had very carefully told her how impossible any escape efforts would be. They were in France; she was in a French jail.

The knowledge that she was being used as bait to trap Sinjun into overstaying warred with her frantic desire to escape the fate M. Beaumont had outlined to her. When she had insisted that she would never be Hervé Richard's mistress, he had only shrugged. It was true, he said, that Hervé would keep no mistress who wailed and wept and tried to escape at every moment. For he was not a brute. But if she did not agree to go pleasantly to Hervé and behave as a woman of her sort should, there were other places he could take her for profit. Places, he had said calmly, where she would be expected to accommodate twenty men an evening rather than one poor devoted Hervé. Places where her weeping and shouting would only be considered piquant by the patrons. And while every instinct she possessed cried for escape, still she knew she would rather suffer her fate ten times over than cost Sinjun his life.

She sat and gazed up at the little square of black, at last admitting it was a full night sky. The tide must have gone out, she thought, and Sinjun and Jenkins must be safely away. She wondered how long they would remember her after they were safe in England again. At last her control snapped and the tears began to flow. He might have at least stopped for a moment on his way to freedom to bid her good-bye.

There could have been nothing, she knew as she sobbed, between a lord of the realm and a foolish girl who had gotten herself in a tangle through her own willfulness. And she had known all the while that she would part from him forever when they reached home. But she had felt that the memory of him would sustain her through all the long years while she stayed and watched her sister's family grow. And now, almost wildly, she regretted her reactions of the night before. For if she had let him make love to her, it might have been a thing that could sustain her in the strange new life that lay ahead of her. She would live and she would go on to things that were now unimaginable, for she was by nature a survivor. But how? She almost cried aloud.

So it was that when her jailer rose and slowly climbed the stairs to a summons she had not heard, she scarcely cared who it was that he admitted.

And when Sinjun saw her, crumpled in a corner and weeping soundlessly, he caught his breath and tightened his knuckles till they were white on the bars of her cell.

"Catherine," he called to her, when he had his voice back in control, "Catherine, come here."

She turned and, seeing him, rose and came running to the bars.

"Oh no, Sinjun, you must not stay here," she cried out wildly, "for that is M. Beaumont's plan, to delay you till it is too late. You must go," she said frantically, her tearstained face striking him to the heart.

He grasped her hand through the bars and tried to think of a way to calm her, for time was short.

"Hush, Catherine," he said sternly. "Quiet. I must speak and you must listen. Listen carefully. Calm yourself, for, as you say, I do not have much time and you must pay attention.''

She fell silent at the cold imperativeness of his voice and listened, her eyes wide and unblinking.

Sinjun ran a hand through his hair and thought rapidly. He saw that her spirit was held only by his voice and that fear and shock had driven all else from her mind. So he spoke rapidly, forcefully, and clearly, knowing that her jailer could not understand the language.

"I have been very busy, Catherine. I have not forgotten you.

"Indeed, no one has forgotten you. Rose could not speak in your defense, for if she had, Beaumont would have accused her of theft as well. She and James wanted to stay to help you, but I persuaded them they could do no more. They had already made sure that the duchess signed nothing, so that nothing she said would be held against you by anyone but Beaumont. The duchess bore you no ill will, Catherine; she was only a frightened old woman. They sailed on the late tide. Violet elected to stay on in Paris with a gentleman of her choice. But none of them deliberately wished to harm you."

When he saw tears start at his words, he quickly went on, knowing now that he could not speak of emotions, or recall emotions to her mind, or she would crumble.

"But there is a way to get you safe from here. There is a way to take you with us. But you must agree and agree at once."

She nodded, clutching his hand tightly.

"You must marry me," he said.

He saw her disbelief and lowered his voice and said firmly, "Beaumont cannot keep you here if you are a peeress of the realm. He cannot keep you if you are a marchioness and we are not at war. Marry me, Catherine, and we can leave at first light and go home, home to England again."

Her eyes searched his face, and he kept his countenance impassive with difficulty as he looked back at her. Now, here in this filthy jail, was no place for him to spout on about love, desire, and future happiness. He doubted that she would believe him, and feared that, even if she did, she would refuse him. For as she did not love him, her sense of what was honorable might override her instinct for preservation. So he said nothing of love and continued, "I have Jenkins here. And a minister. Yes, an accredited representative of the Church of England, trying to make his way back home with his charges. He was traveling with schoolboys when the news of Napoleon's return came to his ears.''

The jailer looked up at the one word he recognized and shifted uneasily. M. Beaumont had said the woman might have visitors and converse with them, but had warned of terrible repercussions if any escape attempt was made. Although the sound of his onetime hero's name had jolted him, he soon relaxed, remembering how many soldiers were above stairs.

''An attaché from the consulate in Paris is here as well, Catherine, though not with me, for his face is recognized by Beaumont's men. He has gotten me the special papers. We can be wed here and now. And then you will be allowed to go free. Say yes, Catherine, for your own sake.''

But she only stood dazedly staring at him.

Sinjun wondered now if any of his words had reached her, so he went ahead in a low despairing voice, ''Catherine, you cannot stay. And I cannot live with myself if I let you stay. So say yes. If you marry me it will be for the best, and,'' he said suddenly, trying a new tack to bring some sort of comprehension to her eyes, ''if it does not suit you to be my wife, we can procure a divorce when we are back home. I promise you that. I will not keep you tied to me forever if you do not wish it. But for now, you have only to sign a paper and repeat some words and you are free.''

At last he saw some new emotion coming into her white face and he pressed on, ''For me, Catherine. So that all my work will not be in vain. For I promise you if you do not agree, I will stay here until I hit upon a plan. But by then it might be too late for both of us. I cannot live with myself as a man if I abandon you here.''

He had to strain to hear her whispered reply:

''Yes, Sinjun.'' Then: ''I will if you wish it.''

Dizzy with relief, he motioned to the men behind him.

''Here, Jenkins, you just stand so that you can hear Mr. Whittaker. And Mr. Whittaker, you cannot take out your little book; you must recite by heart. Can you do that? For though the jailer looks like a fool, the book will alert him to something to be suspicious of.''

The tall, thin, balding man smiled and said briefly, ''If I cannot recite it by heart after twenty-five years in the Church, Your Lordship, I am more of a fool than the jailer.''

''And,'' Sinjun said clearly, taking Catherine's two hands in his tightly, "you must alter the pattern of words. For the cadence of the ceremony might strike a note in our watchdog's mind."

"Let us see," the minister mused. "How about this, then?" And, clearing his throat, he looked at Catherine and said in a friendly conversational tone, "Dearly beloved we. Are gathered. Together here in the sight . . ."

Catherine gripped Sinjun's hand and thought only that she must do this so that he would not be caught. Tears gathered in her eyes when she thought of the sacrifice he was making. What if she were the sort of female to hold him to the marriage once they returned, making him regret his act of gallantry for the rest of his life, tied to a woman he did not want?

Sinjun carefully listened to the weird rhythm of the words so that he would know when to reply, and kept smiling and nodding as if Mr. Whittaker were only chatting and trying to reassure Catherine.

"Live?" asked Mr. Whittaker pleasantly.

Sinjun increased the pressure on Catherine's hands and looked toward the minister.

After a confused moment she said, in a thin voice, "Yes, I will."

Sinjun closed his eyes in relief and hoped only that she would never regret this moment. For although he had forced her to marry him, he vowed he would do all in his power to make her content with her state, to persuade her to one day accept him as husband, even if she could not love him.

And so in a basement in Le Havre, St. John Basil St. Charles, Marquis of Bessacarr, was wed to Catherine Emily Robins in a ceremony signally blessed with complete misunderstanding on the part of the bride, the groom, and the witnesses. As Sinjun guided her hand to sign the paper Mr. Whittaker handed her, and Jenkins assured the guard that it was just for the transfer of some of her property now that she was remaining in France, the ceremony was completed.

Jenkins and Mr. Whittaker left to congratulate each other royally at a tavern near the docks before continuing on the marquis' errands. The groom stayed the night on a bench outside the cell as he told the guard he could not bring himself to leave his *chère amie*. The guard was content—his master had told him it would suit him well if the English gentleman did not leave his prisoner. And the bride sat and watched the sleeping face of her new husband through the night.

M. Beaumont's face was wreathed in smiles when he descended the steps to Catherine's cell in the morning. So it was true, then: The marquis had stayed the night and missed one voyage out to be with the girl. With luck, he thought, he could be maneuvered into staying another. And another, it if was necessary, till the news he waited for came through.

"Good morning," he said happily, eyeing the weary girl as the marquis rose from his seat.

"Good morning," the marquis said briskly. "It lacks half past the hour of ten, Beaumont. You must have slept soundly. And now, if you please, release your prisoner."

M. Beaumont laughed.

"Ah, if it were only that easy to forget crime," he sighed happily.

"I'm afraid it must be," Sinjun smiled, "for you have no authority to arrest my wife, the Marchioness of Bessacarr. If you have any doubts upon that head, I beg you to look at these papers. There are our marriage lines. And there is a very official note from our ambassador requesting that you immediately release my wife from your custody. And the mayor of this city, as you can see from this other document, requests you comply. You would not want to disrupt amicable Anglo-French relations, would you, Beaumont?"

Sinjun smiled as he lay back against the tarpaulin upon the deck of the fishing vessel. He smiled just remembering the look upon Beaumont's face as he took the papers from his hands and read them.

Jenkins looked over from the rail where he had been watching the coastline of France begin to recede in the morning mists.

"Recalling past triumphs, lad?" he asked.

"And present ones," Sinjun agreed, looking down at Catherine as she slept, her head against his shoulder.

"There might be rough seas ahead," Jenkins mused.

"At least we are at last asail," Sinjun replied.

The ship glided smoothly home, and the two men did not break their contented, separate silence till they heard the far-off sound of cannon fire and the distant, almost toylike sound of the tumultuous ringing of many church bells coming from the direction they had so recently left.

"You left it close, lad," Jenkins whistled. "At least, you can never forget your wedding day. It was the day the news of the emperor's return finally reached Le Havre."

"I shall never forget my wedding day," Sinjun agreed, gathering his sleeping bride closer.

Chapter XVII

Catherine trailed aimlessly through the fragrant garden. The spring sun shone so warmly upon her shoulders that she had taken off her hat and held it by its strings as she wandered. She paused by the ornamental pond and watched the small golden fish glint in the sun-drenched water. There was no doubt that Fairleigh was a lovely place. It was well appointed and very commodious. It had delightful gardens filled with unexpected pleasures at every turn. Any path could take one to a statue or a waterfall or a bench overlooking a delightful view such as this one. Fairleigh also had a well-run genial staff of servants and comfortable well-furnished rooms. In fact, it had everything one could wish for in a home, Catherine sighed, except a heart. For its master was away. And Catherine did not know if he would ever return.

A month ago when she had first come here, straight from the dock where their fishing vessel had deposited them, she had been too exhausted to appreciate Fairleigh. Sinjun had traveled on to London to deliver his lists and his news of the emperor's return and future plans. He had sent Catherine straight on to his country seat. She had arrived by night, after a long and weary journey by carriage. But then sleep and ease and the security that emanated from the house had helped to mend her spirit. The knowledge that she was home and safe aided her. But Sinjun's prompt return to her side and having him near her every day had done the most to restore her.

Those first weeks she and Sinjun had roamed the grounds. He had shown her all the secret places of his youth; they had laughed and played together as though they were back in his childhood. He saw to it that the servants acknowledged her as mistress and she was easy in her mind at all times. He was such a clever, attentive companion that he almost succeeded in making her forget that this was but a temporary time for her and that she must soon move on again. He had treated her as a well-loved sister.

She did not know precisely when the change had begun. Before she had even been aware of it, it had arrived. One day he had been her eager friend and the next it seemed his air of polite and icy indifference was upon him again.

It was as if the one night they had dined by candlelight as usual, and there had not been enough hours in the evening to tell each other all they wished, and the next night he had sat listening to her with sedate half-interest until her voice had dried in her throat and conversation ebbed away. He was not cold to her, nor ever rude, but she could feel the distance grow between them. Instead of reassuring him that she was prepared now to be on her way, perversely, cowardice stilled her tongue and instead she attempted to draw his interest back. And the more she tried, the more precisely polite he had become.

But then, only a week past, she had, in a burst of misery-induced bravery, stopped him as he finished his dinner and began to bid her good night before retiring to his room. As no servants were in the room, she spoke swiftly, before any could return to complete the clearing of the table.

"Sinjun," she asked, "is it that you want me to begin the divorce proceedings now? But you will have to assist me, for I do not know how to go about it."

"Whatever gave you that idea?" he asked, sitting back to watch her closely.

"It was only that you have seemed less than pleased with my presence of late. I have tarried here but perhaps for too long. You said our marriage was to free me from M. Beaumont. And so it has. But you also said that you would free me from it when we were home. And so we are. I haven't made a move to go as yet, I know, but that is only because I do not know how to go about the thing. If you wish, we can start it in motion."

His eyes became shuttered during her speech and he sat quietly for a moment and then replied in a colorless voice, "Catherine, lay your mind to rest about that. You may stay on as my wife as long as you wish—till death do us part, for that matter. I only offered divorce if our relationship became unbearable to you. Has it?''

"Oh no," she had answered quickly. "But it is you that I am thinking of. I do not want to constrict you in any way. It would be the devil of a coil," she laughed artificially, "as Jenkins would say, if you wished to be rid of me and I just stayed on."

"You are pleased with our relationship then?" he persisted.

"Of course," she said, "except for the fact that you have been so distant of late."

His shoulders seemed to droop, and then he at last rose and gave her a thin smile.

"It is only some trifling estate matters that have occupied my mind. Well then, my dear, since this form of marriage is acceptable to you, we'll go on just as we are. By the way," he asked, "have you yet written to your sister to inform her of your sudden nuptials?"

She faltered. For she had not as yet. Since her marriage had begun with the promise of divorce, she did not know how long she would be a wife. It seemed impossible to explain all to Jane in a mere letter. And almost impossible to tell Jane the tidings of a wedding, then follow it with an announcement of a bill of divorcement. Yet of all the things she had been able to speak freely of with Sinjun, the precise nature of their marriage was the one thing they both, by some unspoken agreement, never discussed.

"I see," Sinjun nodded as she tried and failed to explain. "Well then, my dear, I bid you a good night. Oh, by the by," he had added, as though he were discussing a change in the weather, "those estate matters I spoke of. I am off to London tomorrow. There is business to attend to. Do you care to accompany me?"

The lackluster offer he made warned her off and she answered in a low voice that she would if he wished it.

"It makes no matter," he said coldly, "but I wondered if you were interested in consulting a lawyer while you were there?"

"Do you wish it, Sinjun?" she asked.

"I have already told you," he answered almost angrily, "that is not my desire."

And then he was gone. Jenkins had gone with him and Catherine had spent the week cudgeling her brain for an answer to her problem. She was the Marchioness of Bessacarr now, but she was yet a maid. Sinjun had never so much as held her hand since their return. She had asked if he wanted a divorce and he had denied it. Still, he made no effort to make her his wife. She no longer knew what it was he wanted or what she wanted. For all her brave thoughts back in Le Havre, she did not wish to leave him. Distant though he was, he was still Sinjun and she could not accept the thought of being apart from him. But neither could she bear the thought of being an encumbrance to him.

And there was also the fact that she knew divorce to be an expensive, complicated affair and one that would put her beyond the pale forever. It was one thing for Sinjun to have laughed at her fears for her reputation when they returned to England. For it was one thing for the duchess's infamous companion to return to quiet obscurity in Kendall, quite another for her to be wed to no less than the Marquis of Bessacarr. But he had laughed her fears away. He had told her that as his wife she would be above reproach. And that few people who mattered to her would have traveled in the duchess's set anyway. And, that having been rescued from the duchess, she would in fact, be a sort of heroine. But being his divorced wife, she knew, could not be easily laughed away.

She watched the sunlight play upon the water and wished she had more understanding and experience. The worst part of her situation was the loss of Sinjun's attention. She wondered again what she had done to turn his friendship.

His room was connected to hers, but she had never entered it. And so she could not have heard the angry conversation the morning of his departure for London.

"Have done, Jenkins," Sinjun had snarled in a voice she would not have recognized. "I am to London and there's an end to it."

"And your wife?" Jenkins asked, lounging against the door.

"Better with me gone," Sinjun said, "for I cannot go through with this masquerade. I am not the man I thought that I was. I cannot be with her every moment, laugh with her, condole with her, and yet be a plaster saint. You cannot creep into the master's bedroom at Fairleigh, Jenkins, as you did in France, and stop the master from forcing his attentions on his legal wife. It's just not done, old fellow," he said with a trace of his old humor.

"And you think she would call for help?" Jenkins asked again.

"Worse," Sinjun said. "She would probably suffer me out of gratitude, and that is one thing I will not bear. No, I am better off away from her. I saved the girl, Jenkins. And now she finds herself trapped in a loveless marriage, at least on her part. I am not so lost to decency that I will take advantage of her gratitude. Nor will I settle for it. Nor can I pretend to be a eunuch any longer. So I'm off to London. Perhaps time will clear the air and we will see what is to be done. And Jenkins,'' Sinjun said slowly, ''if in your self-appointed role of nanny, you think to tell her anything of my feelings on this head, I will slit your throat.''

''I have never betrayed you,'' Jenkins said simply.

''I know,'' Sinjun said softly. ''Forgive me, old fellow, I am not myself.''

''And so you're off to London, seeking the comfort of women?'' Jenkins said quietly.

''Women?'' Sinjun laughed. ''I swear you know me better than that. It is woman that is my problem, in the singular. I am not at all in a plural mood, dear friend. No, I am pure of heart and I wish to remain so for a space. I need time, Jenkins. Catherine needs time. And my trip buys us time.''

He had gone, and Jenkins with him as escort, and Catherine wandered the halls of Fairleigh and haunted its gardens. The morning sun played tricks with the water's surface, but she shaded her eyes with her hand and leaped up in eagerness. For she saw Jenkins strolling toward her through the garden. She flew to his side to greet him.

''Jenkins!'' she cried in pleasure, ''you are back. Is Sinjun back as well?''

''No,'' Jenkins said correctly, ''His Lordship remains in town.''

''Oh,'' Catherine said, downcast. ''And how does he? Does he remain long? When shall he return?''

''As to that I cannot say, My Lady,'' Jenkins replied.

''What is it, Jenkins?'' Catherine asked. ''Why the formality? Have I given offense?''

''No, My Lady,'' Jenkins replied, ''but you are the Marchioness of Bessacarr now, and it would not be fitting for me to call you otherwise.''

''Jenkins,'' Catherine said, fixing her eyes upon his deferentially lowered head, ''you cannot be so proper with me. Not now. Now when I need you as friend. We have traveled together. You have shared my bedroom, Jenkins,'' she said roguishly. ''Do not say it will be 'My Lady' and never 'Catherine' between us again.''

"I am a servant, My Lady," Jenkins said as he studied his boots.

"Oh, you a servant," Catherine laughed. "You are a servant in the same way the prime minister is a servant to his king. Please, Jenkins, if you wish to come all propriety when we are in company, I could accept it as a whim. But when we are alone, surely you can remain my friend? For I do need one, indeed," she said sadly. "I have no other."

"And what of His Lordship?" Jenkins asked shrewdly.

"As to that," Catherine waved her hand, "you see how eager he is for my company, don't you? I've been spending the morning wondering would I do better if I were just to be gone from this place."

"So that we three can chase the breadth of England together this time?" Jenkins said, shaking his head. "No, adventuring days are over for us, Catherine. We must learn to live with peace."

"I know," she said simply and sadly.

"Come," Jenkins said, "if you want to be friends, we must sit and have a chat as we did in the old times."

Once they had seated themselves on the white metal bench that faced the pool, Catherine turned to Jenkins.

"Why has he gone?" she asked.

"Business," Jenkins said. "Why did you not go with him?"

"I don't think he really wanted me to." She sighed, dangling her hat and watching it spin on its strings.

"Do you not know?" Jenkins asked. "A wife should know her husband's mind, not think she knows."

"But I am not truly a wife," Catherine whispered, fearful of a gardener overhearing her, but glad of a chance to speak with someone she knew and trusted. "And you know that, Jenkins. For you were part of the entire plan. He married me only as an act of gallantry, a gesture of kindness. And now," she said bitterly, "he's stuck with me. For I haven't the wit or experience to take matters into my own hands and free him from the consequences of his own good deed."

"I don't know," Jenkins mused, putting his hands behind his head and looking up into the unfolding blossoms of the tree above them. "I haven't met many fellows, no matter how noble, who would give their name to some female as a gesture of courtesy. Seems a mighty high gesture. For example," he went on contemplatively, "I should think it would have been just as easy for him to get those papers mocked up. The curate was a good chap and the mayor such a nit that he believed anything anyone told him loudly enough. Any warm body would have done to pretend to be a minister, for that matter. As I recall, the fellow from the consulate was so flaming mad at the Frenchies, he would have signed anything to dupe them. No," Jenkins said thoughtfully, "it seems to me that he made a highly permanent gesture of kindness when he didn't really have to."

Catherine sat still and blinked.

"But Sinjun's so honest," she finally managed to say, "why would he tell me it was the only way to free me if it was not?"

"I'm not saying he's dishonest," Jenkins said quickly. "Perhaps it was what he believed at the time. I've often found that a fellow believes what he wants to, deep down, when an emergency arises."

"No," Catherine said flatly, after some thought, "that cannot be. For he's never said a word to me about any tender feelings, not since we've come to Fairleigh. And," she said, a blush rising in her cheeks, "he's never made a gesture either. And," she said with hurt in her voice, "he's grown very cold towards me in recent weeks. Oh, Jenkins, what does he want of me?"

"As to that, I couldn't say," Jenkins said mildly, "for he's not one to open his budget to another. But it seems to me, if you'll forgive the impertinence, My Lady, that you're the one that's got the only right to ask. And speaking of such, I couldn't ask Her Ladyship, but I can inquire of Miss Catherine, do you want to stay in this marriage?"

"Yes," Catherine said simply, hanging her head.

"I can't blame you," Jenkins commented. "A lovely home, fine clothes, no more worries about money. It's a soft berth, it is indeed."

"How could you!" Catherine said, suddenly blazing with anger. "You know me better than that, Jenkins. I couldn't care if we had to live in a barn forever, as we did in France. It's Sinjun I love!"

"Love?" Jenkins asked, grinning when he saw her sudden dismay at the hastiness of her words. "Well, there's a horse of a different color. Love. And so then, you are sad because His Lordship rejects his wife's love? Ah now, that I can understand. But I can't understand him turning down such a lovely female."

Jenkins wagged his head slowly. "Well, I don't know what

sort of maggot the fellow's got in his head, turning down the attentions of a lady like you."

"He hasn't," Catherine said guiltily.

"Hasn't," Jenkins said with surprise. "Why, here you are languishing since he's left you, and now you say he hasn't rejected your love."

"He has not," she said in a rush, "because I haven't offered it. Jenkins, can't you see? If I tell him how I truly feel, I know, I just know what his reaction will be. He will feel sorry for me. He will offer me sympathy. Why, he's so kind, he'll stay on in a marriage with me, because he'll feel responsible. And all the while, it will all be only more courtesy. I could not bear that."

"You could always leave if he offered you sympathy," Jenkins reasoned. "But the thing of it is, you don't really know what he'll offer. You've been a brave lass since I've known you, Miss Catherine, I wonder at you not being courageous enough to hear what his offer will be. I should think it would be more comfortable to know once and for all where you stood than just standing on air like this. I should think the only thing you'd have to lose was pride. And that only for a moment, for then you could up and say, 'Well then, thank you, but I think I'll be going along now,' and there's your pride back again."

"It frightens me to death," Catherine whispered, "when I think of the look of sympathy that will come into his eyes. For there's nothing worse than knowing someone loves you, I should think, and knowing that they ask the one thing of you that you can never give them."

"Pride's a curious thing," Jenkins said, as if speaking to himself. "It's a terrible thing to lose, but unlike a heart, once you've lost it, you can always grow it back."

"You think I should bring up the matter once and for all," Catherine stated defiantly. "You don't think I should shilly-shally any longer; you think I'm making too much of my sense of pride."

"I think," Jenkins said straightforwardly, "that the Catherine I knew would rather have things clear and in the open, whatever the cost, than dangle and waver like a puppet, or like that fine bonnet of yours, on its strings. But I suppose that now you're a great titled lady, you've taken on new airs and graces to fit your situation. And if you count a moment's discomfort above a lifetime of doubt, I can't blame you. So if you'll excuse me, My Lady, I'm off to get back to business, for Fairleigh don't run

itself. And I'm sure you've got important things to do, like
watching fish and wondering about when life will straighten
itself out and be kinder to you."

"I'm going to London," Catherine announced suddenly. "Oh
Jenkins, I'm going to London!" she cried, springing up. "Here
and now. For if I wait, I will lose courage and go back to
waiting upon things to come right. And they will not, alone. I
have to go out and face it squarely. And I shall. Jenkins, help me
to go now. If I think about it, I know I'll change my mind
again."

"I'll ready the carriage," Jenkins said, moving quickly, "and
tell your maid to pack like devils were after her sweet body. We
can be there by nightfall if we hurry."

"But, Jenkins," she cried to his retreating back, "you've only
just returned. I can't chase you back again."

"It's as well," he called back across the wide lawn, "for I
discovered I've left my best boots there, and I'm lost without
them."

Jenkins drove the coachman to hurry, as though they were
indeed being pursued by demons. Catherine sat back and rehearsed her speech to Sinjun again and again as the coach fairly
flew toward London. She did not have a word for the happy
young maid sitting across from her.

She only looked out the window, not seeing the spring day
flash before her as she argued with Sinjun in her mind. By the
time they changed horses at the Owl and Cross, she had three
excellent speeches to choose from. And by the time they had
achieved the outskirts of London, there were two she was sure
she'd begin with and two alternates to use, depending on his
answers. She had decided that she would phrase her opening
statements obliquely, to give her room to maneuver away from
an outright declaration of her feelings if he so much as hinted he
would be unhappy to hear of them.

In fact, she had so many excellent speeches, rejoinders, and
face-saving devices at her command that by the time the coach
finally slowed and came to a stop outside of her husband's town
house, she felt as though she had been orating to an unseen
audience for hours.

As she stepped from the carriage, Catherine looked down the
street toward the duchess's house, the first home she had known
in London. The knocker was off the door and there was no sign

of occupation there. As Sinjun had told her, the dowager had retired from the high life and was now residing with one of her sons, happily spending the remainder of her days driving her relatives to distraction. As Jenkins came to give her his arm to assist her up the white steps to Sinjun's door, she drew in a deep breath.

He would be surprised to see her, but, as Jenkins had twitted her when they had stopped for a light luncheon, he seldom threw great orgies at his town house, so she need not worry about interrupting him at anything important. At last I am taking some positive action, Catherine told herself sternly as she mounted the steps, so there's no need for me to keep trembling like a puppy in a thunderstorm. She raised her head high and when the door swung open, she walked in calmly, as befitted the Marchioness of Bessacarr visiting her house in town.

His Lordship was out, the butler informed them unhappily, but he said more positively, since the marquis had not sent orders to cancel dinner, he would most likely be returning soon.

After the staff had made its curtsies to its new mistress, Jenkins ordered a hip bath brought to Catherine's room and told her to go and refresh herself and change. He would, he promised, send Sinjun straight to her when he returned. "Head high, girl," he whispered to her, bowing respectfully and wishing Her Ladyship a good evening.

Catherine washed and changed into a simple white at-home robe and brushed her hair. Then she sat poised on the récamier in her elegant room. She had time to pose herself in a variety of casual fashions and run through her speech several more times. She had time to admire the gracious chamber that was hers and count the exact number of cherubs carved into her bedposts, when she at last heard voices below stairs.

She forgot her pretense at languor and flew to her door to see Sinjun taking the steps of the long, curving staircase two at a time as he came toward her.

He came toward her with a delighted easy smile, but in a moment she saw it slip and by the time he had achieved her room, he wore his habitual cool expression.

"Catherine," he said politely, entering her room, "I am surprised to see you. Is anything amiss? Jenkins said you felt you had to see me straightaway."

"No," she said quietly, with admirable control, "but I felt

that I must speak with you, Sinjun, and I did not wish to put it off till you returned to Fairleigh.''

''Very well,'' he said, standing before her, ''here I am. What is it, my dear?''

She eyed him in dismay. All her rehearsed comments seemed to churn into one insoluble mass now that he stood before her. He looked so formidably immaculate. He wore high mirror-polished boots with gold edgings, clean carefully tailored buckskins clung to his legs, and his jacket fitted closely to his wide shoulders. An intricately folded white neckcloth completed the picture of the aloof aristocrat.

''Well, Catherine, what is it?'' he asked with growing impatience.

''Sinjun,'' she breathed with difficulty, ''it is hard enough for me. But I cannot speak to you as you are now.''

Seeing a look of confusion upon his face, she said hurriedly, ''That is, you are so . . . imperious looking. You look exactly as you did when I first met you and you so frightened me. On this very street. Not at all like the man I traveled with through France. It's as if you were two different men,'' she complained, shaking her head.

He hesitated, then went to close her door. As he returned, he began to strip off his jacket. He flung it to the side and in a moment the white neckcloth followed suit. With his shirt open at the throat, he sat in a fragile gilt chair and took both hands to disarrange his careful Brutus haircut. Then he threw one booted leg over the other and grinned at her.

''I would,'' he said ruefully, ''scuff up the Hessians if I could, and if I dared face the rage of my valet. But if you wish, Catherine, I'll nip below stairs and get some earth from the garden to rub over them.''

She relaxed and gazed happily at him, for he had shed some of his coldness with his garments.

''Now,'' she said carefully, finding it easier to look at her own clutched hands than at his face, for it had been so much simpler to discuss the matter with the Sinjun in her mind than with the vital, handsome actuality before her. ''Sinjun, I must know, exactly why did you marry me?''

After a brief pause, his voice came coolly to her ears. ''Catherine, you know that as well as I. Why did you marry me?''

''Don't answer my question with a question,'' she retorted,

daring to look straight at him. "I came here to see you, to talk with you, for I do not think we can go on as we are."

"That is true," he agreed, which was an answer she had not thought he would make, and which stopped her for a moment.

"And I have been thinking," she said wretchedly, feeling all her resolve fading and all her craven subterfuges coming to her command again, "that we must not go on so. For I have come to realize that we cannot continue to live a lie. It is too hard, Sinjun. It is too difficult. I find that I cannot even explain it to you."

She bent her head and railed at herself, for she did not have the courage to suddenly declare love to this watchful collected stranger.

He came, sat beside her, and wrapped one long arm about her to comfort her, but she kept her face averted.

"I know," he sighed. "It was a bad beginning and you should not bedevil yourself. I do understand."

His nearness and the soothing tone of his voice made Catherine wish to curl up and hide herself.

"It's just," she sniveled, "that now I find that it is too much for me. Especially now when I know my own heart. And what I was prepared to say to you straight out, I discover I cannot say at all, out of fear. Fear of your sympathy, Sinjun. For I do not want that. Nor any pity either," she went on, feeling his body stiffen and his hand pause in its stroking of her hair.

"I do understand, Catherine," he said in the iciest voice she had ever heard from him, "and I do not offer you pity. Quite the reverse, in fact. I congratulate you. And so, do not worry, for you shall have your freedom just as soon as it is lawfully possible. Who is the lucky fellow? He must be a paragon, to send you haring to London to settle matters so swiftly."

She looked up at that, to find him looking at her from eyes that seemed to be narrowed and carved of marble.

A sense of outrage at having so thoroughly blundered in what she had assumed to be a perfectly clear statement of her case made her gasp, "What are you talking about? What fellow?"

"The one you have discovered you love and wish to make your true husband," he said with weary patience.

"There is no other I love," she blurted, "or could ever love. You are the only man upon this earth that I want for a husband."

The enormity of what she had said, the way she had put the whole matter, plain and unadorned, caused her to stop and stare at him with an expression of horrified guilt. She had to restrain herself from clapping her hands over her mouth.

"What did you say?" he asked, incredulously.

"Oh Sinjun," she almost wailed, "it is not how I wished to say it. Indeed, it is nothing like the way I had planned to say it. And you do not have to dissemble. I beg of you, talk frankly to me for I am not a child. And do not be so noble that you will sacrifice your future life to spare me a moment's dismay. For I will not keep you tied to me, indeed I will not," she almost babbled, for now that he had discovered her, she was trying to say all the things she had hidden, all at once.

"Catherine, Catherine," he said, taking her in his arms, and holding her closely, "what are you talking about? Are you mad? Tie me to you for the rest of my life? Why, you have done that already, and so securely that I find I cannot break free to save my life. Nor do I wish to. For I love you, and have done so for so long that I would feel empty without it. As I have done this past week."

"But you left me," she whispered, delighting in the warmth that flowed from him.

"Only so that I could save you from my attentions," he said, "for we have no millpond at Fairleigh to cool my ardors in. And I did not wish to force you to my desire, nor did I want your charity either, Catherine."

"Oh, that. But then, it was only because I did not wish you to think me like Rose and Violet," she admitted, still finding it safer to speak into his ear than meet his knowing eyes.

He laughed and she could feel the laughter deep in his chest, where her hands lay.

"And so you came all the way to London to confess your love," he breathed.

"Yes, and to straighten matters out between us, even if it meant I should have to leave at once. For Jenkins was right, one cannot stand upon air."

"Jenkins?" he asked, drawing back a space. "What did he tell you?"

"Only," she said, at last looking into his eyes fully, "that he did not know how you felt any more than I did, but that I could no longer be such a coward. That I should make a push to settle things between us rather than wait for fate to intervene once more."

The tender look that grew in his softened gray gaze made Catherine's pulse leap.

"Jenkins is a knowing fellow," he smiled. "Catherine, let us have done with pretense for all time. Will you be my wife because you love me, with no hope for escape in divorce, for I love you?"

"Oh yes, of course, Sinjun," she whispered, and then he drew her to him gently and kissed her for reply. She gave herself to his embrace and freed herself to give him back kiss for kiss and embrace for embrace.

But as his gentle hands and mouth threatened to drive all further rational thoughts from her, she placed her hands against his chest again and gently pushed him from her.

"Sinjun," she said, catching her breath, "before we go on, there is something I must tell you."

"Tell me," he said into her neck. "Keep telling me while we go on, for I will listen."

"No," she said, firmly tugging at his hair. "It is a thing you must pay close attention to. It is a thing Rose and Violet told me about marriage."

He straightened instantly and looked at her with dismay.

"I was afraid of that," he muttered to himself and spoke carefully, "Look, Catherine, you must not pay too much mind to what they told you of the ways of love. They are not respectable married females. And many of the things they have . . . ah . . . encountered are not things to which a respectable woman is subjected. So you need not fear, for I will never do anything that I think will frighten or distress you. I will only try to bring you pleasure."

"That's just it," Catherine said with satisfaction, "just as they said. One afternoon Rose and Violet were speaking of marriage. And they said that the reason they had many clients who were married gentlemen was that so many of them treated their wives with nice notions of what is proper between a man and his wife. And further, they said that if a man would show his wife exactly what pleased him, as if she were a paid companion, they would probably be a great deal happier and the gentlemen would save their money, for then they wouldn't have to seek out special females for their pleasures. But, Violet said, it was as well that they did not, after all, for then she would have to go back to the theater again, having no employment left to her. So you see, Sinjun," Catherine continued, sincerely, "you must show me everything that you desire, so that you will never have to go to other women again."

"Everything?" he asked, arching one eyebrow wickedly.

"Everything," she said staunchly.

"Oh Catherine, my delight," he said with a look upon his face that melted her resolve to be logical, "I will, and gladly, for I do love you. I shall do my best to make you my own dear doxy."

"And I love you terribly," she said as she went back into his arms.

Since theirs was to be a marriage built upon laughter, he paused in undoing one of the tiny pearl buttons on her robe and smiled tenderly. "Then I shall have to do something about that. For I want you to love me expertly, just as Rose and Violet wished. It is only that"—he paused—"I hope I do not disappoint you. For I wonder if I know quite as much as Rose and Violet did."

And then he found an excellent way to stop her laughter before it threatened to overcome her completely.

The morning dawned so gray that Molly, the youngest maid in His Lordship's establishment, grumbled to herself as she groped her way into the kitchen to start the fire and greet the day. She yawned as she opened the back door to the kitchen and groggily watched the lamplighter begin his rounds of damping the glow of the new gaslights that lined the street. As she stood stretching and scenting the air, she heard laughter ring out in the empty street. Craning her neck, she looked up to its source.

The sound of masculine laughter blended with the high sweet trill of a woman's mirth. The sounds came from her own establishment, from the upper regions, where the master's rooms were.

Molly shrugged—that portion of the house was not one she had yet been qualified to enter.

"What I'd like to know," she grumbled, thinking of the work that lay ahead of her, and speaking to herself as she often did so early in the morning, "is what folks has got to laugh about at this ungodly hour?"

She started, as she saw she was observed, and then ducked her head in embarrassment. For it was Jenkins, that mysterious fellow who was the force behind the master's establishment. He stood on the lower step, his hands on his hips, and a wide grin on his face as he listened to the merry sounds above him. Only when the woman's laughter had ceased and then the man's laughter stopped abruptly, as if cut off at its source, did he turn his gaze from the upper window. Then he came jauntily into the kitchen bound for the servants' stairs, and a short walk to his rooms. But first he turned and smiled at Molly.

"There's a great deal to laugh about in the morning, little Molly, as you will discover one day if you are a very, very good girl. Or," he added, with a wink, "if you are a very, very bad one."

Molly flushed and went to close the back door, holding it open only a fraction longer to admit the kitchen cat, in from his night's wanderings. The cat sidled in and made quickly for his basket by the stove, glad to be in from the night, in from his weary travels, in safely from the cold gray of dawn.

NEW & FREE

Audio KISSETTES™

Listen to the Romance You Love to Read!

Thrilling original romantic novels recorded live by full cast... with stereo music. With these new full-length audio "KISSETTES," enjoy romantic fantasies whenever you wish, wherever you want—in your car, your kitchen, the quiet intimacy of your favorite room.

Order now—get your first audio KISSETTE in the series for only $6.95 plus postage and handling and you will receive a second audio KISSETTE, "My Haunting Passion," **FREE!** No risk...we guarantee satisfaction or your money back! Use the coupon or call CATI Productions toll-free at 1-800-327-9900. **Do it now!**

CATI ♥ PRODUCTIONS

Dept. NAL-1, 65 Commerce Road, Stamford, CT 06902

Yes! I want to join the CATI Club. Send my first CATI romance on audio KISSETTE for only $6.95 plus $2.95 for postage and handling. And at the same time, send me a second CATI romance FREE. I understand I will be enrolled in the CATI Club and will receive two KISSETTES each month at the regular monthly charge of $13.90 plus postage and handling.

I understand I may return my KISSETTE(S) within ten days for a full refund if I am not completely satisfied. And, I may cancel my membership at any time without obligation.

CHARGE MY ORDER TO ☐ VISA ☐ MASTERCARD

Acct. #_____ Exp. Date_____

Signature_____

Print Name_____

Address_____

City_____ State_____ Zip_____

Please allow 2-3 weeks for delivery.
Offer valid through 3/31/89 unless otherwise extended.
© 1988 CATI Productions, Inc.

OR CALL TOLL-FREE: 1-800-327-9900